NOW YOU SEE ME

D1053941

BY THE SAME AUTHOR

Honour Thy Father
Trick or Treat
Digging to Australia
Limestone and Clay
Partial Eclipse
The Private Parts of Women
Easy Peasy
Sheer Blue Bliss

NOW YOU SEE ME

LESLEY GLAISTER

BLOOMSBURY

First published 2001
This paperback edition published 2002

Copyright © 2001 by Lesley Glaister

The moral right of the author has been asserted

Bloomsbury Publishing Plc, 38 Soho Square, London W1D 3HB

A CIP catalogue record is available from the British Library

ISBN 0 7475 5771 3

10 9 8 7 6 5 4 3 2 1

Typeset by Palimpsest Book Production Limited,
Polmont, Stirlingshire
Printed in England by Clays Ltd, St Ives plc

One

Her last lift dropped her in a small town centre – she never caught the name. The engine's echo died away. It was late. The street lamps fizzed, lit nothing: gratings, palings, geometric shadows. Nothing *live*. The station was closed up. There were no shelters. She tried car doors. A car is fine for sleeping in, especially a big one with a wide back seat. She tried and tried but this was a careful town and all the doors were locked. She set an alarm off, one of those that say *Stop the thief* in a robot voice. She would have laughed if she hadn't had to run.

She legged it through an alley into a car-park full of vans. She tried all the doors and finally a back door opened. She looked around and climbed in quick. She couldn't see a thing at first, but as her eyes accustomed to the dark she saw that the van was full of blankets. She couldn't believe her luck. Not nice soft blankets, they were the sort you wrap things in, stiff and scratchy – but still, *blankets*. They smelled like the insides of cardboard boxes and old smoke. She settled down.

Her bones were hollowed out with lack of sleep. She had not slept since walking out of the loony bin. A thrill ran through her thinking that. But being dirty, cold and empty soon wears that thrill to rags, like waving a torn flag. Freedom is not necessarily the greatest thing.

She knew all about sleeping rough. Been there before. Wasn't scared of that. There are ways to survive, and ways. But last time it all went wrong, what with the cutting up. She fell and landed in the bin. It was OK. You could bath every day if you wanted in a bath big enough for a whale to wallow in, though you couldn't lock the door. It was warmer than the streets but the food was dead and nervy grey and not the sort of thing you want to eat. She rarely did.

She walked out. Just walked out of there, easy as that. Cheesed off with the therapy, trying to get her to face up to things. So, there are things she'd rather not remember. So what? She doesn't *want* to do the facing up. Why should she? Her mind is her own mind and no one else's. Get that? So she strolled on out of there. It was getting boring. And all her scars were healed.

The blankets in the van were a rough cocoon and she was so bone tired she did drift off to sleep. Dreamt she was in the bin again where smoke hung thick and people floated through it slow as fish. When she woke, the smoke was true and the van she was in was moving.

It was cold and she felt sick and shocked. She sat up, her back jolting against a wheel arch. She put her satchel over her shoulder and got ready to jump out the minute the van stopped, ready to run. The drive went on and on. The driver was smoking and talking to himself. Replaying a row, saying the things he wished he'd said.

'You've just contradicted yourself as per usual,' he said. 'And another thing, please stop leaving me those cute notes.' He lit another fag and the van swerved. 'And for God's sake, do you really think you can get away with those jeans? Have you seen your arse from behind?'

She couldn't help grinning even though she felt sick and cold and scared. She lifted her head to try and see the horizon because that is what you're meant to do if you get motion sickness. But she could see no horizon, just rain and motorway and traffic. There were no signs to say where they were, or even which direction they were travelling in. She didn't know how long they'd been going before she'd woken up. Hours and hours, she hoped.

The driver's hair was ginger and matted at the back. His fingers on the steering wheel were bony, two of them stained with nicotine. She shrank down again and her mouth filled up with spit.

There was the sound of a siren. 'OK, OK,' he said, slowing down, 'and if you give me that bleeding hummus in my sandwiches once more . . .' The van turned. Make your own bleeding sandwiches, she thought. He changed gears down and down, the van slowed and reversed. She crouched ready to run.

The engine stopped. The handbrake creaked. The driver yawned, lit another fag, got out. He locked the front door and came round. The handle turned and she crouched. Cold sweat was like a hand on the small of her back. But the door didn't open. The lock turned and it went quiet.

She waited for a while then knelt up and looked out of the front. She was in the car-park of a service station. She climbed over into the front where fag-ends cascaded from a jammed-up ashtray. There was a passport photo of a woman with arched black eyebrows stuck on the dashboard.

'Let him make his own sandwiches,' she said to it. There was an air-freshener in the shape of a pine tree but it stood no chance in all the smoke. There was a Tupperware box on the passenger seat and inside a hummus sandwich, a banana, a sausage roll and a note that said *Just you wait, big boy*, with a purple lipstick kiss. She took the sandwich, since he didn't want it, and let herself out.

It was cold and drizzly and there was miles of car-park but

not that many cars. Her legs felt like paper folding underneath her. She went over to the building and inside.

The Ladies' doors were bright orange and the sinks had taps where you have to wave your hands to make the water come. She had to try loads before any water would come and then it was boiling. She put the plug in a basin, squeezed a pink worm of soap from the dispenser and washed her face and hands. She was starting to feel better already. The good thing about motion sickness is it stops when the motion does. The hot-air drier roared her dry. It was nearly seven o'clock. In the hospital they'd all be sipping their cool grey tea.

She went into the cafeteria, stared at the slippery mountain of fried eggs, the trough of leather sausages. It cost a fortune to eat. £1 for a slice of toast. She had less than a fiver in the whole wide world. She asked for the bottomless coffee and the woman didn't look at her twice. There was an early morning feel, not many people about and those that were puffy and bristled, shut inside.

She sat by the window and stared out at the vast wet car-park. She noticed the man on the next table – her driver. His hair was poking out in all directions like rude tongues. He was puffing away at his fag and between puffs shovelling in forkfuls of the Hearty Start, which was double eggs, bacon, black pudding, sausages, beans, fried bread and tomatoes plus toast and marmalade. Her stomach growled. Not that she wanted anything like that. She got out the hummus sandwich and ate it right in front of him, not caring if he recognised it as his. There was cucumber in it too, very nice actually. She felt like saying.

The man smiled across at her. 'Hi,' he said. His front teeth were crossed over in a goofy way and he had the smallest deep-set eyes.

'Hi.'

'What a place,' he said.

''S'OK.'

'Where you off to?'

'What's it to you?'

The man shrugged. 'Nothing. Just making conversation.'

'Where are *you* going then?' she asked, and he laughed. She liked the way his eyes nearly shut.

'Huddersfield,' he said. 'Got to pick up some gear and head straight back. Lucky I like it. Driving.'

'Yeah.' She looked out of the window for a minute then dared herself. 'Reckon you could fit me in?'

He looked harder, more interested, like *What have we here?* 'You hitching then?'

'Yeah.'

He ground one fag out and lit another. 'I reckon so,' he said. 'Bit of company'd be a change.'

She finished the sandwich, went to refill her bottomless coffee and sat down at his table. His plate was like the wreck of a sunset, egg-yolk, bean juice, ketchup.

'Smoke?' he said. She shook her head. 'So,' he said, on a suck of smoke. 'I'm Greg. You?'

Nothing came into her head.

'No names no pack-drill, eh?' he said. 'Fair enough. Where you heading?'

'North,' she said. 'Leeds maybe. Newcastle. Dunno.'

'Free spirit, eh?'

'Sort of.'

They got back in the van. She remembered not to know which one it was. Greg moved the Tupperware box and nodded at the photo. 'Sammy,' he said, 'the girlfriend.'

They turned back on to the motorway and he talked about all sorts of things – places, music, things he'd done or not done. She didn't say much, didn't need to. He asked if she had a boyfriend and when she said no, gave her a long look and said, 'I'm surprised, girl like you.' *Here we go*, she thought.

She'd been wondering when he'd try it on. His eyes were the purest blue.

The sun came out and flashed off the road in long diamond splashes. Lorries towered past blocking out the light. He drove fast though sometimes they entered the fuzzy glitter of a patch of fog. If he hadn't smoked all the time it would have been fine though the girlfriend's eyes were like sharp pencil pricks that never left her face. He started to talk about Sammy and how they'd been together for five years and how she wanted to get married but he wasn't sure.

'I mean *married*,' he said. 'She wants kids, well that's fair enough but I don't, not yet awhile. Maybe in a few years but she's gone right broody. We can't walk past Mothercare any more without her starting up. How old are you, if you don't mind me asking?'

'Nineteen,' she said.

'Never.' He swerved a bit. 'I'd have guessed maybe fifteen, sixteen at a push.'

'Keep looking at the road,' she said. 'What about you?'

'Thirty-nine,' he said. She thought that sounded old. Quite old enough for having kids.

'Biological clock ticking away for Sam but men, well they can go on for ever, can't they?' he said. 'I mean wasn't it Charlie Chaplin had one in his eighties?'

'Don't suppose he was much use to it,' she said. 'How embarrassing to have a dad who's eighty.'

He laughed. Something strange was going on. She had to keep peeling her eyes away from his skin. There was something about him. It was his eyes and his crossed-over teeth. It was the sandy stubble on his chin, the skinny orange fingers on the steering wheel and the way he spoke out of the side of his mouth, crinkling his eyes. It was even the way he smoked his fags though she hated the actual smoke. His legs

6

were thin in black corduroy with some of the ridges worn away on the knees.

She kept staring at his knees and the easy way his hand would grip and push the gear stick and then he said, 'Oh Christ,' and braked. She looked up. The back of a red car was hurtling towards her and before she had time to think anything at all, there was a smash. And from behind a jolt and booming crash and then stillness. Stillness with things falling and creaking and wispy screams.

A crash. OK. The view from the windscreen was mashed car and a mess of hair. OK. She tried her feet and hands and they still worked. She was OK. OK. Incredibly OK. She looked at Greg. The steering wheel had jammed right up to his chest and the pink in his face had turned to grey.

'Hey?' she said.

He did a long breath and opened his eyes. 'Yeah. I think so. Christ.'

'Yeah.' They sat there for a minute like that just gathering the fact that they'd been smashed between two cars but seemed to be OK. Everything was sharp and vivid. Her mind perfectly clear. His door wouldn't work and they both got out the passenger side. Outside was fog and a petrol stink and someone screaming a high fingernail-on-blackboard sound, screaming on and on.

There was a soft white arm hanging from the wreck with lilac-painted nails and a silver bangle. You could only see the arm and not the body it was joined to. Cars were squeezing past the wreck and hooters sounding and wet stuff, maybe blood, maybe oil, was sliding in a graceful lick from underneath the mash of car and flesh.

'Come on,' Greg said, then he went to the side of the road and puked. He came back wiping his mouth on his sleeve. He lit a cigarette. 'Let's go,' he said.

'What about the van? Your stuff? And my stuff,' she said, thinking fast.

'What stuff?'

'My *stuff*.'

The sirens started.

'No tax, no insurance, no MOT,' Greg said. 'And no licence.'

'What no *driving* licence?'

'Come on.'

'But my stuff!'

'I didn't see any stuff. What stuff?'

'Everything.'

'I didn't see anything.'

'I shoved it in the back.'

He looked at the van. For a horrible moment she thought he was going to go and look but he didn't.

'We'll get you some more stuff,' he said. He patted his pocket. 'Plastic. No problem.' He walked away, head down, hands in pockets. She stopped a minute, looking at the smash. There was definitely blood and oil and petrol and even milk running on the road. *Milk*. The screaming had stopped. Someone was talking into a mobile phone. The first police cars arrived, screeching up the wrong side of the central reservation.

She followed him along the hard shoulder till they came to a concrete flyover. They had to scramble up beside it and over the top into a dead place of wheel-trims and broken mirrors, oil cans and dirty spiky flowers. The air was solid with fumes. If you moved your arm it left a trail. He leant against the concrete of the bridge and pressed his hand into his side.

'Think I've cracked a fucking rib,' he said. She started to shiver, the shock catching up with her. 'Let's get out of here,' he said. They got over a fence into someone's garden. There was a climbing frame and a pink duvet cover drooping damply from the washing line. She couldn't move. It was the same duvet cover she'd had when she was small. The same pink, the same daisy pattern. She couldn't move. The sight of the duvet cover stopped her. She wanted to wrap herself up in it and just stop. Just stop, wrapped in the pink of it. But Greg grabbed her hand and pulled her away from the duvet cover and out on to a street with daffodils and street lamps still on even though it was light.

She could hardly feel her legs or make them go forward at all. She thought she was going to be sick. 'Wanna lie down,' she said.

'Come on.' Greg put his arm round her and they walked along the pavement. It was a dream, the path soft underfoot and shivers running through her like the shivering of trees. Her mouth wouldn't make any words at all. After a while they came to a main road with shops. He led her through a door that opened with a sharp ping and they were in a café. Her legs gave way as she got close to a chair and half fell on it. A woman's voice said, 'She all right?' The cloth was plastic lace against her cheek. There was a chipped saucer near her nose and a squeezy tomato.

'Two teas,' Greg said from miles above.

'Ask no questions,' someone said to someone else. 'Looks like she needs it.'

She didn't care what she looked like. She kept her face on the tablecloth and some time later heard a clinking close to her ear as he stirred her tea. 'Come on then,' he said, 'get it down you.'

She sat up. Her neck was weak and her hand shaking so much she could hardly lift the mug. Her skull felt like it was about to burst. Greg's hand was shaking too and half his tea went on the table. 'Got any aspirin or anything?' she went. Greg asked the woman who said, 'Yes, as it happens, Anadin. OK?'

Greg opened the box and gave her two and took two himself. The tablets stuck and she choked. They scraped bitterly down the back of her throat. She sipped the sweet stewed tea. He got out a fag and she nearly laughed at the way the lighter flame wavered everywhere before he could get it to meet the fag-end. His eyes were small blue chips of stone.

'Is there a loo?' she said. He shrugged. She balanced on her legs to the counter, feeling faint.

'Toilet?' she asked.

The woman sighed. 'I'm too soft me. Through there,' and pointed to a door marked *Private*.

She went down a passage and into the toilet. She sat on the toilet lid and put her head between her knees till the blood ran back. She washed her face and hands and used some of the Nulon handcream that was there. In the mirror she saw that one of her cheeks was printed with the pattern of plastic lace. She combed her hair. She was OK.

There was a crate of milk cartons in the passage from the toilet and milk was leaking out on to the brown floor. She looked away.

'OK now?' the woman asked when she came out.

'Fine.'

There were two more mugs of tea on the table but it was too sweet. 'Sugar for shock,' Greg said when she pulled a face. 'Drink it.'

The sweetness made her feel sick. 'All that and it's only half-past nine,' Greg said and suddenly a laugh came tearing out of her. She couldn't stop it. She laughed and laughed until tears were running into her mouth. Greg tried to stop her but then he caught it too.

The woman came over and said, 'I can't have all this laughing in here. You'll have to leave if you don't stop laughing.' She looked as if she'd been sucking a lemon. They tried their best to stop but couldn't.

'I'll call the police,' the woman warned. But it was as if they were having the laughter wrung out of them. She finally lost patience, opened the door and stood there pointing out into the street, until they got up and staggered out.

'Drugs,' she said to someone as they left. 'Sticks out a mile.'

When they got outside they only managed a few steps before collapsing on the ground. 'It's not funny,' she kept trying to say but every time she nearly got it under control she remembered the way the woman had said *I'll call the police* like there were laugh police to stop you laughing and a whole new squeeze went through her.

'This is hysteria,' Greg said and that started her off all over again, the solemn way he said *hysteria*, but in the end they did stop. And nothing was funny after that. It was a cold day in March. They had nearly been killed. The sky was high and grey and couldn't care less.

'I can't get that arm out of my head,' she said.

'Yeah,' Greg said. 'What we need is a drink.'

But it was too early for a drink so they walked by a river and looked at willows and ducks. They wandered vaguely about. Other things were going on as normal: buses running; people wheeling babies; flowers flowering; birds and squirrels whisking through the trees while they walked by, leaning together to keep each other up.

Later they went into a pub and drank Guinness for a long time and shared a cheese sandwich. She was about as drunk as she'd ever been. She hadn't drunk a thing since before the hospital and wasn't used to it. They walked about afterwards like lovers, their arms tight round each other's waists. They stopped by a tree and he kissed her very softly on the lips. 'I can't believe I've only known you a few hours,' he said.

She looked into his face and said, 'Me neither,' because it

looked so much like the right face. And it did feel like years had passed since she'd sneaked into his van and still more years since the crash.

'You poor lamb,' he said.

'Why?'

'You seem so lost,' he said. 'Can I call you Lamb?'

'Why?'

'It suits you.'

'K,' I said.

We found a department store in the centre of town and he flashed his plastic and got me a rucksack, sleeping bag, knickers, jeans and two sweaters. He must have known I didn't have that much stuff before. All I'd had was my old satchel, and I *still* had that. I didn't feel too bad about it. They were things I needed and after all, he had nearly got me killed. We went in another pub and then to a hotel. The room had thick grey wallpaper like rhino hide and a fierce clanking radiator.

We lay on the bed and drank tea and watched TV. When I could get the arm out of my mind and stop thinking that it could have been me mashed to death – when I could get that out of my mind it was nice to be there with him. But I was worrying because the next thing to do was to have sex. And sure enough, after a while he rolled over and started to kiss me. The kissing was OK kissing with lots of different nips and sucks and licks not just his tongue rammed straight down my throat. It tasted very much of tobacco though, wet tobacco.

I froze. I tried not to. I don't know why or what happened. I kept my eyes open to look at him, his narrow lapiz eyes and crooked teeth, to tell myself I wanted this. He bought me all that stuff. I had to give him something back. But he ground his groin against me till it hurt and his sandpaper chin rubbed me raw. He put a condom on and tried to do it. But I had turned to stone. It was impossible. The trying hurt me and it must have hurt him too. I don't know what was wrong. What was wrong with me that I turned to stone like that? I do not know.

He stopped and looked at me for a minute before he rolled away. The look in his eyes. I couldn't stand to see that look in anybody's eyes again. He didn't thump or shout at me, just *looked* and turned away, groaned and shuddered like a dog and finished on his own. I stared at the matted smudge of hair at the back of his head until he finished.

He fastened his trousers with his back to me. He said he was going out to make a call. He could have made the call from the room but he went out. He didn't say, but of course it was to his girlfriend. After me he'd be dying to get back to Sammy, hummus sandwiches and all. I could just imagine her arched eyebrows winging upwards when he told her about the crash. Or maybe he wouldn't say. Who cares?

He came back and didn't look at me, just lit a cigarette. There was a *No Smoking* sign but I didn't like to say. We watched TV but then the news came on about a fatal motorway pile-up and I heard a din in my ears like drums. He changed channels to some football match.

When I woke in the morning he was gone. Well that's not true because I did wake and hear him leave at five o'clock. I turned over and pretended to be asleep because what was there to say?

Two

Best to be alone. Alone you can balance. You can concentrate. One foot after the other like a tightrope walker. You have to concentrate. You want no one hanging on your arm or your heart because then your balance is lost. Small and private and one thing after another thing with nothing strange. That is the way to be.

I know no one because of that. And that is fine. You meet people of course you do. But you imagine a field around you like radioactivity. And they are outside the field, the shield. Though you have to be prepared. But sometimes a person can slip in when you're not looking, not ready, when your head is somewhere else. Sometimes a person can hook straight in and put it all in danger – the order and the balance.

I keep my balance like this. I clean. I live in the same place. I have lived in the same place for months now and I got the work by lying and writing false letters. It is surprising what people will believe. And it is OK the cleaning, rubbing things, sweeping them, smoothing them. Being in the houses of people and usually alone. And even to have that little money which is clean money earned cleanly. And to rest my head on a pillow that is my pillow and in the same place every night. These are important things. The things I balance on.

I am sitting on the bed in my cellar. If you looked that's

what you'd see. If anyone could see but no one can. It looks like I'm sitting on the bed but I am way up there, balancing. Trying to get it back, the balance. Because someone got to me when I was not ready, not looking out. My arms are spread and my toe is pointed and below me is the deep and dizzy world.

I first met him on a Wednesday at Mrs Banks'. I was hoovering the stairs, watching the fluff whisk into the roaring tube, when I got the feeling that someone was staring at me. I carried on for a minute thinking, *don't be daft* but my skin was prickling with the sensation of eyes. There is no scientific explanation for why skin can feel eyes on it but it can. I switched the cleaner off and looked up. And there he was, standing at the top of the stairs. He was wearing a dressing gown and staring down at me. With the dressing gown and his beard and the landing light shining like a halo behind his head he looked like something holy.

How dare a person be there like that when I thought I was alone? I said nothing, just stood and waited. If you say nothing the other person has to speak first to stop the silence. People can't bear silence. I wasn't scared. The door was behind me. I could run if I had to. I could kick.

He stood there so long I was beginning to lose my nerve but then he broke the spell and said, 'Who the fuck are you?' He took a step down and I stepped back.

'Who are you?' I said.

'She's my mum,' he said after a while.

'Mrs Banks?'

I didn't know what to think. Mrs Banks has got Roy, who's four, but she's never mentioned any other children. Why should she? It's not as if we're the best of mates. She doesn't look that old though, not old enough to have a son with a beard. If it was true though, everything was OK. He had a right to be there. I didn't know what to think.

He started coming down the stairs and I backed down with the hoover. He came a bit too close. His hair and his beard were black but his eyes were light in his olive face. They looked odd, pale silvery grey, like razor blades.

When you're alone in a place that's OK, that's good, long as you know you're alone. But if there's someone there, lurking, specially a strange man with such sharp grey eyes you don't know what to think. No point being mad at him. He was as surprised as me. I didn't know what to do or where to look. I wasn't going to switch the vacuum on again, not with him in the house. It makes you vulnerable. A person could creep up behind you in all that roar and you wouldn't hear till it was too late.

I went into the kitchen and he followed. He stood there watching me while I shoved the cleaner away. What was I supposed to do?

'Coffee?' he said after a minute. I didn't know if he was asking or offering. I didn't know what to do with my hands so I put the kettle on. There was definitely something dodgy about him. You might think he was good-looking. Wild but clean. Drops of water sparkling in his stubbly beard and his toes pink on the floor. But it was the clean hard glint of his eyes that got to me. He kept staring till I said, 'Got an eyeful?'

He nodded and did a slow smile. 'Yeah, ta,' he said.

'Maybe I'll go,' I said. He shrugged, sat at the table and got stuck into the biscuits as if he was half-starved. I took a small sip of my coffee because it was the first thing I'd had all day and I needed it. He said he was surprised his mum would have a cleaner. I prickled when he said that, I mean I *clean*, but that doesn't give anyone the right to call me a *cleaner*. I said that Mrs Banks hadn't mentioned him to me either. He said that was because he was there to surprise her.

I told him my name and he said, 'Fuck *off*?' I asked him

his name and he said, 'Doggo.' *Doggo!* If Lamb is a stupid name, then what is *Doggo*?

He stood up and I was very conscious that I was alone with him and conscious that he'd got nothing on under the dressing gown.

'What you thinking?' he said. I blushed.

My hands were all slippery. I didn't know what to do with them. If he was Mrs Banks' son then it was OK and I had no right to question him – but something wasn't right. I thought I'd try and catch him out. He could have been anyone, a breaker-and-enterer, he could have been dangerous. But he did *look* a bit like Mrs Banks, same colouring and a baffled look as if he can't quite believe what he's seeing. I've been taking that personally from Mrs Banks but maybe it's just a family trait. With him though the look is colder, cold metal scraping skin.

He asked when Mrs Banks would be back. I said, 'Didn't she say?' He said he hadn't seen her yet, this was a surprise visit. He picked up a box of matches and struck one.

'You don't say a fucking word. Right?' The flame flickered in his eyes. He let the match burn between his fingers till the flames reached his finger-ends then he dropped it. It made a little fleck of scorch on the pine table.

'Why?' I said.

He leant forward and I said, 'Right,' quick. He kept striking the matches and when the flames reached the ends of his fingers I recognised the flirt and flare of pain. 'Hey,' I said. But he struck another match and another. 'You're ruining the table,' I said.

'Yeah?' He looked at the freckled patch. 'Oh dear.'

I was starting to get mad. 'I'll get the sack,' I said.

'Shame to lose such a great job,' he said. He went to strike another match but the box was empty. Then the phone rang and he jumped. We both stood there listening to the few rings

17

then Mrs Banks' voice saying *Sorry but we can't come to the phone, please leave a message, do*. There was a click and a high-pitched whine. The other person left no message.

He started moving fast, like *he'd* lost *his* nerve or something. He took some clothes out of the drier. The dressing gown opened a bit revealing the inside of his thigh, soft curly hairs. I looked away quick. I just wanted him to get out and go.

He went upstairs to get dressed. I put the mugs in the dishwasher. I had a weird sweaty feeling, like I'd only just got away with something but I wasn't sure what. If he would go now it would be all right. I could have my bath, I always have a bath when the house is empty. I could get everything done, get everything back to normal, only I didn't know what to do about the table with its freckle of scorches. She was bound to think it was me. And give me the sack and I couldn't afford to get the sack and would *not* get the sack because of someone else. I would just come straight out and tell her.

He came down the stairs wearing a pair of mirror shades even though it was one of those days when it never gets light. He put a ripped leather jacket on and picked up a back-pack.

'See ya,' he said. He went for the door then he turned round. 'Don't fucking say.'

'Why?' I said.

'Just don't.'

'Or what?'

'You'll see,' he said and slammed off out. I went to the window and watched him slope off then sat at the table and picked at the flecks. Maybe I could sand them off or something. Or why not just tell Mrs Banks that he did it? What could he do to me?

I *should* have told her. It's just that I do try not to get hooked into other people or their stuff. Other people and their stuff can unbalance you. You have to watch out. Anyway, what was it to me if he was here or not? None of my business.

I made sure both the doors were locked before I went upstairs to run my bath.

Three

He'd had a shower and left the shampoo on its side leaking out everywhere and a tangle of black hairs in the bottom of the bath, smooth head-hairs and little crinkly ones. I picked them up and examined them. Hair is such weird dead stuff, the way it streams for ever out of the pores of your skin. I chucked it in the bin. He'd left the towel wet and screwed up on the floor.

While I waited for the bath to fill I went into Roy's room to make his bed. You have to climb a ladder to get to the bed and it's hard to tuck the sheet in. I sniffed the child smell on the pillow and tidied up the toys. There's a bear made of rainbow fur with its paws chewed flat and fraying. I went out of that room and banged the door shut.

Mrs Banks has got some aromatherapy oil to pour in the water. It turns the water into silk and smells like heaven. Must cost a fortune. Worth it though, if I was ever rich I'd get some. It says it soothes, softens and lifts your spirits. I stepped into the bath, slid down and waited for my spirits to lift.

I don't like looking at my body. Any of it. Especially the herring-bones of scars that line my arms, silvery thin. They are *all* silvery thin and old now, nothing new for ages because of my balance. My new balance. Which I must maintain. I closed my eyes and tried to see the tightrope but all I could see was the glint of Doggo's eyes.

I should have tried harder to catch him out. I could have done something like ask him if he was going to see Mrs Banks, in her play. A play's the last thing she'd be in so his reaction would have told me. But maybe he wouldn't have reacted at all. I don't know how you read a person like him. But I could read Mrs Banks. She would never be in a play. She wouldn't say boo to a goose – although I bet she'd say boo to me if she caught me in the bath.

I was annoyed that he kept coming back into my head. There was no need to think about him ever again. None of my business. But there was something about his eyes. The table wasn't that bad. If I put the mat and a vase of flowers in the middle it would be OK.

I dipped my head underwater and felt a million tickles as the air bubbles rolled out of my ears. Then I had a sudden thought. I sat up as if someone had dropped a toaster in the water. I remembered Mrs Banks' note. How could I have forgotten that? Mrs Banks works part-time in a building society and sometimes she's there when I come and sometimes she's not. When she's not, she always leaves a note stuck with alphabet magnets to the fridge saying things like *Could you sort the kitchen cupboards?* or *Could you tackle the ironing?*

This time as well as asking me to vacuum she'd said her bag had been stolen with her keys in it. She'd had to use the spare key to lock up and asked me if I could leave her my key till she got another one cut. I hadn't thought much about it except, tough luck, baby, join the real world. I mean bags go missing all the time, don't they?

But lying there in the bath I got a clear image of the bag downstairs. By the kitchen table all the time I was talking to Doggo. I'd been so uptight about him being there and trying to keep control that the oddness of the bag being there hadn't struck me. I lay thinking that it couldn't have been the bag I saw, or not *the* bag anyway. Because how could it be there if it was stolen?

But I couldn't relax after that. I got out of the bath and got dressed. I went down to the kitchen and sure enough, there it was. And it was *the* bag. I looked inside and everything seemed to be there: make-up bag, comb, tissues, purse still with its money and cards – though no keys. I had to sit down to try to work out what was going on.

Maybe Doggo wasn't her son at all but a burglar who'd stolen the bag and used her key to come in and do the house over – and I'd scared him off. But do burglars have showers while they're at it? Or sit down to drink coffee and scoff about half a packet of gypsy creams?

I didn't know what to do. Tell Mrs Banks or not. It was like taking sides in something I didn't understand. The way he narrowed his eyes at me, a kind of threat. Like I should be scared of him. Like he could hurt me. Maybe he could. I remembered the glint in his eyes. He was more like me than like her.

If she came back and found the bag she'd be bound to think it had something to do with me and, even if she didn't find the damage on the table, give me the sack – and I don't want that. She's good to work for. She doesn't leave the place a tip like some people. She's one of the guilty ones and they're the best. They do the dirtiest work before you get there. She can't have had someone to clean for long, because it soon wears off that feeling. They get blasé.

When I went down I put a table mat over the burns and put the salt and pepper on top and it looked OK. I sat there with the bag on my lap not knowing what to do. If you clean for people you have to at least seem trustworthy, otherwise word gets round. I was sitting staring at the bag when I heard her car stopping outside and the door slamming. Then she was coming up the drive with Roy. I shoved the bag inside my jacket and rushed out saying I was late for something and didn't stop even though she was calling after me.

So there I was rushing along with a stolen bag that I didn't even steal. Talk about stupid. I don't steal, not unless you count hot water. I tried to look normal, strolling along and swinging the bag over my shoulder as if it was mine, but I felt as if it was flashing *stolen stolen* in neon lights.

I was about to dump it in a wheely-bin but someone came round the corner so I walked on realising that I didn't know *who* might be looking out of the windows at me. In the end I kept hold of the bag and brought it home. What I call home but with inverted commas round because home is where you feel at home and there isn't a single place in the world where I feel like that. I hid it on a shelf under a heap of old gardening magazines dating practically back to the Second World War and tried to forget.

My *home* is in a big tumbledown house with a room like a tower coming out of the roof. It's got a slippery cobbled drive with moss growing up between the cobbles. There's a lamp post, one of those old gas ones. It doesn't work of course. You go down the drive, beside the house. You go round the back and because the house is on a slope you come to the cellar door, under some stairs that come down from the kitchen door. Well I live in the cellar which is not as bad as it sounds because there is at least a little window. With net curtains. Cobwebs actually but they work the same.

There's a sink with a tap and a toilet outside. What more could a girl want? And it's got electric light. It's damp but I heat it with Calor gas. The house belongs to Mr Dickens. I clean for him two afternoons a week and soon after I started I discovered the cellar. The good thing about Mr Dickens – well not good for *him* but good for *me* – is that he can hardly walk. He has to use a Zimmer frame so he'll never be able to get down to the cellar again. He's half deaf too, so he doesn't hear me and I can even listen to the radio. I've been here months. It's here I got myself together, and really got my balance back.

Mr Dickens has got a whole lifetime's worth of stuff stowed away, all sorts of things. Some of them very useful to me. A canvas bed, a couple of deck chairs, a kettle. It's OK.

I like Mr Dickens. He's ancient and a wreck to look at but interesting. He's full of stories. He hasn't gone soft in the head or anything like that. He does ask me about myself but I'm evasive. Not rude, I answer his questions but I don't give anything away. You can say anything, you know. Who really cares if it's the truth?

I felt furious with the Doggo person when I thought about it. He really dumped me in it. There I was minding my own business, living my own life, maintaining my balance, when he barges in and puts me in a position where I end up having to steal a bag I don't even want. And that slow smile, that eyeful. The more I thought about it the more mad I got. Why was I so easy on him? Letting him go off like that leaving the table scorched and not giving a shit about me or my job. I got so angry I could hardly sit still. You cannot keep your balance if you feel like that.

I think myself up to the wire but I can't put out my foot. It is too deep below me and too dangerous. I am not steady enough to balance. I have to sort this out. I can't have people breaking into my life and spoiling my balance like that. I just can't have it.

Four

When I arrived at Mrs Banks' on Friday a figure lurched out of the bushes. It was Doggo and he nearly stopped my heart. I had been OK. Getting on OK. Though the day before Mr Dickens had told me a really horrible story. You can be safe and steady for weeks, then suddenly everything starts to go awry. Things happen, people turn up, people tell you things you really don't want to know.

Thursday afternoons is Mr Dickens. The obvious way would be to go up the cellar stairs and emerge in his hall, but those steep stairs – there's no light and – and anyway I have to give the illusion of having just arrived.

So I creep out, up the cobbled drive on to the street, then back up his front path, which is broken and lumped up with roots from the trees that stretch across as if they're trying to join hands. I press the doorbell – which is quite something. Mr Dickens had a school kid round doing a GCSE technology project on a doorbell for the hard of hearing. He must have got an A. When you press the button, which is ivory and crazed like an old tooth, you get an ear-splitting blast of what Mr Dickens says is the Trumpet Voluntary which you could probably hear on the moon. Followed by half an hour of dog battering itself to death on the door before Mr Dickens gets there – what with getting up out of his chair and his Zimmer and all. Nowadays I just ring and go straight in, he knows me that well.

I hurry past the boarded-up room. It's one of the big front rooms and it's nailed shut. Literally nailed shut with a plank of wood across the door frame. The curtains of the room are drawn so you can't see in from the outside either. Why would anyone want to board up a room like that? That's the kind of thing I have to keep my mind off.

Doughnut nearly knocked me over in the hall. He always goes berserk when anybody comes into the house. He's a fat spaniel with blind white eyes and matted lumps all round his ears. As soon as he knew it was me he staggered straight back to his place by the fire and keeled over.

When I went in Mr Dickens' face broke into about a million crinkles. He said, 'Ah, there you are, Lamb,' which he always says, then hauled himself out of his chair to make the tea. It takes him so long it sends you round the bend or breaks your heart depending on your mood. His hands are silvery as driftwood and they shake like mad so you're lucky to get half a cup by the time you get it. I once offered to do it and he did let me but it wasn't right. He seemed to crumble and age before my very eyes – though he is actually ninety. *Imagine* being ninety. He's proud of it, tells me every time. *Ninety I am*. And he likes to make the tea himself.

While he was making it, I carpet-swept round the dog in front of the electric fire where the rug is thick with hairs and crumbs. Then I picked the sweet wrappers and pipe dottle off the plastic coals. He chucks things on there as if it's a real fire and I take them off again.

That room stinks of dog like no other place I've ever known. It gets you in the back of the throat like a snarl. It makes you sneeze. Thick, fusty, ancient dog and pipe-smoke. You have to breathe through your mouth at first to give your nose time to acclimatise. Mr Dickens smokes a giant pipe with a runkly black bowl and when he puts it down, brown juice runs out on to his *Yorkshire Post* or the arm of his chair.

He let me carry the tray in for him and we shut the door. Me, him, Doughnut in the unspeakable electric fug. He'd cut a jam Swiss roll into raggedy chunks and when I took one I realised that he must have cut it with a dirty knife so it was smeared with something like sardine or, I hate to think it, but dog meat. I doubt I'd have eaten it anyway but I had to watch him and sometimes when other people eat I get this empathy thing, like I can taste whatever it is they have in their mouths. I sneaked the slice into my pocket and said no when he tried to get me to take another.

He said, 'You want to get a bit of flesh on them bones,' staring perkily at me for a minute. 'When I was a youngster I liked something to get hold of in a lass, can't see the fun in these twiglets nowadays.'

I sneezed and said, 'What do you want me to do?' and he didn't answer. I sat there and waited. Sometimes he just nods off mid-sentence. He had a bit of Swiss roll sticking out of his mouth and I itched to flick it off but I didn't. I started to wonder if he'd actually died this time, but then he spluttered and carried on.

I listen while he talks and drink the tea which is never hot and has big weedy leaves floating about in it that cling to your tongue. To tell the truth I do more talking, or listening rather, with Mr Dickens than actual cleaning. I like it. Sometimes I think I ought to be a social worker. I mean I can see he needs someone to listen to him more than he needs his floor mopped or his draining board scrubbed. Although admittedly they do need doing too.

He got on to the subject of his wife and I was so fascinated I almost forgot myself. I almost forgot Doggo. Mr Dickens is a good talker. If I closed my eyes I could see it all like some old film. His wife was called Zita which is the best name I've ever heard.

He asked me to get his photo albums out of the sideboard. The photos looked like something out of history books. There was Mr Dickens with a sharp young chin, wearing a cricket sweater and pads and leaning on his bat, looking like something off a knitting pattern. It makes you want to weep when you see someone young and handsome like that and then see the wreck of their old face beside you. Does that really have to happen?

Then he showed me some pictures of Zita. When they were engaged, sitting in a vintage car, and when they got married and later. What can I say about Zita except that she was beautiful? I mean *beautiful*. These big sad eyes and a movie-star mouth and a long neck. You know those women from silent movies with hair like petals round their heads and eyes practically bleeding stars. I could see what Mr Dickens saw in her, I could nearly have gone for her myself.

Mr Dickens lit his pipe and told me the story of how they met. Her father was the captain of Mr Dickens' works' cricket team and she used to watch Mr Dickens play and once he scored a century, which apparently is good, just because her starry eyes were watching him. They got married in 1930.

In my favourite wedding picture she is alone. She's standing under a wintry tree looking like a snow queen, very tall and slim in her white dress and white fur cape. Her face is serious, no smile, all the spark is in her eyes and around her the world is a snowstorm of confetti. Or maybe real snow. It was midwinter when they married but Mr Dickens can't remember if it was actually snowing or not.

She made silk wigs. Not for money – her father was rolling in that and Mr Dickens says he's still living off it now – but just for the fun of it. There's a picture of her in one of the wigs, thick and fringey and so white it makes her skin look black.

Like the negative of a photograph. Or maybe some sexy alien. I asked if he still had any of her wigs but he just shrugged, well not shrugged, I don't think he can shrug with his shoulders all seized up, but put on a shrugging expression.

He went on and on and I was riveted. The couple of hours he pays me for were up but I didn't even notice, just sat there listening to him and when he dropped off, I looked at the photos and waited quietly. I love the way he starts and carries on where he's left off as if nothing's happened. Sometimes he drools a bit but I pretend not to see. The afternoon rolled cosily by, the dog snoring and farting, the clock ticking, Mr Dickens occasionally filling his pipe and puffing out so much smoke I could hardly see him.

But then he told me the horrible thing. It was about what happened to Zita in the end. He said that since she'd died he'd hardly been out of the house and that was sixteen years ago. Sixteen *years*. I said, 'God. How did she die?' There was a long silence and I thought he'd dropped off again but then he said, 'Haven't talked about it since inquest.'

'Inquest?' I said, getting a jittery feeling, like maybe I didn't want to know any more. I said, 'It doesn't matter.'

But he said, 'No, no . . . it's natural to ask, since I've bored you all afternoon. Ought to pay you double-time.'

'Not *bored*,' I said. 'And anyway all I've done is sit here.'

He watched my lips, like he does, then he laughed and said, 'You are good,' which no one's said to me since I was about ten. He puffed away till he was lost in a cloud of smoke then he said, 'Look in sideboard, there's another album.'

I got it out. It had a black leather cover. I gave it to him and he flipped through till he found the right page and passed it over. It was full of newspaper clippings and photographs. I looked at the page he'd opened it at and just stared at the headline CHARRED REMAINS OFFER NO CLUE stuck next to a picture taken by forensic scientists.

In the picture there's a room: wallpaper; a lamp with a beaded shade; a table and on the table a cup and saucer with half a biscuit balanced on the saucer; a book with a bookmark sticking out all as normal – and then just this black space and on the edge of the black space two legs, not whole legs, just the shins, like two silly fallen skittles.

'Spontaneous combustion,' he said.

I didn't know what to say. In the end I just said, 'How awful,' and put the album down. It felt as if ash was coming off on my hands.

Doughnut staggered up then and Mr Dickens said he needs to go out so I jumped straight up and said I'd take him. I dragged him off down the road. I was glad to be outside where it was starting to get dark and smelled of wet leaves, fresh and cold. There was no one about, no one I know, anyway. I breathed in that air to try and get rid of the smoky taste in my mouth which is only from Mr Dickens' pipe but still.

On the way back through the hall I paused and stared at the plank nailed across the door frame and the perfectly ordinary door behind it. Which I suppose is where it happened.

When I got back in Mr Dickens said, 'You look pale.' I shook my head and said I was fine. He said, 'It were shocking. Zita going so suddenly were bad enough but . . . but such a horrible . . . there were police and forensic scientist fellas here and questions, questions, questions. Nowt I could tell them. I'd been out for day – and got back to find . . .'

He swallowed. 'In coffin there were nothing but her shins.' His voice cracked then and I thought, please don't cry, but he didn't. He struggled with his face for a minute and looked past me with his watery old eyes. He said, 'Well, nearly TV time. You'd best be off home, duck. Someone must be missing you.'

Well that nearly started me off so I went. A big show of

going out the front and walking up the path then back down the drive at the side.

I got in and lay on my bed for a minute and listened to the bump-shuzz, bump-shuzz of Mr Dickens and his Zimmer frame. Zimmer sounds like something quick, doesn't it? Somewhere between zip and shimmer. I could hear him coughing and spitting in the sink which he never does when I'm there, too much of a gent. Then I saw something I have never seen before. One part of the ceiling is dark. Not above my bed, further away, a big oily-looking stain. Maybe that's the place it happened, the smoke and ash sinking down right through the floorboards. I pulled the covers round me and lay there shivering. Very alone.

I try to see the high wire but all I can see is the mess below. I pinch my skin between my nails but I catch myself and stop it. There are no sharps here so it's OK. I don't keep them around. I don't even like to look at sharp points or edges, a knife left lying around, a razor blade.

But it can be beautiful when the blood comes out. You open the skin and it is such a pretty eager red and you feel fine then. Fine for a while. But I don't do that any more. I do not. The scars are old. It is a sick and stupid thing to do. I don't do it any more and I won't. But I keep away from sharp things when I can.

Five

When Doggo appeared the street lurched and I grabbed hold of a fence. It was a bright morning, had been. I had left an awful night behind me and was trying hard to smile. If you pretend to smile it can cheer you up. Some chemical message goes from your smile muscles to your brain which thinks, *hey she's happy* and you are. So I was walking along smiling all over my stupid face and trying to notice happy things like scarlet berries on a bush and a slinky black cat with lantern eyes – when there he was. I saw him a second before he saw me.

'Hi,' he said. He was wearing the mirror shades and I could see myself twinned in the lenses, cheesy pale with my hair sticking up everywhere.

'Did you say?'

'What?'

'You'd better not have fucking said.'

I looked round. It wasn't like he could murder me in broad daylight in the street. We stood there for a minute. 'What you doing later?' he said.

'Nothing.'

He kept shuffling about and looking over his shoulder, shifty as hell. 'Duke's Head, dinnertime?'

'Do you mean lunch?' I said.

'Oh I do beg your pardon, *lunch*.'

'No way,' I said. I let go of the fence and tried to push past him but he stepped in front of me. We did a kind of shuffling dance.

'Let me go in.'

'Duke's Head. Later on then? Fiveish.'

I couldn't look in his face for fear of seeing my own. I thought about screaming, But what about the police?

'K, then,' I said.

He let me pass. 'Don't fucking say,' he warned and stalked off, his shoulders up to his ears.

I watched him go. The light fizzling on the wet path stung like lime. My smile had fled a million miles away. I kept both footsoles on the ground. Mrs Banks opened the door to bring in her milk.

'Morning, Lamb,' she said. 'Coming in?'

I went inside remembering certain things like her handbag and the scorches on the table. I half expected her to sack me on the spot but she only smiled and said, 'You OK?'

'Yeah ta.' I tried to look normal, whatever normal is these days. It was warm and steamy in her kitchen and smelled of washing-powder and coffee. Roy was in the sitting room watching a Pingu video.

'He's got a bit of a snuffle,' Mrs Banks said, 'so I kept him off nursery.' The cruet set was still on the mat on the table. She didn't mention it. She obviously wasn't planning to sack me because she'd had some new keys cut and gave me one, which is ridiculously trusting. I asked what she wanted me to do. She said, 'Upstairs could all do with a good clean round and other than that just a bit of ironing.' She stared at me for a minute as if there was something else she wanted to say. I stared back till she looked away.

'I'll get on then,' I said but before I could get the hoover out she said, 'Look, Lamb, why not sit down and have a coffee first. I want to have a word.' I thought, uh-ho, here it comes. A vision of the handbag flashed past my eyes so vividly she could probably see it too.

She had a pot all ready, a cafetière, not instant, and she said, 'Hot milk?' putting a little jug into the microwave.

'Black,' I said and sat down.

She gave me my coffee and offered me something to eat. 'Nice piece of toast? Fruit cake?' I told her I'd had breakfast, thanks very much. I get so fed up with people trying to get me to eat. They probably think I'm anorexic. Well I'm not. Maybe I was verging on it once but not now. I just like to be light. I've got small bones and I like to see them and anyway you can't think clearly all clogged up with food.

The microwave pinged and she poured a froth of milk into her coffee and sat down. She blew across her cup before she sipped. 'You look a bit peaky,' she said. 'I don't know anything about you, Lamb. I've been wondering. Do you . . . do you live alone?'

She's never asked me a personal thing before and I didn't know how to take it. I mean whether to tell her to mind her own business or what. Because my business is my business and nobody else's. Right? But it was cosy in the kitchen and her face was very pink and for the first time I noticed a mesh of lines under her eyes so maybe she is old enough to be Doggo's mother after all.

I got the job with her through Mrs Harcourt, who I do on Mondays. I thought they were friends but now I think it's more like mere acquaintances. I only had to write one lot of references for the first woman I cleaned for, the American woman, and after that it was word of mouth. Easy as pie. I would never dare to have a cleaner, even if I had a house. To have someone you hardly know in the most intimate corners of your house. To trust someone, who could be anyone, like that.

They're so completely different in their attitude, Mrs Harcourt and Mrs Banks. Mrs Harcourt treats me like dirt. When I arrive first thing on Monday mornings there's always a tower of greasy pans waiting for me from the night before. 'I don't like to put them in the dishwasher,' she says. 'They've got a very special finish that needs the personal touch,' and she does a charming laugh. I wish she could hear herself. And the vacuum's always full so I have to empty it out before I can even start on the carpets. And once she asked me to change the sheets in the *master bedroom* as she will call it and when I did I found that she'd come on in the night.

Anyway, I sat there looking at Mrs Banks' pink face and feeling guilt expanding like a balloon inside me. She was as good as me at the waiting game though and eventually it was me who cracked and said, 'Yes, I prefer living alone.' She looked down and her hands were jumping about as if electric shocks were shooting through them. I couldn't stop myself staring at the table mat.

She said, 'I don't want you to take this the wrong way, Lamb, but you do . . . you do have *somewhere*, don't you? I mean you're not homeless.'

I tried not to laugh but I did laugh a bit, then I said, 'No, of course not, I have a very nice home,' seeing the inverted commas flashing.

But then I felt insulted. I mean why did she think that? Do I *look* homeless?

As if she was reading my mind she gave a reassuring smile and said, 'Not that you look homeless,' and then I, contrary Mary as my mum used to say, thought, what does *homeless* look like? She said, 'It's just that you never mention anyone and Neville said he asked your address and you were evasive and I asked Margaret Harcourt if she knew and she said come to think of it she didn't. So I just wondered.'

I was starting to feel pretty narked. All these people

discussing me behind my back. Getting into my space. 'Does it matter?' I said.

She thought for a minute. 'Well it might be handy to be able to get in touch if . . . but no, I suppose it doesn't matter very much,' she said, 'just as you like.' I felt like getting up and stomping out of there but somehow I just didn't have the energy. She smiled. 'Sure you won't have something? Nice yoghurts in the fridge.' Her smile was a kind of surrender.

'K,' I said amazing myself. Maybe I was surrendering back. It was a kiwi-fruit yogurt, low-fat, and I have to admit it was good. She smiled with satisfaction as I ate it and I thought, well at least it will shut her up. It really gets on my nerves people trying to get me to eat. It's all about them, that's my theory, it makes them feel better about stuffing themselves if they can see me eat. Then Roy came in asking, 'What's acid indigestion?' and she said, 'Oh dear, has the video finished?' I escaped and did the ironing.

When I left Mrs Banks' no one was out there waiting. It was OK. Just because I'd said I'd be at the Duke's Head at fiveish I didn't have to be. I wandered about a bit. I went for a walk in the park and stood by the duck pond. The water looked hard and green like enamel, with arrow ridges stretching out behind the ducks, as if everything was frozen – but it wasn't. Then a brown leaf circled down from a tree and landed on the surface and everything flinched and got moving again. And noises started though I hadn't realised it was quiet. I thought, *God, Lamb, get a grip.* Does that happen to you? Everything stopping and then starting up again?

There was a baby in a padded suit throwing crusts to the ducks only the ducks weren't looking. They were on the verge of sinking anyway with all the bread they'd already had. Pigeons were jumping round the baby's feet and he shrieked with laughter and overbalanced. He just sat there in the middle of the flock with his legs stuck out in front of him. He started tearing into the bread himself but his mother picked him up under her arm and hooked the bread out with her finger like it was going to choke him to death or something.

Even though it was so cold I sat on a bench. I was thinking about when I first left my mum's friends' house. There is a time which is a blank – but sometimes certain things come into focus. Almost like the shreds of dreams. They swarm below me showing me how far there is to fall. The colours down there are terrible.

There was a warehouse. It wasn't winter but it was cold. I hadn't been sleeping rough long. I met a girl and we got talking. She took me to where she slept. We had to climb through a fence with a sign that said DANGER UNEVEN GROUND! and pick our way across the dangerous ground, holes and oil shimmering rainbows even in the dark.

Inside the warehouse was a great space, like a cavern you couldn't see the edges of, and in the middle a blazing fire. It was so thick with smoke I didn't see how many people there were straightaway. More and more gathered as it grew late. People smoked, shot up, drank cider, dogs scratched and yawned. Someone played a guitar and two girls started dancing, twining a scarf about each other's necks. I lost the girl I came with, she was with some man.

In the morning cold light leaked from the roof on to the sleeping heads. I got up and went out for a pee, picking over the litter of bottles, needles, rags of cloth. I went back to get my stuff and a guy called me over. He was shooting up. 'Give us a hand,' he said. He'd tied a sock round his arm. The needle probed the grey flesh but he couldn't find a vein. I tightened the sock for him and watched the needle pierce a slow green worm of vein. I saw the light come into his eyes. He offered me some crack. I balanced for a moment on the point of saying yes. Trying it. Why not? Wanting what? Maybe to belong.

I looked around. No one would care. But others were waking by then, two smoke-faced girls kissing with wet tongues, an old man pissing against the inside wall. It was not me, not for me. I could not get dragged in. I got up and left there fast.

See, it is best to be alone.

Six

I got my balance back by concentrating and by luck. You can't control the outside things but sometimes they go right. For a week the sun shone every day. Mrs Banks didn't notice the scorch-marks on the table, or if she did, didn't connect them to me. Mrs Harcourt had a Jacuzzi thing installed in the *en-suite* bath. Mrs Brown-Withers bought a much better hoover and even Mr Dickens stayed off dodgy subjects and was quite cheery. I hadn't turned up at the Duke's Head to see Doggo – and nothing bad had happened. He hadn't stalked me or turned up outside Mrs Banks' house again. He'd melted off into whatever world it was he belonged to. I was off the hook.

Helped by all these things, I got myself back on the high wire, arms out, poised, eyes straight ahead, because whatever you do you must not look down. Everything was fine. Fine and balanced. OK, so I sometimes felt lonely. I took the whole Doggo episode as a warning. He had nearly messed things up for me. Or I had nearly let him.

Sometimes I did lie in bed and wonder what would have happened if I *had* gone to meet him. What would have followed from that? Not that I regretted it. Not that I even liked him. It was surprising how often I wondered. But then so little happens in my life I do wonder each thing to death.

I'm not really lonely. It's just that sometimes when I'm free the cellar isn't big enough, the city isn't big enough. I get restless in my bones. One low bright restless afternoon I scuffed my boots on the path all the way into town which is miles. I went to the reference library. I love the serious/sleazy atmosphere in there. Two main types of people – students studying and dodgy old men looking at the racing pages and clearing great chunters of phlegm out of their throats into their hankies.

The old men had all the papers out. I never read the papers anyway. Who wants to know the news? I like to read the books. Not the fiction, the lies – but about things, *real* things in the world. But this time I got a book down without even looking what it was and sat with my chin resting on my hands as if I was reading, but really I was miles away. Couldn't tell you where but it was peaceful.

In the library it's like the world has gone into slow-motion, drowsy and warm with people rustling papers and murmuring to each other. It reminds me of school, how some summer afternoons you could practically drop off to sleep listening to the teacher droning on and on. It's safe too. You're not alone but you're anonymous. Nobody will bother you as long as you are quiet.

This could be my life. An easy job that earns me enough money just to live and leaves me room to concentrate. A pillow on which to lay my head. Peaceful afternoons in the library minding my own business. Small and private and one thing after another thing with nothing strange. There are worse lives than that.

The man next to me smelt homeless. I tried to work out the different elements of that smell. There's old grease, pee and smoke all mixed up, a kind of trousery jumble-sale smell. I sneaked a look under the table. The hems of his trousers were all frayed over his swollen-bunion-shaped tennis shoes. His nose was like a huge hairy strawberry. He caught me looking and leered so I could see the last few pegs of his brown teeth. I looked down and pretended to be engrossed in the book which turned out to be about lighthouses.

It was OK. Then suddenly a voice said, 'Lamb?'

I shrieked. A librarian looked over, her eyebrows shooting into orbit. It was him, Doggo. My mouth went dry. He sat down beside me. I scooted my chair away, screeching it against the floor.

'Shut the fuck up,' he said.

'Go away,' I hissed. He looked up from behind his shades at the librarian and huddled into his jacket. We sat in silence for a minute. The old man had the racing pages open and was marking horses.

'What do you want?' I said. 'How did you know I was here?'

'You think I'm here because of you?' My hands were shaking so I could hardly turn the pages but I flicked through the book anyway, seeing nothing.

'Why are you here then?'

'You mean some dumb-fuck like me who can't even read?'

'I didn't mean that.' There was a pause. I looked at him. 'Can you?' I said.

'What?'

'Read.'

'Oh fuck off. The cat sat on the mat. Yeah, I can fucking read.'

'Congratulations.'

'Sarky bitch. OK, yeah, I followed you.'

The librarian was staring and the old man openly listening. I shut my mouth. I was thinking hard. As I'd walked into town I'd maybe had that feeling that someone was watching me, that sensation between the shoulder blades, that feeling of eyes. I'd even turned round once but seen no one. Thought, don't be paranoid. Who'd want to follow you? Who do you think you are, the centre of the universe? as my mum used to say.

I made sure to keep breathing. I made sure to keep calm, seem calm at least. Not like he could do anything to me in the library.

'I didn't say a thing to Mrs Banks,' I said, 'if that's what you're scared of. But if you don't leave me alone . . .'

'Shhhh,' he went. I looked up. The librarian's face was all pursed up. Doggo was going to get me chucked out at this rate. If I got chucked out they might not let me in again and it was one of my best places when it was cold. I smiled at the librarian but she didn't smile back.

'Come outside,' he whispered.

'No. Go away. What do you want?'

'I want help.'

I looked at him then and got an unwanted glimpse of myself in the mirror shades.

'Help?'

He nodded. His mouth looked very soft amongst the glossy black of his beard.

'Look, let's get out of here. That bitch hasn't taken her eyes off me.'

'Who do you think you are, the centre of the universe?' I said. Then I felt sorry. He was right anyway, she hadn't. He looked younger than I remembered. Maybe not much older than me. Young and jumpy and needing help from me. No one had ever needed help from me.

'You a student?' he said.

'Yeah. Why?'

'What in?'

I focused my eyes on the book.

'Lighthouses.'

'*Lighthouses?* You can't be a student in lighthouses.'

'Lighthouses is only part of it.'

'Yeah?' He pulled the book away from me and flicked through, stopping at a dingy photo. A lighthouse with a seagull in front of it like a flying moustache. He lost the wariness for a minute. 'When I was a kid I wanted to be a lighthouse keeper.' He moved his chair nearer to mine and even though it was warm in the library I shivered. He smelled like tobacco and mushroom soup.

I strained my thigh away from the warmth of his. It was weird though because when he said that about wanting to be a lighthouse keeper I remembered that so did I once. I wanted to live in a lighthouse on a rock, only not be bothered with the lights and shipwrecks. I just liked the idea of being in a tower of rounded rooms with waves crashing against it and nobody else for miles.

'You coming outside then?' he said. He stood up. The librarian had her eyes fixed on us now like she was waiting for a scene. It was a moment of choice, like a hinge, a door swinging this way or that. Saying no might have been the end of it, the door swung shut. On the other hand he might just have gone out and waited for me anyway. I looked at his soft mouth. He needed my help, he actually said that, *my* help. I stood up.

I shoved the book back on a shelf, probably not the right shelf. I couldn't think straight. Old strawberry nose looked up and practically winked, probably thinking I'd been picked up, maybe he'll try *his* luck next time.

It felt very strange to be walking down the library stairs with someone. I'm so used to walking alone with empty air all around me and now there was someone by my side. Someone I didn't know. It felt like the world was tilting.

Seven

When we got outside the library he stopped. There were two dogs tied up. I was about to say how mean of someone to leave two dogs tied up like that but he crouched down to untie them.

'They yours?' I said instead.

He just gave me a look. One of the dogs was tiny and bright-eyed. It did a frisking dance of pleasure; the other one, the same sort only bigger, dragged itself up and yawned.

'What are they?' I said. 'What make?'

'Jack Russells.'

'So what do you want?' I said. 'What help?'

'You never fucking turned up,' he said.

'I'll just go back in if you talk to me like that.'

He stared at the ground for a minute. 'OK,' he said. 'Yeah.'

'So?'

'Mind if we get out of town?'

'Where?'

'Just out of town.'

He looped the leads round his wrist and started walking. I didn't have to follow him. It was another chance. I could have gone back up the library steps, but I didn't. It was OK as long as we were in public. Nothing he could do to me in public. I was in control. And any minute I wanted I could walk away.

We hurried along, taking the whole width of the path, the two of us and the dogs. A woman with a double buggy had to steer into a doorway to give us room. She flicked me the filthiest look I have ever seen.

'Norma!' Doggo said, tugging at the lead of the little one who was skittering about under our feet and tripping us up. The other one just plodded along with his head down. 'What's he called?' I said.

'Gordon,' he said. I nearly laughed. I mean, *Gordon* and *Norma*. We kept on walking for a bit till we got out of the city centre.

'Where are we going?' I said.

'Pub?'

'If it's money you need I can't help you there.'

'Let's get to pub,' he said.

I was watching the way he kept looking round everywhere as if he thought *he* was being followed. His hands were blue with cold. He had LOVE and HATE tattooed on his knuckles. Not the usual blurry home-made schoolboy effect, ink and a compass point, but ornate lettering and in a different colour on each knuckle. The fancy letters were stretched out over his knuckle bones. He saw me staring at his hands. 'Want to take Norma for a bit?' he said.

'K.' It felt nice holding the lead with a live creature on the end of it, like a sort of connection. She didn't notice the change though, just kept looping about and tugging and stopping to sniff at stuff.

We got to the Duke's Head and had to sit outside because of the dogs. It was freezing. We sat in what they laughingly call a beer-garden where there were some kids skate-boarding about.

'So?' I said.

45

'Just get a couple of pints in,' he said.

I don't know why I did. Being ordered about by a complete stranger is not my usual thing. I stood there a minute wondering whether to tell him where to go. 'What about some crisps and all?' he said.

When I got back with the slopping pints and a packet of prawn cocktail, I said, 'What do you want? Apart from the pint.'

He slurped half his drink in one go, then ripped the crisps open. He crammed about half in his mouth and shoved the packet at me. I took a crisp and nibbled the edge.

'Well?'

'You got a place?' he said.

'Yeah, sort of.'

'Not one of them student halls?'

'No.'

'You sharing?'

'No. No. I like to be alone.'

'Good.' He got his tobacco out of his pocket and rolled a fag.

'Why good?'

'What you doing?'

I looked down and saw what I was doing. It was a thing I did as a kid, nibble and nibble round a crisp so it gets smaller and smaller. You can make a single crisp last for ages like that. 'Nothing.' I chucked the half-nibbled crisp to Norma who snapped it up, mid-air.

'So, what do you want?' I said.

'I need somewhere to crash. Lie low for a bit.'

'What's wrong with your mum's?' I could hardly look at him for fear of seeing myself. 'Don't you ever take your shades off?' I said. I hate talking to a person when you can't see their eyes and if you ask me only posers wear sunglasses when it's not sunny.

He looked round then took them off. I'd forgotten his eyes were such a cool sharp grey. They made me flinch. He shook his head and took a deep breath like someone about to jump. 'Look. I'm in deep shit. There's reasons I can't go to my mum's, OK?'

'But why ask *me*? You don't even know me.'

'Yeah well, exactly. No one would come looking for me at yours, would they?'

'But how do you know I won't . . . I don't know . . . call the police or something.'

'Because I know you,' he said, reaching across the table to touch my hand. He took my breath away saying that. *I know you*. His fingertips were slippery ice.

I couldn't help the smile. 'No you don't,' I said.

'So?' He squeezed the tip of my middle finger between his finger and thumb. I pulled my hand away but the sensation stayed there. One finger-end in all the big cold world.

I nearly got pulled in. At that moment I wanted to help. It was a pity I couldn't but no way could I let him in. The cellar was mine and mine alone. I was quite safe and balanced. And not scared. It was quite simple. He just had to lie low for a time, well I know about that. I am the expert. Except I would never in a million years ask anyone else for help. It puts you in their power. There was a kind of glow in me from his words. *I know you*.

I had to concentrate. I took a sip of beer. His was nearly finished. 'Did you steal your mum's bag?' I said.

'What the fuck's that got to do . . .'

'Am I supposed to be scared of all this swearing?' I said.

He did a weird kind of laugh and looked at me hard, a different sort of look as if he was weighing me up. 'How old are you?'

'*I* got stuck with that bloody bag,' I said. 'I saw it in

47

the kitchen after you'd gone. I didn't know what to do so I took it.'

He laughed. *Laughed.* 'Why?' he said.

'I don't know. Because you told me not to say you'd been. She left a note saying it was gone and I thought she'd think it was me that brought it back and then what?'

'Fuck. So where is it?'

'On a shelf,' I said, 'at my place.'

'Which is . . . ?'

I could feel myself starting to get in a stew, partly the effect of the beer which I haven't drunk for ages. I don't drink much and I don't smoke, I don't do drugs or sex. I am a vice-free zone, me. It would be the most stupid thing to take Doggo back to the cellar and I wouldn't. He was a stranger. Even though he knew me. He could have been a killer for all I knew. But I was starting to like the cold clearness of his eyes.

Then, by coincidence, a guy called Simon wandered into the beer-garden as if he was looking for someone. Doggo shoved his shades back on fast. Simon was wearing his usual Metallica T-shirt and reeking of patchouli. I mean coincidence because I can go for weeks without talking to anyone except Mr Dickens and the ladies then all in one day there's Doggo and Simon. Simon is someone I was at school with, then I bumped into him here one day. He came to Sheffield to go to university, dropped out but stuck around. It's amazing to me that people my age are halfway to degrees already. I didn't think I'd meet anyone I knew in this city. I didn't want to meet anyone who knew me ever again. But Si was always out of it at school, and he probably never heard anything about me, if there was even anything to hear. He's that dreamy sort. Lives on his own little planet behind his long hair and thick glasses. Top of everything at school, probably got about sixteen A levels. But he doesn't do anything now except take drugs

48

and play keyboards in an awful band called The Sticky Labels.

'Hey, Jo,' Simon said, squinting at me through his smeary glasses, and I could have killed him. Doggo raised one eyebrow at me and I noticed a scar in it, rucked up like a bit of bad sewing.

'Jo, hey?' he murmured.

'Come to party?' Simon said. I nearly said I wouldn't, then I thought, well maybe if Doggo came too so I said, 'K then. Can I bring my friend?' but Doggo shook his head. 'Nah, you go,' he went. 'Parties aren't my thing.'

I wanted to say that parties weren't my thing either but it was too late so I said, 'Cool,' and stood up. I should have been glad. Now I could go and he wouldn't follow me and that would probably be it for ever. Doggo looked down into his pint. 'You can finish mine,' I said shoving the glass towards him.

'Cheers,' he said. 'See you around.'

'Cheers,' Simon said. His wreck of a Beetle was parked on the road outside all loaded up with amplifiers and Tortilla Chips. The traffic was so bad it took about half an hour to go a hundred yards. He stopped outside someone's house and went in and was in there ages, then he came out and said, 'Sorry, you should have come in too, had to, you know, sample the goods.' He looked as if his eyes had melted.

He put a thundering tape on. 'This is us last Saturday,' he said, thrashing his head around and beating the steering wheel like a drum. I wanted to scream. Of course I didn't want to see Doggo again, it was just that we hadn't finished the conversation. I wanted to get that conversation finished. I hate leaving ends trailing like that. It's the sort of thing that keeps me awake.

Simon stopped the car to get some vodka from Oddbins. I went in with him and just stood looking at all the bottles of chardonnay and Chablis. I thought how the party would be with everybody stoned and drunk and how out of it I'd feel like always. People are so boring when they're drunk and they think everything's funny and it's even worse when they're stoned.

I didn't get back into the car. I said, 'Sorry. Just remembered something.'

Simon shrugged and said, 'Oh yeah.'

I said, 'Yeah.'

He got into the car and slammed the door. 'Shame. But maybe see you around?' he said out of the car window. He gave me a long meaningful look – which was spoiled by the fingerprints on his lenses and the moss growing on the bridge – and drove off. I stood there for a minute trying to think what to do next. It was miles back to the pub and it was coming on to rain. I should go back to the cellar. That would be the safest thing. Doggo was sure to have gone anyway. Finding someone else to help him lie low. But I thought I might as well walk back and just see. Not as if I had anything else lined up.

It was that time in the afternoon just as it begins to get dark when things huddle together and the lit-up shops look cosy and inviting. The rain wasn't actually falling, it just hung in the air soaking everything. I only had my denim jacket and the denim sucked up the rain like a sponge. The road was bumper to bumper with buses and cars, their lights smearing runny colours on the wet road.

A crowd of students came out of the off-licence with clanking carrier bags, all laughing and practically knocking me off the path. One of them called out *Bailey's, Natasha* and they all keeled over laughing. I felt like yelling, I'll tell you where to stick your Bailey's, *Natasha*. I know it's ridiculous to feel left out when you don't even know the people you are left out of, or even want to know them.

I walked along towards the Duke's Head which is a long walk and the rims of my ears ached with cold. I felt weak and thought maybe I needed to eat. I was just going past Tesco when I thought that so I went in to get something for later on.

It was blindingly bright inside and smelt safe and bready. I picked up a basket and walked round choosing things as if I was someone else. I chose a packet of croissants and some Irish butter and French strawberry jam. Then I changed my mind and put back the croissants and got scones and a tub of clotted cream. I even looked at a piece of chicken but there was blood smudged against the cellophane, and anyway, how would I cook it? Then I lost my appetite seeing the greedy baskets of the people. All that stuff that would just go through them and be in the sewer pipes by tomorrow. I left my stupid basket on the floor and went out where at least you could breathe. It was properly dark now and the lights were a scribbly blur.

I kept on walking towards the pub but then a carrier bag got tangled round my feet, I don't know where it came from, it can't have blown because there was no wind. It was just a wet white bag flapping around my feet but it made my heart go wild. I hate the way rubbish is everywhere, don't you? All sorts, even great big carrier bags just lying about in the street. I kicked it away but it clung to my shoe so I had to kick and kick. It was just an empty bag. Nothing to get upset about. But my spirits sank down into my boots. If I found him, then what? It was raining properly now and the damp knees of my jeans were making me itch. Best to be alone, it really is.

Eight

I went back to the cellar. The cobbles glistened greasily and I thought I would slip. The light switch isn't quite by the door so you have to go in in the dark. I go in with my eyes shut and fumble for the switch. Sometimes I can't find it straightaway and my hand scrabbles at the wall, my stupid mind thinking I'm in the wrong place or worse, maybe when I switch the light on someone will be there, waiting.

Lights are meant to make a place look cosy but the light in Mr Dickens' cellar is dismal. A dull cobwebby bulb which emphasises the dark outside its reach and presses shadows into every gap and crease. The bit of cellar I live in is cramped up in one corner and in the day you don't notice the rest but at night you can see that there is a big area where the light doesn't reach. There are ladders, rusty saws, cardboard boxes, saw-horses, fringed lampshades, all sorts of stuff laced together with cobwebs and shadows, and in the day you can stand there and name the things and not be scared at all. Not that I'm scared anyway. What is there to be scared of?

I tried to make it as cheerful as I could. I put the Calor gas on, even though I'm worried about the fumes. There was something on the radio about a girl who died from carbon monoxide fumes. Just dropped off to sleep beside her gas fire, never to wake up. But the cellar is so draughty I don't think that will happen to me. I made a cup of tea and put the radio on for company. I like listening to Radio 4 best, the calm sensible voices telling you calm sensible things, but I always switch off for the news. The sorts of things it fills your head with, you do not need to know.

I could tell it was going to be one of those nights. Usually I'm all right. I read or just sleep or sometimes there's a play on the radio which I love, it's such a rest from myself – but it wasn't about to be one of those nights. I don't put the light off when I go to sleep but that isn't for any particular reason. I just don't.

I felt all tensed up as if my belly was full of question marks and it was mainly about Doggo. The clear vision of my balance was fading. The balance alone. Maybe being alone too much is dangerous? Maybe having a friend would help? The voice was telling me to leave him be. But maybe the voice was *wrong*. Or maybe it was tricking me, tricking me away from a friendship that would be fine. Which is the good voice and which the saboteur?

I heard a voice. It was above me in the kitchen and it wasn't Mr Dickens' voice and there were footsteps too. My heart nearly stopped. There's never anybody there except for Meals on Wheels and they only stay about two minutes. The footsteps were quick and the voice was a woman's. I reached and switched off the radio. There were sounds like running water and things happening in the kitchen. I thought, calm down, Lamb, and I did sit down on the edge of my bed but not very calmly. I thought I should switch off the light but I couldn't do that. I stayed very still with the cup of tea between my hands, just watching the steam rise off it, straining my ears to hear what next.

I heard a laugh and then the bump-shuzz bump-shuzz of Mr Dickens. The back door opened and a girly voice called out, 'Doughnut, Doughnut, come on, boy, time to do your stuff.' I shot up quick and switched off the light because if she went in the garden she would see the light on and then . . . Anyway I switched it off and stood by the door with my hands all wet and the black smothering me, a blanket in my eyes and mouth, and I started to shrink. I think my eyes were shut I don't know. She was out there saying, '*Really*, Uncle,' about something or other I don't know. I waited till I stopped shrinking and I must have opened my eyes because then I saw it wasn't totally dark, some of the kitchen light had spilled against the window and I could see the patterns of cobwebs with all the dry old legs and wings.

The voice kept calling until Doughnut was back in and it seemed like hours later the door banged shut and I heard the footsteps leave the kitchen and then the front door bang and a car drive away. I put the light back on and looked round at the room. Bleak is definitely the word but at least it's somewhere. You just have to focus on the light places and not the dark. Inside you and without. I was shivering. When you're cold and you sweat it's the worst kind of cold and I was still wet from the rain. I took off my jeans and hung them on a lawn-mower in front of the heater and got into bed.

I put the radio back on and tried to listen to some programme about how chimpanzees can have a vocabulary of up to two hundred words. They don't speak but do a sort of sign language like deaf people. They can even make up sentences. One said *Why have you put me in prison?* when he was locked up in a cage.

I listened to that as hard as I could. It was no good trying to sleep. Maybe I simply wasn't tired enough. I lay stiffly in the bed for ages before I gave up trying. Anxiety can make you itch, really, cause your skin to crawl. I got up and put on my damp clothes and opened the door into the garden. A thin smear of moonlight lit up a tangle of twigs. I went round the front. A slit of light showed between Mr Dickens'

54

curtains but all the other houses were dark though one had left a pumpkin lantern burning in the window and its grin flickered like it was licking its jagged lips. I felt I should tiptoe through the sleeping streets. The only other living thing was a cat. It glanced at me with startled sizzling eyes and sped away. I was an intruder in its world.

I wonder where in the city Doggo is, inside or out, awake or asleep? How far away from me, maybe quite near. Maybe in a doorway somewhere with his dogs. I don't like that thought. It brings back the lost feeling of not knowing where to lay my head. For two years I had nowhere certain to lay my head. And then the hospital with the green honeycomb blankets you could stick your fingers through. There was a woman there, still as a statue. She was marbly blue and it was wonderful how still she was. When her husband came to visit he'd put a fag between her lips and ages later smoke would trickle out.

People in there were fish or dogs or puppets and a clown. But there was one real man, he was called Russ. He always wore Hawaiian shirts. He made me laugh, wiggling a caterpillar eyebrow at me in the therapy group. And when I laughed the taste was bright in my mouth, bright as his Hawaiian shirt, bright as a fruit I had forgotten. It was when he left that I decided to leave too. Said goodbye to no one except the statue woman, who said nothing, of course, but let a thread of drool escape her lips. I dabbed it off for her and tucked the tissue up her sleeve. And then I strolled on out.

Now I have to keep myself safe. I can't tell if Doggo's safe for me or not. Of course he isn't safe. The voice is good and right. But something in me lights up when he comes into my mind. He *knows* me. Nothing in the world has lit me up like that for years.

I walk along a kerb, my arms out, balancing. I walk on till

my feet ache and I am too tired even to think. When I get back I stand and look at the house where Mr Dickens lives and I do. Though nobody knows I do. And then I go back in to wait.

Nine

M onday was Mrs Harcourt and Mr Dickens. The right way round. I could have my bath first and do some actual cleaning – some work is essential for my peace of mind – then relax with Mr Dickens. As long as Mr Dickens would stick to cheerful subjects. Being with Mr Dickens in his warm and fusty room was probably the most relaxed I ever got.

Mrs Harcourt had left me this note which is a typical example:

> *Dear Lamb, please vacuum hall, stairs, landing, master bedroom, Simon's room, spare room. Pay particular attention to stair edges, please!! Please mop bathroom (inc en suite) and kitchen floors – kitchen floor needs to be well rinsed or tiles look dull. Please turn out cutlery drawer and under-sink cupboard if you've time. Fresh shelf-lining paper in big kitchen drawer. Money in envelope.*
> *Best wishes, Myra Harcourt.*

Best wishes, hahaha. And in the *en suite* which is hideous brass and peach someone hadn't even flushed the bog. First of all (after flushing) I ran myself a bath. The bath is triangular, deeper than most baths. I tried out the new Jacuzzi effect. It was strange and wonderful, the bubbly swish of it, milky with the Clarins stuff sloshed in, like being in a milk-shake machine. I shampooed my hair and started the chores in Mrs Harcourt's silky dressing gown while my clothes did a short cycle in the machine.

While I was drying my hair I stared in the mirror which has little lights round the edge as if she thinks she's a superstar. I looked hard, wondering what Doggo had seen when he stared at me but it was just me and nothing more special than that. I do look young, even to myself, as if I haven't lived the last couple of years at all. A kind of space in the eyes. Cheek-bones pitted from teenage acne, cracked lips, dark fluff above the top lip, shadows underneath the eyes. The longer you look, the worse it gets.

I plucked my eyebrows and rubbed some of her wonder cream in my skin, but the only difference was it made me shiny. It took me ten minutes over my time to get the jobs done because of the long bath but I did them and got out before anyone came back which I took to be a good sign.

At lunchtime I walked past the Duke's Head and looked in the garden but there was nobody I knew. I had a Perrier and a packet of peanuts and sat at the same table outside that Doggo and I had sat at even though it was freezing. Nobody else was sitting outside. The wind was blowing a crisp bag round and round in circles making a scrapy fingernail sound and I stared at it till I was almost hypnotised. Then I went back to Mr Dickens. It was a bit early but I knew he wouldn't mind.

I rang the bell. I thought maybe the woman from last night would come to the door and tell me to go away, but it was just the usual transformation of Doughnut into a hell hound. I let myself in before he could brain himself on the door. Mr Dickens was sitting by his fire with a tray of dirty plates and stuff beside him. It took me a minute to breathe properly in the doggy air so I couldn't speak at first. Doughnut collapsed on the floor and Mr Dickens beamed. 'Ah, there you are, Lamb.' His hair is thin and fluffy like baby hair and it was all lit up from the standard lamp he was sitting under.

'Is that new?' I said. Usually it's a bit gloomy in there with only the overhead light in its brown glass shade.

'No . . . it's from front. Niece lugged it through. Nice to see you, duck. Take a seat. I'll fetch tea in a minute.'

'Niece?'

'Great niece actually. Sarah. Nice lass, you'd get on.'

I felt real danger then, like a cold grassy ripple down my back. 'She staying with you?' I said. I held my breath till he shook his head.

'No, no. She were visiting some friends – just dropped in to visit. Nice lass. She cooked me something what was it . . . risotto with some sort of bits in, nuts, get all up in my denture but didn't like to say. Not half bad otherwise. Bit of kick to it. Which you don't get with Meals on Wheels, I can tell you.'

'Didn't know you had a niece.'

'Brother's daughter's girl.' He started to struggle up.

'Sure I can't get the tea?' I could have bitten my tongue off. The day he can't do that himself any more will be a tragic one. I picked the tray up though and followed him at a Zimmer pace through into the kitchen.

'I didn't know you had a brother,' I said.

'There were three of us,' he said. 'Bob and Wilf are both . . . I'm only one that's reached ninety. Only the one offspring between three of us and we were all randy as hell. A right liability.' He gave a dirty snigger. I wondered if he'd been drinking. He does keep a bottle of Scotch tucked down by his chair. 'Nice lass, Sarah,' he added, which *had* sunk in by then. He'd got his Zimmer near the sink and was leaning perilously out to fill the kettle.

'I'll wash these things up,' I said when he'd moved out of

the way. There were little bits of rice in the sink from the risotto. 'How old is she?' I asked.

'Twenty,' he said, 'or thereabouts.'

'Same as me,' I said.

He turned. He can't turn his head so he swivelled his whole body. 'No!' he said after peering for a minute. 'I'd have put you down for sweet sixteen.'

I don't know why people think you should be so pleased to look like a kid when you're not, even if you do feel like one. 'Actually I'm twenty next week,' I said.

He turned back to his teapot. 'Flesh on her bones though,' he said. 'Nice pair of Bristols.'

'What!' I went. I couldn't stop myself. I mean, *Bristols*.

He did his dirty laugh and starting hacking at a ginger cake with a potato peeler. 'She did me a mop-round,' he said, 'so there's no need for you to lift a finger this afternoon. Just keep me company.'

'Great,' I said thinking she could at least have washed up. But I had no heart for cleaning. Really I just wanted to think about Doggo. Or, to *not* think about him. I didn't know what to talk about so I asked if I could look at his photos again. He asked why. I said I was doing a thesis about fashion.

'Thesis?' he said.

'For my degree.'

'Didn't say you were a student,' he said.

'Art school,' I said and he looked surprised. I don't why that should be so surprising.

He nodded at the sideboard. 'Help yourself, duck.'

But it is rubbish about art school, that's the last thing I would ever do. Since I was about three all I really wanted to be was a doctor. I used to toddle about with one of those plastic hammers banging people on the knee and bandaging their fingers together. Then when I got older I could see myself in a white coat, rushing importantly from ward to ward, stethoscope slung around my neck. In a way I *still* want to be a doctor but I do realise I've totally blown it now.

Mr Dickens poured the tea and rabbited on while I turned the pages of the album very slowly, watching the tissue flutter between the stiff card. I stared and stared at Zita in all her fantastic dresses and hats and especially the wigs. When I got to the page with Zita holding the baby I stopped.

'Whose baby?'

'Ah . . .'

I could have kicked myself when I saw Mr Dickens' face cave in. His eyes went dull as if there'd been a power cut inside him.

'It's OK,' I said.

But he swallowed and said, 'Belinda, our little lass. We had her three weeks. It were what they now call a cot death.'

We sat quiet for a minute then listening to Doughnut wheezing and the clock ticking. I was thinking back to what he'd said before, that there was only the one offspring between the three brothers. I wanted to ask if he didn't count Belinda just because she had died. Do you count babies that have died as offspring or not? It seemed like an important question. I wanted to ask that but how could I?

'Two tragedies of my life,' Mr Dickens said. 'Cot death – and then Zita. I do wonder if their deaths had been more run of mill it might not have been so . . .' He stared at the plastic flames then he did a long sigh like he was going to breathe his whole soul out. 'On the other hand,' he said, 'they would still be . . .'

'Yes,' I said fast to stop him saying it.

He looked up. 'Sarah says I must get someone on to garden,' he said and I breathed out. He's good like that, Mr Dickens. Brave. He took a long slurpy sip of tea. 'Know anyone?'

I shook my head.

'She reckons tree roots'll be getting in foundations. Eat your cake. It'll be hers one day.'

'What?'

'This.' He patted the arm of his chair and I thought, *that* old thing. Then I realised what he meant. He meant it all.

We talked a bit more about this and that and then I let Doughnut out into the back garden, stood there looking into the brown leafy mess as it got dark. A bird was warbling on the wet branch of a nearly-bare tree. Somewhere there was a crackle and a bang and a skinny silver streak in the sky. Someone having an early firework party.

'When's she coming back?' I asked as I put my jacket on.

'Who?'

'Sarah.'

'Don't know,' he said. 'She comes and goes, you know. Take it.' He nodded at the album. 'If it's useful for your whatsit.'

'Thesis. Sure?'

'Long as you look after it. You haven't touched your cake.'

I picked up the crumby lump and the album.

'Ta,' I said. His eyes were bright as a child's. I had a stupid desire to kiss him. I mean the *cleaner* kissing him.

'And if you think of anyone . . . for garden.'

'Course,' I said, thinking, that's a laugh, *me* know someone.

I went down and stared at Zita and made myself stare at the baby which was just a blur in a bonnet and a shawl. It was only seven o'clock. I couldn't eat the cake but I needed something. I fancied some beer so I thought I'd go to the pub. It's an OK pub, the Duke's Head.

I sat inside because it was wet and empty in the beer-garden, no sign of a single person there. I drank half a pint of beer and ate a packet of prawn crisps. I flicked through a

Sunday-supplement magazine someone had left on a seat. There was an article about artificial human parts, how they can now grow them, bits of bone and stuff. How one day they might be able to grow a whole new human heart. I thought about it, how maybe you could have a shiny clean new heart put in, a heart that had never beaten in a chest before, or felt anything, that had never fallen in love or been broken. But there was no one to say it to so I finished my drink and went.

Ten

It was a Mrs Banks morning. Doggo didn't show up. If he'd wanted to find me he would have been lurking about like before. I'd woken with a feeling in my bones that he'd be there but my bones turned out to be wrong, there was no one, only an old bloke with hedge clippers giving me a funny look. I went in, thinking how glad I was. Mrs Banks was out but she'd left a note:

> Dear Lamb, there's some left-over curry in the fridge, do eat it up. Would you tidy the living room and water all the plants, please, and yet again there's ironing. I'll pay you on Friday – but call this evening if you're short.
> Take care. Marion.

I did everything and then stuck around for a bit in case she came back. I wouldn't have minded seeing her. I kept looking out of the window to see if anyone was out there. It's natural to be curious about someone when they've said they *know you* in that way. When they've squeezed the tip of your middle finger and made it glow. Not that I expected to see him ever again, or even wanted to. I cleaned the kitchen worktops and emptied the bin because there wasn't enough in what she said to last me two hours. I tried some of her lipstick but it was too sugary pink for me, too pretty, it made the rest of me look worse. I scrubbed it off.

I stared at a picture of Roy, a nursery-school photo with a cardboard frame, trying to see Doggo in him – and there was something apart from the dark hair, I don't know what, just a look, like you wouldn't be surprised to hear that they were brothers.

I only had the quickest shower, using the minimum of shower gel, but I scrubbed the bath after me and picked all the hairs – most of them not even mine – out of the plug-hole. I scooped the curry into an ice-cream carton and put it in my satchel, not that I wanted it, but I didn't want to seem ungrateful.

When I left the house I looked up and down the road but there was no one and nothing, just an empty street and a pile of rusty hedge-trimmings where the man had been. I felt just about as empty as that street.

The afternoon was free. And the day stretched ahead of me so far I couldn't see the end of it. Being free isn't as great as people make out. It can be the saddest and most tedious thing. I wandered along to the Duke's Head and through to the beer-garden just for the hell of it. And you will never guess – he was there. Doggo.

I got a jolt right through me, seeing him sitting there. My feet stuck to the ground. He looked different with his beard grown thicker and different sunglasses. Better ones. I could have darted off before he looked up, I would have done but by the time I could move again, Norma had seen me. Her mouth opened in a doggy smile and she wagged her stumpy tail. Doggo was drinking a pint of Guinness and smoking.

'Like the shades,' I said.

'Fuck me.' He jumped a mile, spilling a creamy lick of froth down the side of the glass.

'Nice to see you too,' I said.

Norma frisked round my ankles but Gordon just raised his eyebrows and did a long-suffering sigh, like oh God not *her* again.

'You alone?' he said, looking behind me. 'Meeting anyone?'

'No.'

'Drink?' He got up.

'I'll get it.'

'You got the last one.'

'K.' I sat down and watched him go in. Norma twisted her lead right round the table to put her head on my foot. I don't know what was going on. He could buy me a drink if he wanted. Nothing wrong in that. My heart was like a stupid trumpet.

There was an old woman at one of the other tables. She'd tipped all the money out of her purse and was counting it in piles of silver and copper. I heard her get to two pounds thirty-three, before Doggo plonked my drink down. 'Got you some crisps,' he said. 'Like crisps, don't you?'

'They're OK.' I thought, Jesus I'm going to turn into a crisp at this rate. We sat and stared across the table at each other. What now? I thought.

'Why did you do that thing,' I said, 'with the matches?' But he shrugged that subject off. We sat in an awkward silence till the old woman, who had got to three pounds seventy-six, stopped counting. She came over and petted the dogs.

'Do you know what I'm reduced to?' she said. 'After a lifetime of sturdy service?'

'Three pounds seventy-six?' I said.

'It's not on,' she said, 'it really is not on.'

'No,' Doggo said, 'it is definitely not on.' He nudged my knee under the table and an electric shock shot right up my leg.

'I'll leave you young lovers to it,' she said. 'A lifetime of sturdy service, I ask you.'

I went scarlet. Young lovers! *God.* When she'd gone I sneaked a look at Doggo but he was staring deeply into his pint. I said I needed to go to the toilet, went in, locked myself into a cubicle and leant against the door. I stayed there until the riot in my chest had calmed down. When I was sure there was no one else in there, I went and looked in the mirror. I blotted my shiny face all over with a bit of bog-roll. I wish I hadn't picked my spots. That's why I've got the craters like Mum warned me I would. My skin is terrible. I know why. I haven't eaten a vegetable for weeks unless you count crisps as vegetables.

I went out again. Norma was sniffing at my satchel. 'It's got food in,' I said. 'From your mum.'

'She OK?'

'Go and see for yourself.'

He lit a fag and shook his head as he blew out the smoke.

'I prefer those shades,' I said.

'Yeah?'

'Where's your old ones?'

He put his hand in his pocket and pulled them out.

I picked them up. 'These are so naff,' I said.

'Have them if you want,' he said. I laughed. It was cold sitting there and there was nothing to say. That was good. Not like there was any rapport going on between us. I thought I'd just finish my pint then go. Maybe to the library. A sparrow hopped on the table, pecking at a speck of crisp.

'Did you find somewhere to crash?' I asked. 'Who are you lying low from?'

He tipped his head back and lipped a perfect smoke ring.

'Very clever,' I said, as it rose and thinned and disappeared.

'What's she like these days?' he said. 'What's her old man like?'

'K, I think,' I said.

He looked cold and dishevelled. A tuft of his beard was sticking out and I wanted to smooth it down. I wanted him to squeeze my fingertip again. The voice was telling me to back off, quick, finish up my drink and go. The sun came out, not far off warm. I took a sip of beer and it tasted like autumn leaves. A breeze riffled the litter about. I looked at the scar in his eyebrow. His eyebrows are black as black and thick, nearly joined up in the middle. I like the way his beard starts out thin at the edges, on the high-up slopes of his cheeks like the start of a forest, and then thickens around his soft pink lips. But what with the sunglasses there's not much of his face you can actually see.

'Got to go,' I said, standing up.

'You haven't finished your pint.'

'I've had enough.' I picked up my satchel. 'I'll take these and chuck them for you,' I said, putting the old sunglasses inside. 'See you.'

I walked away. It was hard. I felt rude. The voices were quarrelling and I was losing track. A strand of warm toffee had attached itself to my belly, stretching out to him and the beer and the sun. The street was shadowy and cold like a different climate. I walked on and didn't stop or even look back. Not once did I look back.

I walked for a long while without breathing. I walked to the Botanical Gardens which is my favourite place on earth. Except it's usually full of couples holding hands and people pushing buggies. I like it best on weekdays, specially when the weather's wet and there's hardly anyone about. I go there to soak up what time of year it is – is it buds or roses or falling leaves? The squirrels come out from between the tree-trunks like little puffs of smoke, they'll eat out of your hand if you take some nuts.

I walked till the strand of toffee set hard and cold and broke in a spike. Then I sat down on a bench. The cold stripes of wood chilled my thighs. I put my head back and squinted at the ivory smudge of sun. Looking at the sun always makes tears come. The bare twigs squeaked like fingers against the glassy sky. I closed my eyes. Someone sat down beside me on the bench, a wet nose snuffled against my hand.

'What do you want?' I said without even opening my eyes.

'You know,' he said. A human hand took mine. It was even colder than my own but between the two cold palms a little warmth started, a spark struck between stones.

'I don't know who you are or what you've done or who you're hiding from,' I said. 'Where I live it's . . . I can't let you in. I can't let anyone in. I would help you if I could.' I opened my eyes and looked down at our hands. 'I *might* help you, if I could, but I can't. I really can't.'

I was amazed to have said so much and sounded so sensible.

'I could always follow you,' he said. 'I could follow you home.'

I tried to pull my hand away but he squeezed till the thin bones rubbed together then suddenly let go, grinning.

'I wouldn't go home then. That hurt.'

'Never?'

'Not if you were following me.'

'How would you know?'

'I could . . . call the police.'

'But you wouldn't do that.' His voice was coaxing, a smile on his lips.

'Oh wouldn't I?' I sounded so childish I couldn't bear it.

A woman in a fur coat walked past and smiled at us and the dogs. Doggo smiled back, charmingly. She left a trail of chemical perfume that jarred in the fresh air. Gordon put his paws over his nose. I'm glad I'm not a dog and assaulted by these smells all the time.

'You're right pretty,' Doggo said.

'Oh *yeah*.'

He took my hand again and this time it was really hot between the palms like magic, and warm in my belly too, melting toffee again, thick and sweet.

'Your eyes.' He tilted my face to his with his finger and looked into them. I screwed them up tight.

'I won't follow you,' he said, 'if you don't want me to.' I jerked my head away before he could kiss me. I don't know if he would have kissed me. I wanted him to kiss me. No I didn't. I would have hit him if he had. I pulled away from him and got up.

'Sure you don't want me to?' he said.

'What?'

'Follow you.'

'As if!'

He laughed. 'Too cold sitting here,' he said. 'Walk?'

'I've got to go in a minute.'

'Walk for a minute then.'

The dogs pulled and he walked just ahead of me, his shoulders hunched up round his ears. From behind he seemed smaller, skinny, his jeans baggy over his bum. It was cold, raw, the sun soaked up in a sudden grey wad of cloud. I shivered. I wanted to go back to the cellar and have a cup of tea. The voice was telling me to do that. Not to walk about with him or be with him a moment longer. Certainly not to take him back. But he needed somewhere to go, anyone could see that. I could help him. He liked me. It was cold. He was cold. He did seem to like me. I'd never taken a soul to the cellar. Too much of a risk. What if he messed it up for me, wrecking the place or inviting hordes of people round? I don't know him. But he knows me. He said so. He likes me.

'Have you noticed?' he said, waiting for me to catch up.

'What?'

'I haven't sworn all afternoon. It's nearly fucking killed me.'

I didn't laugh. A flock of pigeons scuttered upwards before our feet. What about your balance, one voice said, but the other laughed and said how stupid, what a baby I was being, what a little scaredy cat. Of course you need other people in your life. Everyone has people in their lives. How can it be balanced to always be alone?

We stopped by the fossilised tree root that looks like a dinosaur's foot.

'This has been here for millions of years,' I said.

Doggo squatted down to look. 'How was party?' he said.

'Huh?' Then I remembered. 'K. Just a, you know, party.'

'That guy called you Jo.'

'Yeah.'

'Funny that,' he said in the end. 'Why do you call yourself Lamb?' He handed me Norma's lead but I shook my head.

'Got to go,' I said.

'Where?'

'Dentist,' I said. 'Not that it's any of your business.'

'Good,' he said.

'What.'

'Good to look after your teeth.'

I pulled a face at him, not sure if he was taking the piss, but he looked quite serious.

'Teeth are important,' he said.

Teeth are important. I couldn't believe he'd said that. Who could ever be scared of someone who said *Teeth are important*? I started to walk away, a big toothy smile on my face. I turned round, he hadn't moved. He wasn't following but he wasn't walking away. A cold spot of rain dashed my cheek. He looked small and cold and hunched. You can't be human and always be alone. I beckoned him.

'K,' I said.

'What?'

'You can come back to mine.'

'Nah.'

'Why not?'

'You don't want me.'

'I . . .' A spot of rain trickled down the black lens of his glasses. I wasn't going to beg. 'Suit yourself,' I said. I shoved my hands in my pockets and started to walk. He could follow me or not, up to him.

Eleven

'Sure?' he said, giving me Norma's lead.

'Yeah.'

'Thought you were off to dentist.'

'Later.'

We walked down the road towards Mr Dickens' and the nearer we got, the slower I got, till I was hardly moving at all. Norma looked over her shoulder at me and tugged and whimpered.

'Something up with your feet?' Doggo said.

I stopped. 'Oh no.'

'What?'

'I forgot I've got to . . .'

'Wash your hair,' Doggo said like he'd heard it all before. 'Fair dos. No big deal.' He took Norma's lead. 'See you.'

'Wait! It's just . . . I need to explain something. About where I stay.'

'Yeah?'

'It's not exactly *official*. I mean nobody knows I live there, *nobody*, I'm kind of squatting. In the cellar of a house that someone lives in. And he doesn't know I'm there.'

The rain lashed sharply against my cheek.

'We going or what?' he said. 'I'm getting fucking soaked.'

We picked up speed again, Norma tripping me up every

second step. 'He's old,' I said. '*Really* old, and he can't get out or down his cellar steps. And he's pretty deaf so he doesn't hear me. He's cool,' I said, not wanting him to get the wrong idea. 'He's ninety. In a funny way I don't think he'd mind if he did know but I can hardly say, can I? Just drop it in, oh by the way, Mr Dickens, I've been living in your cellar for a few months now, that's OK, isn't it?'

'So no one knows?' he said. 'No one?'

'You have to be very quiet.' I wanted to say, And very respectful but I couldn't quite bring myself to say that.

I nearly died when we went in and I saw it through his eyes. So depressing. The bits of dead insect spattered all over the windows, and even with the light on a desperate clinging gloom.

'Fuck me,' he said. He took his shades off and walked around, looking at my camp bed and my Calor gas, the brown sink, the radio, all my childish pathetic belongings huddled together like refugees. Then he turned and grinned.

'Neat,' he said, 'this is really neat.'

'Yeah?' I looked again and saw that maybe it wasn't so bad. Not as bad as nowhere, anyway. Clever of me to think of it really. You could see he was impressed. Norma snuffled everything while Gordon sat by the door looking definitely underwhelmed. Doughnut went off into a sudden volley of barking upstairs.

Doggo jumped. 'You never said there was a fucking dog.'

'Going to start swearing again?' I said. 'Tea? Doughnut's nothing to worry about.'

'Doughnut? What about that curry. I'm f . . .' He grinned so sharply it scratched me. 'I'm famished.'

I turned away and lit the Calor gas to warm things up.

'Nobody knows?' he said again.

'How many more times?'

'What about your mates?'

'Don't have that many mates. Mind it cold?' Nothing I could have done about it anyway. I've only got a kettle, nothing to cook on. I gave him the curry in the box, with a fork.

'Silver service, eh?' he said. 'What about you?' I didn't want *him* starting on about me eating so I did eat some, just a few mouthfuls, then he scoffed the rest. It was only vegetables in bright-yellow sauce and not bad. I thought it might do my skin some good. I made tea – luckily I do have two mugs.

When he'd finished eating he picked up Mr Dickens' album and flicked through. 'Who's this?' he said stopping at one of the pictures of Zita. I said it was my granny, then I changed it to great granny. Would that be right? I couldn't think straight, anyway what does it matter? He kept looking from me to the photo and back again.

'You look a bit like,' he said. I knelt beside him to look. Zita on a shingly beach under a sunshade, looking up at the camera, her eyes dark and burning.

'Do I?'

He put his arm round me and I froze. I'm not completely stupid. If you ask a guy back to your place he's likely to think he's in there, isn't he? I didn't mind his arm round me, it was warm. But I pulled away.

'What's up?' he said.

'I don't do sex.' It got out of my mouth before I could stop it. I was horrified but he laughed. *Laughed*.

'Well I'd better watch myself then,' he said. '*Don't do sex*.' He narrowed his eyes at me. He kept staring till I didn't know what to do. 'Why Lamb then, and not Jo?'

'No big mystery,' I said. I was looking at Mr Dickens in some sagging knitted swimming trunks. 'I just hate Jo so everyone calls me Lamb.'

'Who's everyone?'

I shrugged.

'Why *Lamb*?'

'Why *Doggo*?' I said, turning the page to a view of grey hills with a grey car parked in front. 'Anyway, Lamb's my surname.'

'So who's Joanna Vinier then?'

It was like he'd punched me in the gut.

He nodded at my satchel which was lying on the floor with the flap up where I'd taken the curry out. It had that name and an old address printed in big biro letters, old but still showing among a load of stupid scrawls about who loves who and STING 4 EVER and phone numbers. It had been there so long I didn't even see it any more. The name was in my mum's writing, she must have done it when I was about eleven, starting secondary school. I got a pang right through me thinking about her, a scribbled flashback of her face, last time I saw her. Years ago when I was still that person.

I flipped the lid of the satchel down with my foot. The silence was long. My throat was burning from the curry. I wanted to tell him to go away but I couldn't say a word. He got up and starting poking through some of Mr Dickens' stuff.

'What's in there?' he said, nodding at the door.

'Just more cellar. Coal.'

He picked up an umbrella and tried to open it but a shower of moth wings and rust cascaded out. He put it down and wiped his hands on his jeans. 'You gay?' he said.

'No,' I said.

'Just don't fancy me, eh?'

'It's not that . . .'

'You do fancy me then?'

'I dunno.'

'Little girls, eh,' he said, as if to someone else.

'I'm nearly twenty,' I said. He stopped and looked a minute, but made no remark. He went off through the door and I could hear him switch on a light and rustle about in places I had never been. It was strange and chilly, the feeling of someone else in my space which isn't really mine at all, but still, it gave me an uneasy feeling like someone's fingers in my brain. I sipped my tea and tried not to feel sick. You're supposed to look at the horizon if you feel sick, car sick anyway, but what horizon is there in a cellar?

When he came back he had cobwebs in his hair and a bottle of wine in his hand. 'There's fucking racks of the stuff,' he said.

'It's vintage,' I said. 'Mr Dickens used to collect it once, as an investment.'

'Got a corkscrew?'

I shook my head.

'S'OK,' he said and got out a Swiss army knife with a corkscrew attachment. I just sat there feeling helpless and watched him open it, a cold sinking in my gut. He was going to wreck everything, starting now.

'What's up?' he said.

'It's not yours,' I said and my voice came out like a mouse's.

'Oh dear.'

'But it's probably worth about a hundred pounds,' I said.

By this time he'd got the cork out. 'Any glasses?' he asked, and he wasn't joking. He looked like he expected me to suddenly produce a crystal decanter set.

'You'll have to use your cup,' I said. 'Don't you want your tea?'

He tipped it down the sink. The wine glugged thickly out of the bottle. It was almost black. 'Château something or other,' he said, rubbing the crud off the label. 'Here goes.' He sniffed at it and swilled it round his mouth like mouthwash. He didn't spit it out though, he swallowed and said, 'Mmmm,

77

interesting. Try it.' I didn't want to but I did anyway and it tasted like Tarmac melting in a heatwave.

'S'OK,' he said. 'Wouldn't pay a hundred pounds though. Maybe three ninety-nine if I was feeling flush.' He took another swig and I saw his Adam's apple bob. I hated him. What was he doing here, making fun of Mr Dickens' wine, drinking it like it was lemonade? He wiped his mouth and held the mug out to me. I put my hands behind my back. 'What's up?' he said.

'I just don't think you should drink his wine, that's all.'

I wished there was a button like a rewind button I could press and get us out of there, back to the street, back to the pub, back to last week, not to have done this, not to have let him in, not to have ever even met him.

Then I heard the back door open above us. I nearly had a fit. I leapt for the door seeing it was still open a crack but it was too late. Gordon and Norma were out there yapping and snarling and I could hear Mr Dickens' poor old voice through it all calling out, 'Here, fella, Doughnut, here, fella.'

I lunged out and grabbed one lead and Doggo grabbed the other. Doughnut was slavering like a hell hound but quite enjoying himself I think.

I looked up the kitchen steps and there was Mr Dickens holding on to the door frame and peering down. 'Lamb?' he said, in a quavery voice. 'Is that you, duck?'

'Oh hello,' I said, making my voice jolly and normal, not *normal* because I'm not normally jolly. I stood where he could see my lips and shouted, 'Hope you don't mind. I was just showing my friend your garden, he's a gardener. We er didn't want to disturb you.'

Mr Dickens nodded his head and said, 'Grand, grand. Why not come up and have a cuppa.'

I looked at Doggo and he looked at me. 'Quick thinking,' he said.

'Just go,' I said, 'now. I'll say you changed your mind.'

But he didn't go. He stood for a moment, flexing and unflexing his hands, thinking.

'You say he lives alone?'

'Yeah,' I said.

'Interesting. Let's go up.'

'No,' I said, 'please . . . just go now. He didn't see you properly.'

'But I'd like to meet him.'

'Please.'

'Why not?'

'No. If you don't go I'll tell him . . .' But what could I tell him without letting on about the cellar? Doggo was grinning. Nothing I could say. But Doggo could, that was the message in his grin.

'Come on,' he said. I had no choice. My spirits were so tangled round my ankles I could hardly walk. He shut Gordon and Norma in the cellar and we went up the steps into the kitchen. It was strange to be in there with Doggo. He looked the wrong scale for the room. Too big and rough, though he wasn't really that big, just bigger than Mr Dickens and me. The room was cold and smelt of dog meat. There was a low sun shining through the window over the sink and you could see how dirty it all was, a sticky film everywhere.

Mr Dickens stuck out his hand and said, 'How do.'

'This is Mr Dickens, this is Doggo, Doggo, this is Mr Dickens,' I said feeling like a traitor.

'Doggo?' Mr Dickens said.

'It's his nickname.'

'Dog-lover are you?'

'Yeah.'

'Grand.' Mr Dickens' face folded up into a laugh. 'Doggo and Lamb,' he said, 'sounds like a couple of blinking glove puppets. Go and get sat down. I'll make tea.'

I led Doggo through.

'So, you're the cleaner,' Doggo said, raising his eyebrow. He was perfectly right. It was a mortifying tip. You could hardly see the pattern of the carpet under the long black-and-white hairs.

Doughnut stared blindly up at us, the tip of his tail still wagging away from all the excitement. Neither of us said a thing. Doggo's hands just lay on his lap in loose fists and I could see LOVE and HATE and wished he'd turn them over before Mr Dickens saw too.

When I could hear Mr Dickens loading the tray I went and carried it. Three cups and a hill of brown crumbs. I put the tray on the low table. I poured out the weak tea and handed Doggo a cup. 'Ta very much,' he said. He grinned and I could see the stain of red wine on his teeth.

'So, a gardener, eh?' Mr Dickens said. 'Well what do you reckon to it?'

'No problem,' Doggo said. 'What you thinking, couple of hours a week or what?' He was a different person with Mr Dickens. Eager and deferential and completely false.

'Much as you can do to start off,' Mr Dickens said, 'it's a right jungle out there. Then whatever's needed to keep it up to scratch.'

'I'll think about it,' Doggo said.

I looked down at my knees. I needed to wash my jeans. I needed to have a bath. I couldn't bear to watch Mr Dickens being taken in.

'We should go,' I said. 'You've got to be somewhere, haven't you, Doggo.'

'No rush.'

'Cake?' Mr Dickens nodded at the plate and Doggo scooped up a handful of crumbs. 'Ta. Lamb?'

I shook my head. My belly already felt like a balloon with the curry in it. And the regret. I thought I wouldn't be able to eat for a week. I'd got a tea-leaf stuck between my teeth and I tried to pick it out.

'What's your hourly rate?' Mr Dickens said.

'A tenner,' Doggo said.

I nearly laughed. *A tenner an hour?* But Mr Dickens didn't even blink. He just said, 'Fair enough. When can you start?'

'I've got an immediate window as it happens,' Doggo said trying to exchange glances with me but I would not meet his eyes. I just wanted to go away and cry. 'Tomorrow suit you?'

'Tomorrow,' Mr Dickens said and put out his knobbly hand to shake.

Twelve

I tried to shut him out but he was right behind me. He squeezed through and leaned back against the cellar door.

'Fuck off,' I said.

'Who's swearing now?'

'Please go away. This is a mistake.'

He pretended to consider this. 'Go where?'

'Please,' I said. My voice was cracking but I would not cry. All crying does is make you ugly and wet. This was like a bad dream getting worse. Him here in my space, him in Mr Dickens' cheating. 'He's a poor old man,' I said.

'He's loaded.'

'I don't mean in money.'

He sat down on the deck chair. Norma curled up on the floor beside him. He stretched his legs out and put his hands behind his head, so at home already. More at home than I could ever be. I could not look at him. I went outside. It was dark now and the sky was clearing. A fragment of icy moon caught up in a net of twigs. I listened but could only hear the outside noises, cars, water gushing from a drain. My breath was a sluggish cloud. No voices or only a thin sigh saying *See*. I should have listened when they spoke to me.

If this was a dream and I could wake, I thought, make it be a dream that I can wake from. I pinched my forearm. It hurt, good. Something honest about pain, something straight forward. The bit of moon was like a shard of broken glass. If only I could reach it down.

The thing to do was play along. I ran my hands over the skin on the front of my head, making a smooth face, and went back in. Doggo was smoking.

'Drink to my job,' he said. 'Get us another bottle.'

I looked down at his sharp shadowy face. 'No. Anyway, you're not really going to do it?'

'You never know.'

'I thought you were meant to be hiding. What do you want a job for?'

He shrugged. 'What does anyone want a job for?' He unfolded himself out of the deck chair. I backed towards the door but he just went and got another bottle of wine. He opened it without even looking what it was. I waited with my nails slicing into the palms of my hands.

'You can't stay here,' I said.

'No?' He sloshed wine into the mugs.

'No.'

'You going to chuck me out then?'

He handed me the wine. I took it even though I didn't want it. I took a sip and tried to get my mind still. There were little bits of cork in the wine. Tried to get the balance. What would a balanced person do?

'Good thinking this,' he said, waving his hand. 'I'd never have thought of it. Living in someone's cellar.' He laughed. 'Like a rat.'

Oh Mr Dickens. The way he trusted me and trusted Doggo. Trusted Doggo was a gardener without any proof at all, just *trusted*. I think it's a gift, trust, but whether a good or a bad gift I can't decide. You leave yourself so open to abuse.

He picked up one of the gardening magazines. 'Ought to get a tip or two before I start,' he said.

'You're really going to do it?'

He wobbled his hand backwards and forwards. My mind was scrabbling about trying to think what to do. Not call the police. There was no one I could call. I went along with him while I tried to think. I pulled out some more magazines and the handbag fell out.

He glugged back more wine and frowned at a magazine. I tried to seem helpful. I read out to him that you prune in the autumn and anyone can see there's lots to prune so that is easy. It's what things are that he doesn't know. He's somehow managed to get through his life so far hardly able to recognise a rose. I showed him pictures: hydrangea, forsythia, lilac, lupin. We drank down through the wine and the magazines got fuzzy. He picked up the handbag. '*What* did you take it for again?' he said.

'What's this one?' I pointed at an iris.

'Will you take it back?' he said.

'Why not you?'

'You took it.'

'You did first.'

'But *you* stole it again.'

'Not *stole*.'

'Crap.'

He'd drunk much more wine than me because I don't drink, not really, I only drank at all out of nerves. He'd had most of two bottles to himself. He opened the handbag and took things out. A comb, a purse, a lipstick. He took off the lid and wound up the blunt pink stick. He drew a line of it on the back of his hand. It was that same sugar pink she always wears. In the purse, along with her credit cards and money-off vouchers, there was a photo. Neville holding a baby Roy. Doggo stared at it for a minute, blinked, slid it back, stuffed everything back in the bag. He rolled another fag. The smoke and clouds of sour winter breath were crowding the dismal air, like a kind of fog. He pinched the fag between his lips, struck a match, watched the flame till it touched his finger and thumb then dropped it on the floor.

'Don't start that again,' I said but he struck another and another. Even though the floor was concrete I was scared he'd somehow set the place on fire. '*Please*.'

'Nice manners,' he remarked.

'*Please*, Doggo.'

He struck one more and watched it burn out on the floor. 'Tell me something then,' he said.

'What?'

'Why you don't *do sex*.'

'I – ' I opened my mouth but I couldn't answer.

'Ever done it?'

'None of your business.' He struck another match. 'OK, yeah,' I said. He dropped the match and the flame died on the floor.

'So, not a little virgin then.'

'No.'

'Well then . . .'

'No!' I couldn't keep my smooth face on, it started to twist out of shape the way it does when you want to cry but I would not cry. He watched me for a minute, like he was really watching. His eyes were like the smoke.

'OK,' he said. 'Something else.'

'What?'

'I dunno. Tell me about your dad.'

'My *dad*.'

'Yeah.'

'Why?'

He shrugged. 'Why not?'

I hadn't thought about my dad for ages. What is the point? I don't like remembering him not because it's bad but only because it's all so faint. It's so faint I don't even know if it's

85

real or if I've made it up from what I've been told and from photographs. The more times I disturb the memory the more worn out it gets. But this is it: brown hair, brown-rimmed glasses, a tobaccoey smell, a warm handkerchief wiping my face when I cried. Once he rolled a corner up into a twisted point to poke a dried-up bogey from my nose. Imagine doing that for someone. I remember a tweedy scratch against my cheek or maybe it was bristles.

Once he gave me a doll's tea set and I set out a tea-party on the bedspread. The cups kept falling off the saucers because of the hills of his knees and feet. There is a photo of that tea-party. He was very ill, bone fingers holding a tiny china cup to his lips, black spaces in his smile. There's a cake and a bit of crumpled wrapping paper and in the background, bottles of pills and a jug of water. I am holding up the teapot, my round face beaming at the camera. My birthday. Maybe my second or third. Not old enough to understand that he was dying. And that's it, no memory of being told he was dead, no memory of a funeral. Once I saw his feet and they were bluish and the toe-nails long and yellow and disgusting. I don't even know if they were dead feet or alive.

'Dead,' I said. 'He died when I was a baby.'

'What about your mum?'

'Her too.'

'Fuck,' he said.

I was startled by the soft sound of his voice. My cheeks went hot.

'Why have you got that?' I said looking at the LOVE and HATE on his knuckles. He spread out his hands and studied them.

'Bit naff, eh?' he said.

'Totally,' I said and looked away.

I was tired. My eyes were stinging from the smoke. All I wanted was for him to go so I could get some sleep. My whole life was out of order with him there, panic rising again. Something broken and he was there. Breathing, smoking, *being* in my space. Like a stranger dabbling his fingers in my head. Before I could think of what to do, Norma did it for me. She scrabbled at the door and whined. Even though Doughnut's blind his hearing's fine and it set him off barking.

'You'd better take her out,' I said. 'If Doughnut barks at night Mr Dickens calls the police. He's got one of those panic buttons.' It was a lie but he believed me.

He tried giving Norma a bit of a smack, not hard, just to shut her up. But she wouldn't shut up, she just whined louder and Gordon started growling too. 'I'll take them round block,' he said. Doughnut was going demented up there. I was scared Mr Dickens really might get up and have a look out the back.

'*Please* go, quick, before he calls them,' I said. 'The police come fast round here.'

'Won't be long,' he said. He grabbed the leads and went off, quick and quiet into the dark. Easy as that. When he'd gone I leant against the door frame, dizzy with relief. But it lasted only a minute. His bag was on the floor. Because he would be back. If there was a way to lock the door I would have locked it but there is no way. There is a keyhole but no key. Nothing I could do to stop him coming back.

I was shivering. I made myself get into bed. My head a messy fuzz of stupid half-thoughts and my heart as heavy as a rock. I shouldn't have drunk the wine. Two stolen bottles lying on their sides. All the choosing Mr Dickens did and all the saving. His investment. But bottles can be smashed.

How could I stop him coming back?

I listened for his footsteps, straining for the sound. I couldn't. But I could go. Pack my stuff – which would take about two minutes – walk out, never looking back.

It's not hard, I've done it before. That is what I'd have to do.

I got out of bed, looked around the dingy space. The cold smoke had settled like mist on the floor. But then a thought struck me, stopped me. If I left now Doggo would move in. He might do anything. Poor Mr Dickens up there unaware. I couldn't leave him to that. So I was stuck. And there was no one, no one I could ask for help. *Your own fault*, the voice told me. *Your own blind and stupid fault.*

Inside my eyelids I try to find the tightrope but it is not tight any more. Someone has cut it and it is dangling down but I open my eyes quick before I catch a glimpse of what is down there. Back in bed, I curl around the empty ache. It comes on nights like these, moves into the soft triangle between the bottom of my ribs. Not good clean pain, a dirty empty ache which can be cured with the let of blood. But I don't do that. I could smash the bottles but no. I am cured of that. See how I am cured? I lie and listen for the sound of footsteps in the night.

Thirteen

The sunlight through my curtains was like *rosé* wine. My duvet was pink with daisies. I snuggled down waiting for Mum to call. It was only Mum and me and we were close. I didn't have friends. Mum was my friend. We looked like sisters, people said.

She died fast. A backache, a cough. A test and then another test and suddenly she was in hospital. Nobody even said the word cancer and next thing she was gone. Like a conjuring trick. Now you see her, now you don't. I was nearly fifteen. I stayed with her friends till certain things. I stayed there till I left.

The sunlight through the curtains was like *rosé* wine oh no it wasn't. Sometimes when I wake, as I am waking, I still expect the pinkness with the sun shining through. But then my eyes are opened to the cobwebs and the leak of deadish light.

It took a moment to remember last night. But Doggo wasn't there. I hauled myself upright and looked. The bottles on the floor, his bag, the stale tang of smoke in the air proved it had been real – but he had not come back. And I had actually slept all night. I never thought I'd sleep a wink. For a moment I was glad until it all seeped back. The guilt. Poor Mr Dickens up there unaware. My head throbbed from the wine. And Doggo would be back, there was no doubt of that.

I got up, peed and splashed cold water on my face. Maybe I'd go out before Doggo did come back. But when he did come, shouldn't I be here? I looked at myself in his mirror shades. My hair like string and a wild look in my eyes. Before I could decide a thing, I heard his feet come tramping down the side of the house. He barged right in with the dogs like he owned the place. He whipped his shades off and grinned.

'Oh God,' I said.

'Good morning to you too.' He reached out and tried to ruffle my hair but I dodged away. His nose was shiny from the cold and his beard looked dewy. 'Any tea going?'

'What are you so up about?' I said.

He grinned and shrugged. 'Miss me?'

'Sorry?'

'Last night.'

'Oh *yeah*.' I put the kettle on. I was going to anyway. I couldn't bear to look at him. He was *rosy*. He seemed so young again. When he was pink in the face and smiling he didn't seem much older than me. Nothing to be scared of.

'Found a fucking van, didn't I? Camper – bed in it and all.'

'You want to be careful of vans. I got driven away in one once.'

'Yeah?' He squatted down to take the dogs' leads off. The smell of outside clung to him. He looked up and snagged me with his eyes. 'What happened?'

'Not a lot.'

He stood up. 'Lamb?'

My heart flickered. His eyes were on my lips. 'What?'

'Got any grub?'

'No.' I turned away and made the tea. He cupped his hands round his and blew and slurped like he'd been desperate. I almost wished I had some toast to give him. He looked cold right through. In the morning he didn't look so dodgy. He was only a person.

When he'd finished his tea, he stood up. 'Right, I'll make a start.'

'You're *really* going to do it?'

'Yeah.'

'But you haven't got a clue.'

'Nothing else to do. Tell you the truth I'm bored witless.'

I went out with him to watch. And then I got stuck in too. The sky was the colour of apricots and the powder of frost sparkled the colour back. We ended up working together all day ripping down bushes. My head was throbbing and I could hardly bear him to look at me at first, knowing what a sight I was. After I'd dodged my eyes away from him a few times he asked me what was up. I said I had a headache. He laughed and said it was a hangover and he had one too. He made it sound so normal, I started to feel better.

He was a person. I was a person. It was normal to be with someone, working together. That is normal. I only had to keep my mind away from what was going to happen next.

Despite the frost which hung around all day, we got hot working and peeled off till we were just in T-shirts and jeans. Doggo was thin, but through his T-shirt you could see the muscles. Mr Dickens came out to see the progress and was surprised that I was there. I said I'd come to keep Doggo company and he said, 'Long as I'm not paying double.' I thought, *you are paying double* but kept it to myself. Norma and Gordon roamed round sniffing and peeing, then Gordon lay down with his nose on his paws with his bored-out-of-my-skull face on. He's a hard dog to impress.

There were old bird's nests and bits of rubbish stuck up in the branches, plastic bags and even a bicycle wheel. How on earth did that get there? I found myself *laughing*. It's a huge garden and there must be weeks of work. While we were working things were easy between Doggo and me, as if we knew each other. Although he didn't say much and nor did I. Funny how working hard can feel so good.

Halfway through the morning Mr Dickens opened the door and called out did we want a cuppa. We went inside and he looked at Doggo, winked and said, 'Can't you get a bit of flesh on her bones?' I did not know where to look.

Doggo went through and I stood with Mr Dickens in the kitchen. I watched his hand waver as he spooned the tea into the pot, the scattered grit of tea-leaves on the draining board. I wondered how many times, how many spoonfuls of tea he'd spooned in his life, how many gallons of tea he'd made and drunk. Then I noticed something. On a nail by the door was a rusty key. 'What's that for?' I said.

'What, duck?' He squinted and reached out his hand. He held it up and frowned. 'I can't rightly say. Might be for cellar.' I carried the tray for him, sliding the key up my sleeve and later into the pocket of my jeans.

Mr Dickens gave Doggo a tin of Pal and he went out to share it between Gordon and Norma. While he was outside Mr Dickens patted me on the arm and said, 'That's a fine lad you've got there, Lamb.' I didn't know what expression to have but my face decided and split into a stupid grin. Then I remembered the wine and the way I'd lumbered Mr Dickens and the smile just sank away. I sat there feeling awkward which I never feel with Mr Dickens. I had broken some invisible thing by letting Doggo in. Didn't know if I could ever mend it.

But the day was so crisp and shiny bright it was hard to stay down for long. We cleared the long grass away from a clump of spiky purple flowers with yellow middles. I asked Mr Dickens what they were called and he said Michaelmas daisies. So that's one we know for definite. I liked gardening, better than cleaning. Maybe I should change direction.

We pulled down an ancient crusty bush and found the skeleton of a cat curled up in the roots. More than just a skeleton, there were bits of skin and ginger fur stuck to the ribs and over the top of the skull. There was one of those little round bells you get on cat collars. I picked it up and it jingled and that spooked me, the bell jingling next to the greenish bones. I went and asked Mr Dickens if he'd ever had a cat but he said, 'No, we never were cat people, give me a dog any day.'

We decided to bury it and I suggested we buried the handbag while we were at it. Doggo gave me a look. 'Why?'

'Just that I don't like harbouring it.'

'*Harbouring?*' he said and laughed – but without smiling. 'You can't bury it,' he said, 'it's got her stuff in.' I started to argue then I shut my mouth. It was one of those stalemates between us. He didn't say a word while we buried the poor cat which fell apart a bit when we moved it. I wondered whose cat it was and where they thought it had gone. To tell the truth I like the way cats creep away and find a secret place to die. Dignified.

We got on fine all day. Doggo and me. Had a laugh even. He loved the ripping down, you could see that, putting all his strength into tearing things apart, splitting branches off trunks, hauling roots out of the earth. I thought there'd be nothing left the rate he was going. A funny sort of gardening. I thought gardening was more about growing things than wrecking them. But Mr Dickens wasn't complaining so why should I? We got on together fine all day. But when the end of the day came, it was as I feared. I couldn't make him go.

Fourteen

'Can't you go back to that van?' I said miserably, when he'd got settled on the deck chair with a mug of tea and a fag. Sitting on the bed I could feel the hard shape of the key pressing into my thigh but I hadn't had a chance to try it.

'Only a couple of nights, then I'm moving on.'

I bit the edge of my fingernail, thinking. Maybe a couple of nights would be OK. Only I didn't know where he'd sleep.

'Where're you going?'

He shrugged. 'Something I've got to get sorted first.'

'What?'

'A mate to see. Then I'll be offski.'

'Honest?'

'God's honour,' he said, doing a salute thing which is maybe Boy Scouts' or something.

I stared. He was so different. Not like someone you'd be afraid of. Maybe he *wasn't*. Maybe it is only me. Scaredy cat. Scared of anyone. Scared of my own shadow.

'You can maybe stay for a night or two,' I said.

'Ta,' he said.

'Long as that's all it is. If you don't do that match thing. And don't keep drinking his wine.'

'Any more rules?'

I thought about it. I'm sure there were but I couldn't think of any straightaway.

'Bit selfish, isn't it?' he said. 'Keeping a place like this to yourself.'

'*I* found it. Anyway, I really like Mr Dickens,' I said. 'I don't want to . . .'

He nodded and put his head back, opened and closed his mouth like a fish and blew a stream of smoke rings that rose like bubbles into the cobwebs.

'Are you on the run?' I said.

'Brilliant.'

'From the police?'

He narrowed his eyes at me. 'Are *you*?'

'Are you an escaped convict?' I said.

He gave a hard-edged laugh that made me jump. 'You kid,' he said. 'Shut it, will you?' He muttered *Escaped convict* like it was something funny.

I had to get out of there to think. Funny how I can't think straight with someone there. I can't get him clear in my mind. It's like looking in a kaleidoscope. Soon as you think you see one thing, it's changed to another. Or maybe it is just me. Not used to people any more. Maybe people *aren't* that simple, one thing or another. I know I'm not.

I said I was going out to get some food. 'Fetch us back a couple of cans,' he said. I wouldn't normally let myself be ordered about but I was so glad he was going to drink beer instead of Mr Dickens' wine, I said I would.

It was the Saturday nearest to Guy Fawkes night and all up and down the streets, in their little back gardens, people were having parties. The air smelt of gunpowder and the wet paths were stained orange from the street lights, slithery with mulched-up leaves. And from everywhere there were explosions and whizzes, and brilliant waterfalls of sparks. It was like war, except instead of being frightened people were cheering and laughing and saying, 'Oooooo!' even though some of the noises were exactly like guns or bombs. If you want to shoot someone you should do it on Guy Fawkes night. No one would turn a hair. I wondered what it was that Doggo had done.

The cellar was a good place for him to hide. The gardening was a way of making a few quid. If it was only a couple of nights, it would maybe be OK. It wouldn't hurt Mr Dickens and he would at least get the garden started. I went to the off-licence and the newsagent's. They didn't have much food, but I bought a couple of Scotch eggs, then stood and looked at the fireworks. I stared for ages at all the boxes of Catherine wheels, Roman candles and splintery rockets. They made my teeth feel funny, the buzzy colours of them, the memory of the smell.

I bought a packet of sparklers. I don't know why. The thin feel of the wires through the paper and the itchy smell of them whipped me back to feeling about five again. I couldn't take them back to Doggo, he would probably think that I was just a kid. I didn't know what to do with them. Halfway back I stopped and lit one. It took ages to light and when it did the sharp silver fizz of it made me start. I waved it about like some lunatic and it went out. Maybe too damp. I put the rest of the packet on a wall for someone else to find.

Doggo gave the Scotch eggs a funny look but ate one anyway and I ate the egg out of the other and fed the dogs the greyish scoops of sausage. We listened to the fireworks, and when it got late enough for Mr Dickens to be in bed we stood in the garden for a while watching the rockets.

'What did you do?' I said. 'If you're staying you could at least tell me what you did.'

'I got away. That's all you need to know.'

'Was it murder?' A screaming silver streak shot up and exploded overhead.

He got hold of my arm so suddenly I yelled. 'Shut it,' he said, opened the door and shoved me in. He stood with his back against the door.

'What do you want to hear?' he said, grabbing me by the wrist. He spoke in a stupid girly voice. '"Was it murder?"' He gripped my wrist so tight I could feel the blood throbbing in my hand.

'Please,' I said.

'Please what?'

'Please let go.'

He shoved me away so hard I nearly fell. But I didn't fall I just sat down on the bed. My heart was banging in my ears. I glared down at my knees to keep them still. Although it was icy cold my ears were burning. Norma yapped round Doggo's ankles. I thought he'd kick her but he didn't. He just stood there till she stopped. Doughnut was barking above us. I was shaking but I sat on my hands so he couldn't see. I was scared that he would hear my heart. He stood for a minute flexing his hands. He looked up at the ceiling but the barking was dying away.

He suddenly slumped down in the deck chair. There was a fierce hiss as he opened a can of beer.

'Sorry,' he said. I swallowed but I couldn't speak. He licked the foam that came down the side, then put his head back and shut his eyes. His throat was white and vulnerable, the skin smooth. There was a small pulse between the sinews.

'How old are you?' I said. He opened his eyes and looked at me like I was mad and then he laughed.

'Aren't you scared?'

'No,' I said.

'Well you should be.' He swigged the beer and netted a delicate line of froth on his moustache. He smiled. 'I could be a serial killer for all you know. It was round here they caught Yorkshire Ripper, weren't it? Can you roll fags? Roll me a fag.' He chucked me some tobacco and papers. I just looked. I may sometimes be a cleaner but I'm nobody's servant.

'Go on,' he said. He blinked at me, his lashes making shadows on his cheeks. I've never rolled a cigarette. I thought it wouldn't hurt to try but I was useless at it. 'Crap,' he said when I finally handed him a loose and wonky tube.

'Tough,' I said. 'Do it yourself then.'

He shook his head at me. I gave him back his stuff and in a split second he conjured himself a tight and spindly fag. What was the point of that? Just making me feel stupid. He lit it, breathing in with narrowed eyes.

'I want to go to bed now,' I said.

He raised his eyebrows tauntingly. 'No one's stopping you.' But I sat there. There was only the one small bed. And I wasn't about to get undressed with him there. My mind had changed. I had to get him out.

'I'll sleep here,' he said, nodding at the deck chair. 'I'll take dogs out first.' He smiled, the nice smile again, the young one. 'Give you your privacy.'

As soon as he'd gone I leapt up and tried the key. It wouldn't turn. I hurt my fingers trying to force it. When I pulled it out of the keyhole there was a clot of rust and filth. I wiped it off on a rag. On the shelf by the door was some oil. I dripped a bit on the key and tried again and this time, after a bit of wiggling, it suddenly gave between my fingers, turned, the latch jumping into place. I gasped with the shock of this success. Stood looking at the locked door, feeling dizzy.

It was a risk, I knew. He might come back and hammer on the door or shout, but I didn't think he'd dare. I touched my wrist where he had gripped so hard. I could just make out the prints of his fingers on my skin. I took some clothes off and cleaned my teeth. I got into bed and waited, listening for his footsteps through the slamming of my heart.

He did come back after a while. He tried the door once or twice and he called my name. It was strange to hear my name being called out in the night like that, 'Lamb, Lamb.' He called it softly, didn't yell or bang. I saw his face against the window but I lay flat on the bed. I heard him hesitating a bit, muttering to the dogs, and then he went away. His footsteps growing fainter up the side of the house until I couldn't hear them any more. I felt almost sorry. I did feel sorry for the dogs.

Fifteen

I let myself in through the back door of the Harcourts'. The kitchen table was stacked with the 'special finish' greasy pans as usual. Everyone was out so I stripped off and shoved all my clothes in the washer on the wash 'n' dry cycle. I was dying for a bath after all that gardening. I didn't even bother to look at the note which would just be the usual list of orders. I ran up the stairs, through the dark 'master bedroom', and turned on the taps in the *en suite*.

I sloshed some plant essence into the bath, switched on the Jacuzzi effect and slid down into the warmth, the bubbles swirling round me like the confusion inside my head. I tried to get my mind to still, to get the balance back. Doggo hadn't returned last night and I'd locked the cellar so he wouldn't be there now. He was maybe miles away by now, going wherever he was going. It was over. I held my frothy wrist up and watched the faint beat of my pulse. Everything was OK.

I closed my eye to see the high wire and I did see it – but I saw other things too, things I hadn't noticed before. Things that looked exciting. In a circus there are more acts than just the high-wire act. The thought of Doggo was more like a trapeze, the high and dizzy swing of it, the swoop. That gasp when the two pairs of hands grab each other and one swings high, swooping above the applause, high and safe in the other's hands. Imagine the trust of that. But anyway he had gone.

I slipped down, my head under the water, and held my breath imagining something crazy. You can imagine anything you like, doesn't do any harm. I imagined Doggo in the Jacuzzi – not that I'd do that, let him in, not in a million years. It is just so gorgeous, the bubbly feeling. You have to give it to the Harcourts, they have some good facilities.

The water started to get cool and I made myself get out. I did mean to do *some* of the cleaning. I was getting dried when the door swung open and there stood Mr Harcourt.

I had the towel up to me at least. We just stood staring at each other. I was too stunned to be scared. Not right away. He was wearing pyjamas. It was like a knife spreading something horrible on bread the way his face changed from blank to a smarmy smile. 'Aaah,' he said. 'Been enjoying yourself, sweetheart?'

'Just cleaning the bath,' I said.

'Not an abuse of your employer's trust then,' he said and stepped closer.

'Don't think so,' I said.

'Drop the towel,' he said coming towards me. I backed away. 'You didn't read the wife's note, I take it?'

I shook my head, still backing till I could feel the edge of the bath against my legs. The pyjamas were those naff silk type with a monogram on the pocket in swirly gold, *BH*. It was close to my nose and I just stared at the initials till my eyes went funny then he started to unbutton himself. 'Imagine my surprise when a naked sylph came flitting through my bedroom.' His voice oozed out like grease. 'Needless to say I pinched myself and, yes, I was awake.'

His head was huge with longish golden hair like a lion's mane and his chest was thick and fleshy. He grinned and I leant back as far as I could then he let his trousers fall down and his stiff prick, all pink and whiskery like a prawn, jumped up and pointed at me. He got so close it rubbed against the towel. So close I caught a whiff of fish.

'This could be rather nice,' he said.

'Don't think so.'

'Oh come come. Listen, if you drop that silly towel' – he got hold of the edge of it and tugged – 'I'll give you fifty pounds.'

I didn't have to think about it. I just kneed him in the balls and when he doubled over I ran down the stairs only I couldn't leave because my clothes were still churning about in the washer.

All I could find to put on down there was Mrs Harcourt's apron and my denim jacket that I hadn't put in the washer but I still had a bare bum. I wrapped the damp towel round me and even though the house was hot I was shivering. I looked at the phone and thought about dialling 999 but what could I say? Mrs Harcourt's note was there on the table:

Dear Lamb, Mr Harcourt is unwell and is upstairs asleep. Therefore please be quiet and considerate. There is no need to go upstairs today. Please do not use the vacuum cleaner. This would be a good opportunity to tackle woodwork, skirting boards, window frames etc. Please remove ornaments from alcove by fire, wash in warm soapy water and polish shelves. Be especially careful with the Shepherdess – sentimental value! Money in envelope.
Myra Harcourt.

I should have smashed the Shepherdess. I should have just run off but I couldn't go without my clothes. I was giddy and weak in the knees with the shock of it, the thought that I'd walked naked right through the bedroom where he was in bed, the bed all rumpled, the curtains drawn, and into the *en suite*. I couldn't bear it that I'd been in there, the door not even properly shut, wallowing in the bath with him next door all the time, probably having some porno fantasy, playing with his prick.

Then I heard his feet creaking down the stairs. I got hold of a cast-iron grill pan. It weighed a ton. You could brain a person with it easy, if you could lift it. I rested it on the table while I waited. My legs had gone like string. It seemed like hours by the time he finally opened the door and stood there. He'd got the smarmy look back but strained this time like a mask that didn't fit. He was wearing a dressing gown now but no pyjamas. His bare feet were plump and babyish.

'Still here?' he said.

'Waiting for my clothes,' I said. The washing machine sloshed and churned. He laughed, actually *laughed*, throwing his mane back and roaring. His teeth were huge and yellow inside his thick red lips.

'That somewhat hysterical response was unnecessary,' he said.

'Don't think so,' I said.

'Not to say hasty,' he added. 'Just as a matter of inter-est, if I'd said a hundred pounds what would the response have been?'

I didn't even bother to answer.

'Two hundred? Five? It's my theory that everyone has their price.' I shrugged. 'A grand?' he said.

I opened my mouth to tell him to fuck off, then stopped. A thousand pounds. I was thinking about a thousand pounds. What I could do with a thousand pounds. My hands loosened on the grill-pan handle.

I left and walked for ages, gulping down the fresh air. I walked through the Botanics. It was a damp day, not raining but if you closed your eyes you could hear a million faint dripping sounds and smell the wet of earth and rotting leaves. There was no one else around, not even a gardener, but a lone magpie jerked about and a flock of pigeons took off in front of me, sounding like a clever card-sharp shuffle.

I needed someone to tell. If I saw Doggo again and told him, what would he think? What would he say about it? I felt sick in my heart and the pain was there between my ribs again. I would pay a thousand pounds *not* to be fucked by Mr Harcourt. If ever I told anyone that is what I'd say. Would Doggo say that was stupid or was brave?

Instead of just kneeing him in the balls I should have pushed him in the bath and held him under the water until he stopped struggling, all his bubbles lost in the Jacuzzi-effect bubbles. No one would have known it was me. I could have said I never went upstairs, I'd read and obeyed the note. I could have done a murder just like that. The perfect crime. When you look at murder like that, it doesn't seem so bad.

I sat down on a wet bench and squirrels gathered round me sitting up on their haunches expecting some monkey nuts but I had no monkey nuts to give. I cried a bit feeling completely pathetic sitting alone on a bench crying for no reason at all. Then I remembered it was a Mr Dickens afternoon and I was glad.

Sixteen

I went back to the cellar and unlocked the door. Everything was just the same. I'd thought Doggo might have slipped a letter under the door or maybe not that but *something*. Been back and left some sort of sign. But there was nothing. Which was for the best. Of course he would be mad with me. He'd probably hate me now. I did feel guilty about shutting him out, after I'd said he could stay. Going back on my word. He only wanted to stay a night or two. The relief had gone now and I just felt bad.

I wanted to talk to someone. All the things that could have happened. Maybe I did it with Mr Harcourt, maybe we got into the Jacuzzi together, had a ball. Ha ha. All sorts of things happen in this world.

I came over suddenly tired, too tired to go straight up to Mr Dickens', my legs like lead, the air almost too heavy to get into my lungs. I needed someone. *Needed?* No. To talk to. No. Anyway there was no one. I flopped down on the bed. Before Mum died it was her I talked to, told things, almost everything. Would I have told her about Mr Harcourt? But if she was alive it would never have happened so that thought is a waste of space.

After she died I went to stay with her friends, the people we spent Christmas with each year. I had hardly ever been to their house apart from Christmas and it looked strange in the summer sun, with no Christmas tree or decorations. It was my GCSE year. I was supposed to get on with it and do my exams as if nothing much had happened. I was still supposed to want to be a doctor.

The friends were very kind but I could hardly bear to look at them. They decorated a room for me and put up bookshelves. They said I must have my friends round and think of it as home. They thought it would be good therapy to talk about my mum. They put photos of her up and talked about her every day. They said it was all right to miss her, it was normal. It would be all right to cry.

I couldn't tell them that I didn't want to cry. I couldn't tell them I was angry. I was angry with her for dying. Furious. I was furious with her for allowing me not to have other friends, for being my only friend. I was furious with her for dying so quickly, of *nothing*, of a backache. What a stupid thing to die of. Furious with her for giving up like that and being dead. She didn't even say goodbye. Last time I saw her she said, 'See you tomorrow,' and it was a lie.

While I was at the friends' house, the man had his fiftieth birthday. They had a party to celebrate. They said I could invite my friends. Ha. They hired a caterer who did a whole salmon with a lemon in its mouth and a pyramid of profiteroles. They had champagne cocktails and sounded like they'd gone into their second childhoods from where I was sitting on the stairs.

Then someone came out to see me. He was the son of a neighbour and had seen me about, he said. He had some grass and said did I want to go outside for a smoke. I didn't want the smoke but I went with him anyway. He sneaked back in and got a bottle of champagne. He smashed a greenhouse window with the cork. The smell of tomatoes in a greenhouse always reminds me of champagne.

We swigged it from the bottle. He said how tragic it was in there, how tragic to be fifty. He wouldn't be celebrating if it was him, he would probably be dead by then. Then he kissed me. Although I was fifteen it was the first time I'd been kissed. It tasted of champagne. After a while he started touching me. I didn't feel anything like the passion of a person in a book.

We brushed away the glass and lay down in the greenhouse on his coat. Looking up I could see a half-moon through the glass, cut up by tomato leaves. His hand fumbled with my breasts then went down my pants. I felt his dry finger stab in. I said we better not go all the way but he had a condom so we did. He bucked about on top of me a bit and groaned and that was that. When he'd pulled out he said, 'Oh shit,' and jammed his fingers back in where it was sore now. He fished a milky little stocking out and peered at it in the moonlight. 'It should be OK,' he'd said.

My mother's death freed me to do the things I never could have told her.

I stirred myself. I was late for Mr Dickens. I couldn't let him down. I went wearily through the performance of going out the side way and back up the path to press the Trumpet Voluntary. When I finally got in I offered to do some proper cleaning. I thought maybe I'd feel better if I did something real.

'No,' Mr Dickens said, 'you've been working like the devil all weekend, you and your lad.'

I nearly said he's *not* mine, then I thought, oh well. 'But you pay me to clean,' I said. 'I feel guilty if I don't.'

'Well just do carpet then,' he said.

'Ta very much,' I said. He blinked at me and went off to make the tea. I ran the sweeper round the room, getting up so many dog-hairs you could nearly see the pattern on the carpet.

'How's study going?' he asked when we were finally settled down with our tea.

It took a minute then I said, 'Oh great thanks, the photos are really useful. Want them back?'

'No rush.' He paused. 'You've got me thinking, you know.'

'About what?'

'Past. Zita.' That's all he ever *did* think about. He pulled a wad of baccy out of his tin and filled his pipe. I watched the grainy wrinkles of his face, the concentration it took to get the thing lit. Everything takes him so long. I will never have the patience to be old.

'When you get to ninety odd, past is all you have,' he said, his eyes all watery. 'Ninety-one come June, you know.' I nodded. I did know. 'If I'm spared,' he added through a coil of smoke.

Doughnut sighed and I heard another dog barking somewhere. I got a sweet shock right up my spine thinking, is it Gordon? Is it Norma? Is Doggo back? I hadn't locked the door. If he was back I'd let him stay. Just for one more night.

He gazed at me for a minute. 'You know, your eyes are like hers,' he said. 'Bright brown and quick. I always loved her eyes. Even when she got older she still had them same eyes.'

He put down his teacup, picked up his tin and looked inside. 'Same colour as this,' he said. He took a pinch of tobacco between his horny old finger and thumb and held it up to his lips. I thought he was going to kiss it but he just dropped it on his lap and gave a cheeky smile. 'You're about half her size though, Lamb. My Zita were a bonny woman, well covered.'

I thought, please don't go on about Bristols but he didn't. He sucked on his pipe and went blank for a moment, as if he was tuning into another channel. He had gypsy creams on a plate which I know that Doggo likes. I picked a couple up and put them in my pocket for him, just in case. I was dying to go and see if he was there but I couldn't just abandon Mr Dickens.

'What was she like as a person?' I said.

'She were that quick-witted.' He smiled. 'Kept me on my toes. Never got bored. She were always that one step ahead. Always some surprise up her sleeve. Not easy though . . . not what you'd call easy-going. After . . . after she'd gone I thought about other women of course, whether I should remarry. I even kept company with a lady or two, very nice lady in particular, Gwen. Widow, couple of boys. She were a looker, intelligent, everything but . . .'

'She wasn't Zita,' I said.

He did a great gurgling puff and nodded. 'Nail on head, there. She were too . . . I missed . . . I don't know, she were too . . . like drinking milk after whisky . . . all very well but by God you miss the bite.' He shook his head in slow motion and I could hear the vertebrae grinding in his neck. 'Typical of her to go the way she did.' He managed a miserable smile. 'That were my Zita all over.'

He sighed, then he started asking me about Doggo, like how long had we been courting, *courting!* and if we had marriage in mind.

'Dunno,' I said. I cleared my throat. 'Mr Dickens, he might not be . . . I mean, about the garden, I don't know how long he's sticking around.'

'Uh? That's shame. Well, long as you let me know.' He regarded me for a minute. I was expecting questions but he rustled through the pile of newspapers and letters by his chair. 'Got something for you here,' he said, 'just a little token.' He handed me a blue envelope with *Lamb* written on it. I had no idea what it would be. My fingers trembled and I tore it open. Inside was a birthday card, one of the crappest ones you will ever see, flowers and twiddly gold writing and a verse to make you chuck up – and folded inside a ten-pound note. He'd written in very shaky biro, *To Dear Lamb, with thanks for your companionship, very best wishes, Kenneth Dickens.* I couldn't look up. My mouth was twisting around like someone was fighting it. I couldn't look up till I could control my voice then I managed to croak, 'Thank you.'

'Got Meals on Wheels to fetch it,' he said. 'Is it today?' I didn't know the date but said it was anyway. Then I looked at the date on the *Yorkshire Times* and saw that actually it's tomorrow. Because I'm a Scorpio, scorpion, couldn't you guess? Dirty great sting in my tail.

It's the first birthday card I've had for years. Because for years no one has known me well enough to know my birthday, or hardly even known me at all. It was only a card but it was like a treasure. Sitting there I suddenly had this vision of Mr Harcourt and the sleazy thing that happened and I felt dirty. I felt like filth. I wanted to spill it all out to Mr Dickens . . . only I didn't know how to put it, what to say.

Just as I was thinking about leaving he gave me a shock. 'That Doggy fella of yours . . .'

'Yeah?'

'How long have you known him?'

'Oh, ages.'

'Hmm. Just that he's got a bit of a look of that young wanted fella.'

My mouth laughed while the rest of me fell away.

'Sorry?'

'That wanted fella in paper a while back.'

'How funny,' I said. The room had gone into a dizzy blur. 'Wanted for what?'

'Murder. He were a murderer. Escaped from jail, just a few weeks back.'

My mouth was so dry it felt like it would tear if I spoke.

He laughed wheezily. 'Course it's not him,' he said. 'Don't look like that, duck.'

I forced myself to behave naturally. It was like torture to think of a few normal things to say, to wash the cups, drag Doughnut out and wait for him to do his stuff. Just as I left Mr Dickens caught my hand in his. He held surprisingly tight, his skin dry and slippery. 'Course it's not him,' he said, 'but you just watch yourself, duck, won't you? There's some right funny uns about.'

'Yeah,' I said, 'yeah, thanks.'

I rushed back to the cellar but it was dark and empty. *That wanted fella.* I was in a whirl again, fear swooping in my stomach, fear and guilt. Should I tell him or not? If I ever saw him again. If I told him he might bolt. A murderer. It might not be him, not necessarily. I stalked about the cellar like something in a cage. I stood the card up on top of the gas heater but it kept falling off. I held the ten pounds up against the light and saw the secret Queen face and the stripe of foil. I put it in my purse then I suddenly felt tired again, drained, thinking I'd rather have Mr Dickens' ten pounds than Mr Harcourt's thousand. I wanted to tell someone that. It's horrible having a good thought and no one to tell it to.

I thought about going out to the Duke's Head to look for him. But he might have been on his way to see me and then we'd have missed each other. Anyway, I felt like I could hardly move. I looked in the sunglasses at my stupid pop-eyed face. My skin was grey. The cellar was a hole and only fit for rats. He had said that, laughing, *like a rat*. Maybe I did look like a rat. I stuck my teeth out over my lips and wrinkled up my nose.

I wanted him, to see him. Yes I did. But the police wanted him too, if it was him, and maybe they had got him. My fault, it was me that locked him out. I turned the radio on. I hate the news. I hate to hear the sad things in the world but I listened for the whole night and there was not a thing about a murderer caught.

Seventeen

Days went and he didn't come. I hardly dared to leave the cellar, except for once or twice, for things I had to do. I was dying to get back to Mrs Banks' to try and get a clue but they weren't her days. I bought a paper and scoured it but found no mention of the capture of a wanted man. My mind wound round and round, tight tangled nonsense, what if and what if not and memories of Mr Harcourt and his lion's roar. Maybe I had done it with him on the kitchen table, then brained him with the frying pan. I drove myself half mad looking at my stupid face in Doggo's mirror shades. They were the only thing I had of his. There was the tiny whorl of a fingerprint on one of the lenses which might or might not have been his.

In the end I just had to go out and do something. I took the wine bottles to the bottle bank. They were bugging me. All that glass in its safe compact shape. As I shoved them through the holes I said sorry to Mr Dickens for the theft. I love the way they smash, that sound.

I saw a hairdresser's with a sign that said *No appointment necessary* and, on impulse, walked in. A woman sat me down without a second glance. She had a pink crew-cut and perfect ebony skin. I stared at myself in the mirror. It was even worse than I'd thought. I didn't look like the same species as the people in here. But I stared at my eyes to see if they really are like Zita's and they are. Well they are as big and round and dark anyway and I can make them squeeze out stars.

The stylist said really short would suit my bone-structure. She said she'd kill for cheek-bones like mine. I couldn't believe my ears. But it will just be part of the job, compliment the clients so they give you a big fat tip. I let her cut it really short in a style she called gamine, and put red highlights in that hardly show but in the sun they will she promised. What sun?

It takes *ages* for highlights. I drank coffee and read magazines while I sat there with rows of space-age foils in my hair. I read about relationships and being positive. Say a positive thing to your partner every day instead of moaning, for instance: I do love the way you smell *after* he's had a bath rather than You stink before it. Positive reinforcement. I tried it on myself. At least you're *alive*, I said. At least you've got cheek-bones.

When I came out it was like some of the compliment stuck to me for a while. I saw myself in a shop window and my head did look a good shape with the way the hair was cut. And I looked older. Not like a silly little girl, a stringy mop-head. Doggo should have seen me like this. Though the rest of me was crap as usual.

I went shopping. I bought black moleskin jeans and a padded waistcoat and a dark-red, nearly black polo-neck sweater. I even bothered to try them on. The light in the changing room was practically neon and seeing my body illuminated like that smashed me straight back down to earth. Whenever anyone says a nice thing I start to get sucked into a delusion that maybe I'm not as bad as all that. But see me undressed and you'd laugh. That or throw up. Don't you think there must be something wrong with Doggo if he fancied me? I think he did, the way he squeezed my finger that time, the way he said he knew me. Men will do it with anything, though, won't they? Anything with a heart-beat. Some men will, I know. Doggo felt horny and I was there, like Everest or something, that's all it was. Anyway he had gone. Alone again. I could get balanced. I could hardly remember the balance. I bought stomping black boots and socks and knickers. All the new clothes made my old ones look like rags so I bought some spare things too.

I walked round the streets, big swishy carrier bags in both hands, neck cold from the new short of my haircut. Auditioning for being a normal person. You do need money for that. But I was wearing out, my legs melting under me, needing to sit down.

I didn't think I'd make it home so I went into a café and had a Diet Pepsi. At the next table was a boy with his mother. They were arguing about pocket money. 'Anyway, Gregory Podsmore does get one pound fifty, so there,' the boy said and turned his lip inside so you could see the shiny pink. The mother sighed. 'Lucky old Gregory Podsmore,' she said and opened her *Hello* magazine.

The thin tinny taste of the Pepsi was making my teeth go soft. I gritted them together. I should have had tea or something hot. The mother had a little silver pot of tea and a toasted tea-cake. What normal person would have Pepsi on a cold afternoon in winter?

The boy kicked away at the table leg for a minute then started trying to do origami with a paper napkin. His fair fringe flopped into his eyes, he kept pushing it back, wrinkling his beaky little nose. He was maybe five or six. I took in every scrap of him. His jeans had a hole in them and you could see the rough edges of a scab on his boy-bony knee. He had a pink milk shake and every so often he pursed his lips round the straw, took a noisy slurp and wiped his mouth on his sleeve. I wished that I had a pink milk shake too.

I realised the mother was giving me a funny look. Probably thinking I'm a paedophile or something, staring and staring at her child, so I smiled. She half-smiled back as if wondering, do I know her?

'Hi,' I said.

'Oh, hi.'

'How are you?' I said.

'Much better now.'

'Oh good,' I said sympathetically.

'Who are *you*?' the boy said. His blue eyes were about ten sizes too big for his face.

'Tom!' The mother gave him a look.

'It's all right,' I said. 'That's good.' I looked at the crumpled napkin.

'It's a dinghy.' He held it up.

'I can see that. It's brilliant. How old are you?'

'Nearly six,' he said.

'Well that's very good for nearly six.'

'How old are you?'

'Tom!' the mother said again but I could hardly hear her.

'I've got a little boy,' I said.

'Does he go to my same school?'

'I don't know,' I said.

'Why don't you?' he said. My hands were wet and trembling. I shoved them under the bones of my bum and pressed down against the chair until they hurt. The mother was looking at me strangely and I was strange. I could feel it coming over me, all the proper-personness slipping right away.

'Must go,' I said. I got up and the chair fell over behind me with a sound like a gun-shot.

'Excuse me,' the mother said as I went out the door. I didn't stop. I walked fast. I needed to pee and my face was swelling, I had to get away and get some air in my lungs. It was like I couldn't breathe and I needed to be alone to breathe. All the confusion, the lurching unbalance, all the worst things, as if I was being ambushed by the night right in the middle of the day. My face was falling off. I had to be alone. I heard the little boy shouting after me *Hey, hey,* and I ran. I ran till the last echo of the voice was gone, bumping into people and making them shout but never looking back.

I ran till I got to the public toilets. You have to plunge down steps into the swimming-pool smell where the hand-driers roar. I shut myself in a cubicle and rested my head against the painted door. My heart was going like a jack-hammer, beating right up till I thought my skull would split. I waited till it slowed down, listening to the voices and the flushing, the hand-driers and the voices. One voice said, 'If you can't trust a sausage what can you trust?'

There was all sorts scratched on the door about people loving each other or being stupid fucking bitches and slags. I sat on the cold toilet seat and peed. Someone had changed the sign that said *Dispose of soiled dressings in the receptacle provided.* Crossing out *soiled dressings* and putting *jam-rags.* How could anybody be bothered to do that?

I came out and washed my hands and dried them on my jeans. Then with a shock that jolted through me like electricity I realised something was missing. The shopping, all the brand-new clothes in their swish bags. I'd left them behind in the café. All those carrier bags left behind.

I started walking back but I couldn't do it. I couldn't face seeing or speaking to another person. So I lost the clothes. It was all just a game anyway, make-believe. They weren't meant for me at all, they were meant for someone else. A possible version of me.

I stopped and swivelled round in the street and got tangled up with a crowd of little kids streaming off a coach outside the theatre. There was a pantomime on: *Dick Whittington.* A popcorn babble and smell. The teachers with scribbled faces gestured and grimaced at each other over all the different-coloured heads. All these other lives going on and on, every single smallest one of them much realler than my own.

A carrier bag caught in a tree flapped at me. I looked away quick and got walking, walked all the way back from town. When I got there there was nobody and nothing had been moved since I left. Doggo's cup was still by the bed. It was cold and the dark had crept in again and got its stain all over everything but it was best to be in there alone. I didn't even care that Doggo had gone or if he was in prison or what. I had to be alone to give my face a rest from all the masks and expressions of the world. I had to let it slide right off. I curled up underneath the covers and tried to make my mind go blank.

Eighteen

There was a fog of days and I gave up. The police had got him or maybe it wasn't him, Doggo, the wanted man, the murderer. Sometimes the world outside is as much a fog as inside your head, nothing really real, believe what you want it's all the same. I lay under a grey blanket or maybe it wasn't a blanket but only my cloudy breath, my cloudy life. I don't know how long, then I did start to get myself together.

There is one thing that is real and clear and that is pain. I had to get real to start to get my balance back. It felt so high to climb now, the high wire too high above me to even see. I had to feel the pain to see straight, to even start the climb.

I don't do it any more. I don't keep sharp things, razor blades or knives. I even took the bottles to the bottle bank and let them smash safely inside the bin. But there is always something. I broke a biro and forced the sharp plastic under the skin above my wrist. The pain was sharp and real, the first clear thing for days, and the blood trickling was pressure running out.

I do know it's a stupid, ugly thing to do. I had therapy at the hospital and I do know that. The worst time, the last time, I lost too much blood. They thought I was trying to kill myself but I would never do a thing like that. And the wound got infected. I was moved to a proper hospital.

Watching the doctors with their stethoscopes slung round their necks I thought *I* should be training to be one of them, not needing a doctor to stop me harming myself. Such a stupid waste of time. I felt embarrassed. That is when I stopped. I have stopped. This was just the once to help me get my balance back.

But while I was pushing the plastic into my arm I heard footsteps coming down the side of the house and then he was there, Doggo. Coming in in that bold way like he owns the place. The pain jammed a smile on my face. I pulled my sleeve down quick. There were tears on my cheek I hadn't even known were there. I wiped them off. He didn't see, the shades still on. He took them off but didn't look at me properly, or at all. He dropped his bag and flopped down on the deck chair, the dogs beside him.

'Where've you been?' I said.

He looked grey and wrecked. He groaned and looked blearily up at me. 'Any tea going?' I put the kettle on and went outside to the toilet. I pulled the plastic out of my arm, the blood flowed bright. The brightest thing in the whole wide world. I wadded up some toilet paper and put it in my sleeve.

I didn't know what to say to him, I felt shy. When I handed him the tea he cupped his gloves round it and hunched over.

'I thought you'd gone,' I said in the end. 'I thought maybe the police had got you.'

'You said anything?'

I shook my head. 'Doggo. Sorry I locked you out. I won't . . . I won't do it again.'

He nodded, blew across his tea and slurped. 'Had to see someone. He owed me. Meant to be getting me a passport and some dosh.'

'A passport for where?' I said.

'The fuck out of here.'

'What about the dogs?' The way he looked at me you'd think that was a really stupid question.

'Anyway he never fucking showed, did he? He owed me. I'll fucking kill him.' A fleck of spit came out of his mouth when he said *kill*. I think he meant it. I didn't dare to say another word. After he'd finished the tea he smoked a fag. He was miles away, his black eyebrows scrunched together. He was shivering. I put the Calor gas on for him. The cellar was crowding with the smell of cigarette, damp man and dog.

He stubbed his fag out on the floor, nodded his head forward and shut his eyes. I think he went to sleep. While his eyes were closed I rolled up my sleeve and looked at the gash in my arm. The blood was slowing down. It soon loses its brightness, blood. It was ugly and sore, a new wound across the safe old scars. Stupid. Pain *can* help. But *he* was here now. I know he only came back because it was a place to hide. But it did prove he trusted me. He had come back to *me*.

He woke when Mr Dickens started moving about upstairs. We could hear the Zimmer frame, the toilet flushing and soon the kitchen tap. We had another cup of tea. Doggo washed his face and stretched. When he reached up his fingertips brushed the ceiling. I tried but mine were miles away.

'Hey, like the hair,' he said. 'It's really . . .'

'Ta,' I said, I'd forgotten all about it. I ran my fingers through it, tried to fluff it up, wishing I still had the new clothes. But I could always get some more.

'Might as well do garden since I'm here,' he said and squeezed out a bitter laugh. 'While I was waiting for my mate I was planning garden, killing time. Thinking what could be done with it – if there was time.'

I opened my mouth to tell him what Mr Dickens said about the wanted man. I thought maybe if I could say it with a laugh, like, how ridiculous is that? it might be OK. But if it *was* him

. . . but before I could decide he'd gone outside. I followed. Maybe it was best to leave things be. Outside in the daylight he took another look at me but this time said, 'Christ, you look wasted.'

'Not as wasted as you look,' I said.

We had to dig out the roots of a dead shrub and it was amazing, all the things in the soil, fat white grubs and worms, millipedes and a bent teaspoon all clogged up with earth. It reminded me of something I heard once: in one teaspoon of soil there are more living organisms than people on the entire planet. I took a handful of the damp earth and stood there thinking that. It was like I was holding a whole universe in the palm of my hand. My mind reeled just to think it.

Doggo frowned as he worked, ripping and wrenching the poor trembling bushes and slicing the spade down into the earth. Gordon came outside with Norma following. Doggo said Norma was poorly and off her food. I looked. She was quiet, lying down instead of frisking around in her usual way. I said why not take her to the vet but Doggo shook his head.

'In case you're spotted?' I said.

He did an unwilling grin. 'It's as much the . . .' He rubbed his fingers together. 'Vets cost fuck of a lot.'

'I'll pay,' I said. 'I'll even take her for you if you like.'

He gave me a funny look. 'I thought you were broke as me.'

'I could take her Monday,' I said.

We heaved up the last bit of a great knobbly root and looked into the crater it left, which was hairy with fine broken-off fibres and the pink end of a worm sucking back into the earth. It looked so cold in there I shivered. I went to pet the dogs but Gordon growled and Norma didn't even look up.

'Maybe she should see vet,' Doggo said, 'if you *could* spare the dosh. As a lend.'

'Sure,' I said, knowing what that meant. That he would have to stick around for at least a couple of days, 'whatever'.

Mr Dickens called us in for tea. My mouth went dry, waiting for what Mr Dickens might say, thinking I was mad not to warn Doggo, but when we got in Mr Dickens' mind wasn't on that at all. He looked awful. He must have been feeling rough too because he asked me to make the tea – a much better idea since it meant we got to drink it while it was still hot. He hadn't got his teeth in. I'd hardly ever seen him without his teeth before. It was awful the way his voice lost its edges and his face caved in. I was embarrassed looking at him, thinking he must be embarrassed to be seen.

Doggo didn't seem to notice any difference, well he doesn't know him like I do. It was amazing how Doggo came to life and raved on about his plans, even getting out a notebook with a sketch. He can really draw, I was surprised. It had paths and flowerbeds marked out, and stepping stones across the lawn to a seat.

Mr Dickens gave us lunch of bread and sandwich-spread. Doggo ate it with his filthy gloves on. When we'd finished eating we told Mr Dickens we were going for a walk before we got started again. We went out the front and back round to the cellar.

When we got in I made some tea and he skinned up. It was so great to have someone else there. All the dark corners disappeared, as if light was shining out of Doggo or something although actually he was dirty, dark and hairy. If you didn't know he was a criminal, you'd guess. A murderer. I liked the way he just came in and made himself at home as if it was nothing strange and the way the dogs settled down too. It's not a bad place actually. It could be worse.

He still didn't take his gloves off and in the end I couldn't help asking why. He gave me a long look and took one glove off, as slowly as if he was peeling the flesh off the bones. There were sticking plasters all over his knuckles. 'What have you done?' I said. He said nothing. He pulled up the corner of one of the plasters. It came up gradually, sticking and lifting the dark hairs and the thin skin on the back of his hand. Underneath was a raw red circle with wet oozing off it. 'What have you *done*?' I said and then I knew. What he had done was get rid of the LOVE and HATE. It took me a minute to take it in. Then I asked him how.

'Fag,' he said and I nearly passed right out thinking of the shocking burn and sizzle of that.

I swallowed. 'Who put the plasters on for you?'

'I did.' He got a strip of Band-Aid and a spray of Savlon out of his pocket. 'Could you help me change them?'

I felt so chuffed that he asked me, like Florence Nightingale or something. I knelt down in front of him and carefully peeled off the old plasters. It must have hurt like hell but he didn't say anything, there was just a little catch in his breath. The burns were shiny red and runny, not with blood but with clear stuff. On the puffy edge of one you could still see a tiny bit of blue lettering, but I didn't point that out. I didn't want him burning himself any more.

After I'd sprayed the Savlon and put new plasters on I looked up. Our faces were very close together. Only maybe six inches from a kiss. We stuck like that for a breathless moment then he said, 'Ta,' and leant back.

I stood up. 'You can't work like that,' I said. 'Let's tell Mr Dickens we can't do any more today.'

'I'll be right.'

'Why did you do it?' I said and his eyes met mine with a sort of pang.

'Because they were naff.' A long moment hung there. He said, 'Your birthday?' noticing Mr Dickens' card.

'Last week.'

'Should have said. Drink tonight? Buy you a pint.'

'K.' I had to turn away so he couldn't see my idiot face. 'Only I'll treat you – Mr Dickens gave me some birthday money. But . . . what if you're seen?'

'Nah. Anyway, a man has to have his pint.'

We got back to work. I don't know how he could bear it. And my arm was hurting. Maybe a bit of plastic left in. They're splintery as hell, biros. But still the fog had gone and it had all come clear. I have not been happier, not for a long, long time. It was me that said that the LOVE and HATE were naff. Does that mean he burnt them off for me? He should not have done it, but still I have not been happier since I don't know when.

I just loved the way his beard looked so soft around his lips and the little prong of lines at the corners of his eyes when he smiled. Murder? It was hard to believe, seeing him out in the fresh air like that, gardening. I loved the way he breathed when he was lifting something heavy. There was pale sun so I think my red highlights would have been showing and I was glad I'd had them done. Nice eyes, nice hair, that's two things anyway. Oh, and the cheek-bones.

Then a female person came round the back.

'That was quick,' she said.

Her hair was silver in the sun, long and straight, pushed back from a high white forehead. 'I'm Sarah,' she said, 'Mr Dickens' great-niece.' The blue sky cracked quietly like an egg.

Nineteen

We all stood staring at each other for a moment that went on far too long.

'Hi,' I said eventually. Doggo darted me a panicked look. He didn't even have his shades on.

'You must be Lamb,' she said. She turned her eyes on him. 'And Doggo. Hi. He's told me all about *you*.' Doggo and I froze, but she seemed oblivious. She came closer and I saw that her skin was like cream. Her lips were very pink and her teeth square and white when she smiled. She smiled at Doggo.

'I said to Uncle he should get a gardener but I never thought he would. Not so fast anyway. Look what you've done already . . .' She shook her head at the chopped-up garden like it was some kind of miracle.

She was wearing jeans and a white sweater that was tight over her big tits. When she went up the steps and straight into the house without knocking, her thighs were like pork chops. I would never wear tight jeans if I had those hips and thighs. But Doggo kept on watching even after the door had shut.

'Shit,' I said.

'Yeah.'

'What shall we do?'

He shrugged. 'Just get on with it.' He went into the cellar

and came out wearing the shades. I thought it was a bit late
for that, but didn't like to say.

Doggo had planned a rock garden to make use of the rocks
we kept finding in the long grass, rocks with a trail of glitter
through them, I don't know what kind. It was hard work
lugging them about with a cronky wheelbarrow and Doggo
changed his mind twice about where the rock garden should
be. I was getting fed up. What did it matter where it was? Not
like it would ever get finished anyway, the garden. I wanted
to say that to Doggo. *Remember, you are on the run.* The
rock garden ended up in a dingy corner under the shadow
of a tree. I couldn't see what he could see. He could see what
wasn't there yet, flowers and stuff, all I could see was a heap
of mucky rocks.

'What will grow in the shade?' I said.

He shrugged. 'Them little white things.' I gave up. Every
time there was a noise from the house he flinched. He'd got
the hunched and dodgy look back again. I wanted to hold
him. I was his protection. I got a blooming feeling in my belly
thinking that. Only it would be good to know exactly what
he'd done.

'Are you worried,' I asked, 'about her?'

He stopped and pushed his hair out of his eyes. His glove
left a smear of earth across his forehead. He was acting like
his mind was somewhere else but I didn't want it somewhere
else I wanted it right there with me.

'Where do you fancy tonight then?' I said. 'Duke's Head?'

'It's crap on a Saturday,' he said.

Sarah came out again. Her forehead was furrowed like
someone had pulled a fork through the cream. 'I'm worried
about Uncle,' she said. 'He's not himself at all.'

'I thought that,' I said.

'Anyway shall I bring you out some tea?' Her brilliant
smile swept over the two of us like some kind of searchlight.

She brought out a tray with two cups and some biscuits. 'Here.' Gordon trotted up to her, followed by Norma. 'Hello.' Sarah's voice went babyish. 'Hello, you two.' She squatted down to pet them and I thought her jeans would burst.

'Norma's a bit off,' Doggo said.

'Norma!' She let out a trill of laughter. 'I've heard some good ones, but I like that!'

'After my great-aunt,' Doggo said, which was news to me, 'and Gordon.'

'Her husband?'

'No, the gin.'

I smiled knowingly.

'So what's wrong with Norma?' Sarah ran her hands over the little dog and she whimpered. 'All right, girl,' she said, petting and feeling. 'She eating?'

Doggo shook his head. 'Not much, not last couple of days.'

Sarah smiled up at him. 'Actually I'm a veterinary student,' she went. I thought she was joking but she wasn't.

You should have seen Doggo's face then. You'd think an angel had landed. 'Could you do anything for her?' he said.

'I'm taking her to the vet on Monday,' I said.

'I'm only first year,' she said, 'but I've a mate who's qualified. I could pop her there now if you like. Want to come?'

'What *now*?' I said looking at Doggo, but he was nodding.

'Sure?' I said.

He looked irritated. 'Course I'm sure.' I was only thinking of *him*.

'I'm afraid there's not room for the three of us.' Sarah pulled a face at me.

'Well Doggo can get on with the garden,' I said.

'No, I'll take her,' he said.

What could I say?

So they left Gordon with me and went away. I watched them get in the car and she was telling the truth, it was full of boxes and stuff and Doggo had to cram up with Norma on his knee. It seemed like a funny sort of lying low to me.

I shut Gordon in the cellar and went up to see Mr Dickens. He was asleep in his chair with a trail of drool stretching like a wire from the corner of his mouth to his shoulder. Doughnut was keeled over by the electric flames and Mr Dickens' tea was cold beside him. I took the tea away and washed the cups up. Mr Dickens woke up. I could hear him saying, 'What . . . what . . .'

I went and sat by him and said, 'It's OK, Mr Dickens.' I told him Sarah and Doggo had taken Norma to the vet and he smiled an empty pumpkin smile and said, 'Good lass, she is.'

'Shall I make more tea?' I said. 'Only yours got cold.'

'Must have dropped off,' he said. He looked at his Zimmer frame and then changed his mind. 'Please.' I turned my face away and switched the lamp on to try and make everything seem brighter.

'Feel poorly,' he mumbled.

'What's up?'

'Can't rightly say.' He creaked his head from side to side. I went and put the kettle on.

I sat by him again so he could see my lips. 'So Sarah's back,' I said. 'She staying?'

'Didn't I say? Could of sworn I said. She's thinking of packing her course in.'

'She didn't mention *that*,' I said. 'She must have only just started it.'

'And coming to Sheffield to work at a kennels. She's staying with a friend for a couple of days, thinking it over. It's in bag if she wants it, connections, you know. And she's a looker,' he added, irrelevantly. 'Got a way with animals, she has. Ever since she was knee high to a sparrow always rescuing baby mice and feeding them with eye-droppers.'

The kettle started whistling so I went to bring the tea through.

'Going home for Christmas?' he said.

It was like someone had suddenly got hold of my guts and squeezed. 'Dunno,' I said, which was true because I hadn't let myself think about Christmas, even though the shops were all choking up with tinsel like some sort of mutant weed.

Last Christmas I minded my American lady's house – not one of my ladies any more. I was only meant to be going in twice a day to feed the cat, switch the lights on and off and draw the curtains to fool any watching bur- glars. Instead I stayed in the bath practically all week or in bed watching TV. When I was in bed I kept the electric blanket on and the warmth got right into my bones till they almost melted – which made it all the worse when she came back. I got the sack after that. She knew I'd been staying, someone must have said. But what difference did it make? Surely it was better if there was someone there? Not the sack exactly. She just said they'd be moving back to the States soon and she could manage herself till then so she'd have to let me go. Only they didn't move. I kept walking past to see and she even saw me once and looked away quick.

Christmas makes me think of my mum and I can hardly bear to think. We used to have Christmas lunch with the friends. The morning always started off the same right up till I was fifteen. I'd take my Christmas stocking into her bed really early and we'd take everything out together. We'd drink tea from her Teasmaid and unpeel and eat the tinny-tasting chocolate money. Then we'd have bacon sandwiches for breakfast because they were our favourite thing and she'd mix up fizzy white wine and orange juice to drink while we opened our presents. We'd put on our best clothes and lipstick even though it was only us and still early in the morning and we'd take turns to watch each other open the presents and make noises like fireworks going off though we already knew what half of them were.

We'd walk to the friends' house which was a long walk but we always did because it was good for us and so that she could drink. We'd take bags of presents and bottles of wine and spot the kids playing out on their new bikes or roller skates, spot the new hats and scarves. The lunch would be long and hot and noisy with crackers and silly jokes and a flaming pudding.

Walking home was always the best bit. The friends always said for goodness sakes get a taxi but we would love to be walking with ringing heels in the frosty dark, our breaths puffing out in front of us and the path glittering in the street lights. We liked to peep in windows where the curtains hadn't been drawn yet and see snatches of other people's Christmases, televisions flickering, streamers flopping down, someone snoring in a chair. The moon would be a flung-up silver threepence and cats would prowl and we would link arms and hardly need to say a word.

Anyway this Christmas I don't know what yet and I don't really care, to tell the truth. It's just another day in a line of days.

'What about you?' I asked.

Mr Dickens said, 'Don't fuss with it myself. Meals on Wheels usually drop off a cracker.' Which made me laugh.

It seemed like hours before Doggo, Norma and Sarah came back and when they did there was a look between them which left me out. I couldn't look at Doggo. I wondered what he'd told her. After all that they hadn't even got to see her friend. The surgery was closed, and Sarah had decided that anyway Norma wasn't seriously ill. They were going to try again tomorrow.

'Back to work then,' I said, but Sarah said, 'Oh no, let's have a cup of tea first.'

I said, 'Well we've just had one.'

But Mr Dickens said, 'I could do with another, Sarah makes a good cuppa,' which I know was only him being polite but still made me think, what about *me*, don't *I* make a good cuppa too?

I have to admit she's pretty even though she's big. She's got the kind of smile that makes you want to smile too, just some trick to do with a dimple and a look in her eye. She told us a story about her friend who had to do an operation on a goldfish and operated on the wrong one. Imagine operating on a *goldfish*. It's a mad world, isn't it? One end of the street there's someone frying great hunks of slaughtered cod and haddock and at the other someone fiddling about taking a lump off a goldfish.

I needed to pee after all that tea. I went out into the hall to what Mr Dickens calls his cloakroom which is a toilet with coats hanging in it – including a blue fur-collared one of Zita's – and a washbasin with a cake of leatherish cracked soap.

When I came out I stood in the hall and listened to their voices sounding happy, sounding like they were part of something and I wasn't. I stood by the nailed-up door. I put my nose against the wood and sniffed to see if there was any smell of burning left. It seems wrong to me, to nail it up like that and leave it burnt. If it was my room I'd clean it up and use it, fill it with light and flowers, not nail a plank across the door and leave it empty. I think that's what I'd do.

When I went back in they were sitting cosily round, drinking a second cup of tea. Norma hopped up and sat on Sarah's lap which she has never done with me. 'Uh-ho,' Doggo said, 'she's fallen in love.'

'She's always had a way with them,' said Mr Dickens, giving Doggo a dirty twinkle. 'Animals I mean.'

You *have* perked up, I thought.

We finally managed to get away. It was always worse when you first went into the cellar, the dismal light, the cold and damp. It got better when you were used to it. I lit the Calor gas. 'You didn't tell her about the cellar – or anything?' I asked.

He flicked me a look like I was stupid. 'She's cool,' he said.

'Sure?'

'She's OK.'

'Yeah?' I didn't really mind. I was relieved. And pleased to think we had our secrets, Doggo and me and no one else.

Twenty

It's hard to have someone always in your space. You might want to be private. You might have things you need to deal with without another person there. He asked me if I'd fetch him some chips. I should have said yes but I said no. I said *Fetch your own chips*. I mean if he could go to the vet's and go to the pub he could go to the chippie, couldn't he?

Soon as he'd gone, I rolled my sleeve up to look at my arm. The blood had stopped but it was sore, the toilet paper sticking to the scabs. There was plastic left in but I couldn't pick it out, it hurt too much. Not like the clean first hurt, this hurt is dirtier and more like guilt. I washed it and put fresh toilet paper on.

Doggo came back with chips and a pickled egg. I ate a few chips which were cold and tasted of the paper they were wrapped in. He scrubbed his beard with his fist.

'Here,' he said, looking embarrassed, shoving me something.

'What?'

'Happy Birthday.'

It was a silver pendant shaped like a hand with fine-etched lines like the lines on the palm of a hand. I didn't know what to say. 'Indian,' he said. It still had the price tag on. 'You might want to take that off,' he said. He grinned and snapped it off with his sharp side teeth. There was no bag or wrapping paper. I think he stole it. I wanted to ask, to tell him off. What a stupid risk that was. But a risk taken for me. His gloved fingers fumbled the nape of my neck as he fastened it.

'Well ta,' I said.

We held one dog-lead each and he took my arm as we walked along but it was my sore arm and I yelped. 'What's up?' he said. I said I'd hurt it.

'How?'

'Dunno. It's nothing.'

'Let's see.'

'No.' I would rather die than have Doggo know what a stupid thing I did.

He had his shades on because we were out in public. I said it made it look obvious that he was disguised, wearing sunglasses at night in the dark. He thought about that for a bit but he kept them on. A police car cruised past and I watched his face but he didn't look any more dodgy than usual. You'd think if someone was lying low they'd stay in all the time, under the bed or crouching behind a sofa, but it isn't like that. People in hiding keep a low profile but that doesn't mean they don't go to the pub or walk in the park just like anybody else. They go about a sort of life. I know all about that myself.

The pub was brown inside and there was folk music going on in the back room where we had to take the dogs. A haystack of a man was whining through his nose with his finger in his ear. But I didn't care. We found a table and the dogs curled up underneath it. Doggo plonked a couple of pints down in front of me. 'Finished your essay?' he said.

A sip of beer went down the wrong way. He thumped me on the back. When I'd finished choking he kept on. 'On lighthouses, wasn't it?'

'Oh *that*,' I said.

'What kind of stuff? History or what?'

'Just a kind of general survey,' I said, 'you know, the meaning of lighthouses in . . . books and you know art and that.'

'Sounds interesting,' he said and he was right, it did. Maybe someone really has done it, I don't know. 'You must be fucking clever.' He stared at me till I could nearly make out his eyes through the dark plastic. I shrugged modestly. 'At university then?' he said.

'Yeah, sort of,' I said. 'Mr Dickens didn't look too great today, did he?'

Doggo drank his beer about ten times faster than me. He got up to get another but I said I'd get it.

I hated standing at the bar, knowing he was watching me, watching the way I stood and the way it took me ages to get served, as if I was invisible. I could just imagine how Mrs Harcourt would deal with it. She'd burst in saying, 'Excuse me,' in her loud posh voice, pushing in and getting her Campari-soda or whatever before anyone else.

Thinking about Mrs Harcourt reminded me. I'd gone back to the Harcourts'. I wasn't going to but something made me. I let myself in and there was the note on the kitchen table as usual. This time I read it. It said:

Dear Lamb, I'm afraid I'm going to have to terminate our agreement as from today. Please leave your key behind. No wages, which under the circumstances I'm sure you'll understand.
Myra Harcourt.

Fuck you, I wrote at the bottom which was a bit childish so I screwed up the note and chucked it in the bin. I didn't care anyway. I crept upstairs really quietly just in case *he* was tucked up in bed again and he wasn't. It was messy and dark with the curtains drawn. 'Who's going to pick up all your shit for you now?' I said to the bed.

I went in the *en suite* and had a last bath. I used up all her bath milk and dried myself on three towels. I slapped on half a bottle of body lotion. Then I went. I didn't empty the bath, flush the bog or hang up the towels or anything. I thought about smashing the sentimental Shepherdess but I didn't. I just went, left the key on the table and went.

I wonder what Mr Harcourt told her? Not that I give a flying toss. Don't need that job anyway. Don't need to clean for anyone any more. I'll keep Mr Dickens on but I'd do that whether he paid me or not. I'll keep Mrs Banks on too because she's Doggo's mum but apart from that I'm not doing it any more, anyone else's dirty work. Not for a while, anyway. The Harcourts and the Brown-Withers can get stuffed.

Doggo and I shared a packet of crisps and I tried to eat them in normal big crunches. There should be a law that everyone has to clean their own mess. If everyone did that there would be just one lot of cleaning for each person and that's not too much to ask, is it?

'Why are you doing that?' Doggo said.

He was looking at the beer-mat I'd shredded up into a million pieces, like a pile of snow. I am always ripping things up without knowing.

'Dunno,' I said.

We listened to a man play the concertina for a minute then Doggo started going on about gardening.

'It's ace,' he said, leaning forward so I could feel his warm breath on my ear. 'Never even thought about gardening and that but I fucking love it. Never even used to notice plants and trees and that but now they're everywhere, know what I mean? I wish . . .' He looked wistful.

'What?'

'Oh fuck it.'

But I know what he was going to say. In another kind of life he'd like to have a garden. To have time to watch a garden grow. I smiled. See I was getting to know him now, to understand. I was wondering if you could count this as a date.

The evening was going fine then someone jolted right into my bad arm and it hurt so much I yelled. I was on the edge of tears. But you should have seen Doggo in action. He leapt up, spilling his beer, and took a step towards the harmless twitching little man who was blurting, 'Sorry, mate, accident, sorry.'

Doggo raised his fist and went, 'You watch it, right?'

'Right, right,' burbled the man. 'Can I buy you a drink, both of you?' So Doggo let him buy us both another pint. It was the first time anyone's stuck up for me for years and for some reason that nearly set me off crying too, but I was worried that he was drawing attention to himself. Another risk for me.

We smiled at each other. Just looking across the table and smiling straight into each other's faces. It's not often you do that. It was like a sunrise in my chest. The man brought us our drinks.

'Ta,' Doggo said, not even looking up. Then he said, 'What about that Sarah then?'

'What about her?' I said.

'She's something else, isn't she?'

'Hmm,' I said. The sun set at once. Did I mention he was *still* wearing the shades. In a pub at night? If I didn't know him I might have thought he was a prat what with the sunglasses and the woolly gloves and a kind of fugitive hunch in his shoulders.

'She's not a student vet any more,' I said, 'she's given up. She gave up before she'd hardly started.'

'She hasn't decided yet,' he said. 'She were finding it hard-going. If she takes job managing kennels she'll be earning right off. We were discussing it in car.'

Discussing. That is not a Doggo-type word. *What else were you discussing?* I wanted to say. But didn't.

There was a long silence. 'Tell me about the murder,' I said. 'Have you escaped from prison?'

'Einstein,' he said.

I felt like walking out of there. Sometimes his voice has such a horrid scornful edge. I was losing him again. I didn't know what to do. He downed his beer and got up to get another. Sometimes I hate the way he walks, kind of cocky, like his whole body is swinging from his shoulders. You'd never see a woman walk like that. He sat down with his beer. He hadn't even offered me another drink. Fair enough I'd hardly started mine, but still. He took a long swallow and I watched the bobbing of the Adam's apple in his soft white throat. He said, 'What about you, *Lamb*?'

'What?'

'Who are you hiding from?'

My throat went so knotted I couldn't breathe let alone speak.

'Go on,' he said.

I looked down and saw another beer-mat was in shreds. My fingers were trembling. I tried to take a sip of beer but my lips wouldn't bend the right way. Someone started playing the bagpipes.

'Christ,' he said flicking his eyes over to the bagpiper and back. He smiled and put his gloves out to cover my hands and keep them still. 'Come on,' he said. His voice had gone soft and coaxing. I looked up at him. Trying to imagine the dagger or the gun. I could not imagine. There was nothing I could tell him. The moment stretched between us till it broke. He took his hand away. We sat there a bit longer, listening to the dreadful racket. I found I was fingering the silver hand. He saw and smiled. I dropped it.

The music was really getting on my nerves. The company was shit, the smoke was thick, the beer was horrid and even the crisps were stale. I got up. Gordon heaved himself to his feet.

'We going?' Doggo said.

'I am,' I said, 'you do what you like.'

I walked off and he followed. We walked along and after a while he grabbed my hand. It's the first hand, well glove, I've held since I don't know when. We didn't say much. As I walked I was trying to let all the tension go. It was still him, Doggo. And he was still choosing to be with me. He needed to be with me. Nothing had changed. It was him and me against the world.

He had Norma's lead and I had Gordon's and I liked the patient way Gordon plodded along unlike Norma who skips all over the place only not so much when she's poorly. It was like we were a kind of group or even family, all joined together by hands and leads. OK, so there were things about each other we didn't know. There are always things you don't know about other people and most of all about yourself. You don't know what you would do in certain situations. It makes me laugh the way people sound off about how they'd never do *this* or how *that* is so wrong because they simply do not know. But me and Doggo, even though we knew there were no-go areas between us, were still holding hands and I suddenly got a feeling inside which is *happy* and I squeezed his hand but he yelled and yanked it away.

'Sorry,' I said.

We carried on walking. I didn't know what to say any more. It was misty, the mist thick and fuzzy orange round the street lights. I didn't dare get hold of his hand again and he didn't reach for mine. Him yelling about his hand had reminded me about my bad arm and that whole sickening subject.

'Sarah's great, isn't she?' he said. Probably just to break the silence. That would have been OK. But then he kept on. 'I mean it was great of her to try and take Norma to the vet like that.'

'Yeah.'

He suddenly guffawed, making me jump. 'You should see the way she drives!'

I laughed grimly.

'What about asking her to look at your sore arm? If she treats animals she could maybe treat you.'

'Thanks very much,' I said.

'Didn't mean it like that,' he said. 'Fuck it, you're touchy. What's up?'

'Nothing.' Nobody said another word all the way back to the cellar. I was half thinking of locking him out again. I don't know why he had to bring Sarah up at that moment. And why he had to sound so *tickled* about the way she drives. There's nothing clever about bad driving if you ask me. OK so it was a good idea getting her to look at my arm. I couldn't go to the doctor's because I haven't got one. You probably have to be an official person to have a doctor, with an official name and address. If they saw my arm with the scars and the new wound they would know about me. And I do not want to go back to hospital again. I do not and will not. And there's no need anyway because I'm not getting into that again. It was only that once.

Doggo looked ridiculous in the lamplight with the beard and glasses like someone who'd bought a plastic face from Woolworth's. I couldn't lock him out. We got to the cellar and went in. I locked the door behind us.

I got into bed fast as I could and turned my back on him. He didn't come near me though my heart was beating with a kind of fear wondering if he'd try. But after washing his face and moving about a bit he sat down on the deck chair. He whispered, 'Are you asleep?' but I didn't answer. It was hard as hell lying so still but after a while I heard him snore and then I could relax.

Twenty-one

B ut I couldn't sleep properly. I couldn't lie on my arm and Doggo kept snoring and creaking about in the deck chair. Was I sleeping in the same room as a murderer? I was cold in bed so God knows how cold he must have been with only a thin blanket over him. I fell asleep near morning and woke to hear him moving about, making the kind of noise people trying to be quiet make. I pretended to be asleep. Then the key turned and he went out with the dogs. I squinted at my watch, it was before six and not even light. I sat up. But it was OK. His bag was on the floor. I fingered the warm silver hand. I lay back down and slept soundly for an hour or so.

When I woke there was a strip of sun on the floor. You never get sun in the cellar. Maybe it's the time of year, the sun slanting unusually low. It reminded me of the strip of metal a burglar might use to break in with. Not that there's much to break in for. I just lay watching it slide along the floor till it was gone.

I got up to put the kettle on and the floor was so cold it burnt the soles of my feet. It took ages for the water to come through the tap but in the end there was a freezy trickle.

The row with Doggo hung about in my stomach like an undigested meal. Not *row*. The ill-feeling. It was only because of Sarah. I got back into bed with a hot-water bottle and stayed there for as long as I could, drinking cup of tea after cup of tea and reading about aphid control till my bladder was practically bursting.

Outside it was one of the sparkly days. The air so cold it hurt my lungs. No garden has ever sparkled more and my heart lifted. Doggo would soon be back and we would get sorted out. The water in the toilet was frozen and my pee froze on top of it instantly, yellow with a little wisp of paper like a sail.

While I was waiting for Doggo I listened to the radio. There was a service on, the gloomy-sounding shuffle of a congregation, the bellow of an organ, a mumbled prayer to God Almighty. There isn't a God any more than there's a Father Christmas. But you can still pray if you want something badly enough. You can pray to God like witches make spells, like shamans kill chickens or whatever it is they do. You can believe in a kind of magic or intervention. So I prayed for Doggo to come back and for everything to be OK between us, for Sarah to go away and leave us be. And before I'd even finished praying there was the sound of his boots clunking down the cobbles.

When I heard him my heart opened like a fist but when he came through the door I could hardly look at him. I made more tea and we crouched down in front of the heater looking at the magazines. I wanted to say sorry but I wasn't sure what for.

'Where've you been?' I said instead.

'Walked to Ringinglow,' he said.

'That's *miles*.'

'Got restless. Carried *her* halfway back.' He nodded at Norma who was flaked out.

'Good job she's small,' I said. ' Ouch.' I'd banged my arm on the heater. It really hurt. I wanted to roll my sleeve up and see. Yesterday I'd done Doggo's hands for him, changed the plasters. I wanted to borrow his Savlon and spray it on but I couldn't ask or he would want to see.

'Your arm?' he said. 'You should get that looked at.'

'What, like your hands?'

'You know why *I* can't.'

'Yeah.'

'Let me look.'

'No.'

He opened his mouth then shut it again and shrugged. 'Won't get a lot done today,' he said. 'Ground's frozen solid.'

'Like iron,' I said.

'Yeah.'

It made me think of the Bleak Mid-Winter carol, my favourite one, the bit that goes 'Earth stood hard as iron, water like a stone'. Whenever we sang that at school I would get a lump in my throat like the stone.

I wished it would snow, proper sticking lasting snow. Snow on snow on snow.

'Do you think she's OK?' I said, crouching down to pet Norma.

'Think so, just too long a walk for her with her little legs. Love walking, me, clears head.'

'Me too,' I said.

He started on about the garden again, what he'd been planning on his walk. He'd had the idea of putting in a fountain. I thought he was getting carried away but I didn't like to say. I just said, 'God!' thinking Mr Dickens would never consent to a fountain, all he wanted was the garden kept tidy not turned into frigging Fontainebleau. He rambled tiredly on a bit, then yawned and stretched.

'Mind if I lie down for a bit? I didn't sleep right well.' He could hardly keep his eyes open. He got into my bed and shut his eyes. Norma tried to jump up beside him but couldn't make it. I lifted her up and sat on the edge of the bed watching Doggo fall asleep. If someone watched me like that I wouldn't be able to sleep a wink but he didn't notice or care and soon he was making a wiffly noise that made me sleepy again too.

I got closer and studied him, knelt down by the bed learning every single thing about his face. The scar is thick and jagged and stops just under his eyebrow. He's lucky. Whatever happened to him nearly got him in the eye. Maybe it happened during the murder, someone fighting back.

If you look really closely at someone you can see each pore and see where each bristle comes out of the skin. You can smell their hair and their breath. His eyelids were veined and bluish. After he'd been asleep a while they started to twitch which meant that he was dreaming. I wanted to know what was happening in there, to lift up his eyelids like sheets, to crawl inside and watch the dreams.

My knees got cold and I got up and back on the bed, pushing my feet inside to soak up his warmth. I heard Sarah arrive and walk about upstairs. I wished she would go away. Not wishing any harm to her but just that she would go away because she was a danger. I tried the prayer again. Sooner or later she'd find out Doggo was a wanted man. Maybe Mr Dickens would say. Or she'd see something in the paper. And any moment she could come down the stairs and find me living in the cellar or if I was out, find my stuff. Nothing wrong with *her* legs, nothing to stop her. Sooner or later she would. If she was going to stick around I would have to go and where would I go?

It's never bothered me before, moving on. Maybe it would be OK, if Doggo came too. But we might end up on the street. I have never done that. I've slept in all sorts of places but never in the street. Even with Doggo I didn't want to do that, to huddle in a doorway with people passing by and flicking their eyes away quick. I didn't want Doggo doing that either. It was so warm and so sweet, the sealed way he slept, the little puffs of air coming out between his lips.

Then a vehicle stopped outside, footsteps hurried up the path and there was a sudden blast of the Trumpet Voluntary. Doggo jerked straight up, his eyes on stalks. 'What the fuck's that?'

I shot up and switched off the light. Doughnut was barking and Sarah's voice shut him up. We sat close together on the bed. I was shivering. Doggo put his arm round me and that was great, like he was holding the bones of me together.

The dogs seemed to understand the danger. They didn't bark, even Gordon only did one controlled little growl. We all huddled there like a family or something. I would have stayed in that moment for ever if I'd had the chance. There was this *us* and *them* feeling and for once I was part of the us.

Doggo pushed his feet into his boots. Ready to run if he had to run. A sour smell hung around us, the smell of fear. I was getting dizzy from lack of breath, expecting at any moment the police to come storming down. But after a while, the front door slammed, the voice went off up the path and the vehicle drove away.

'Fucking hell,' Doggo said and gave a long breath out. We didn't move. We remained still as if we were posing for a photo until Gordon broke the spell by scratching.

'It's OK,' I said, trying to sound sure.

'Christ,' Doggo said.

'Shall we . . . shall we go round and see what's going on?' I said. 'We could say we're turning up early for the garden.'

We left the dogs curled up on the camp bed and went up the side and back down the path to ring the bell. Doggo laughed at the bell this time. 'Fuck!' he said. 'What a wacko idea.'

Doughnut went into his usual orgy of barking and after a

minute Sarah opened the door. Her eyes were red and she had a balled-up tissue in her hand.

'Hi,' she said and we followed her into the house. The fire was turned up high – Mr Dickens never had it high like that – and the pretend flames beat like trapped wings against the plastic coals. She saw me looking. 'I was cold,' she said.

'Where's Mr Dickens?' I asked, noticing his empty chair.

'He's had a stroke,' Sarah sniffed. 'I came in and took him some tea this morning and he was all . . . he couldn't move his arm.' She lifted up her own left arm. 'An ambulance came and took him away.' There was a tremble in her voice. Doggo and I exchanged glances. 'It's funny,' she said, 'I woke this morning thinking something's up. And I was right.'

'Serious?' Doggo said.

'Course it is,' I said.

'Well it's not a huge stroke – but it's not good.'

'When I was a kid I used to think that a stroke was a nice thing to have, like a stroke of luck or the stroke of an angel's wing,' I said. They both looked at me as if I was mad.

'We'll go,' Doggo said. 'He won't want garden doing today.'

'No,' Sarah said, 'but please, stay and keep me company for a bit. Tea?'

I would have said no, having drunk about a gallon already, but she'd gone to put the kettle on. 'How's Norma?' she called.

'OK, I think,' Doggo said.

I flexed my fingers. It must drive you mad not being able to move. Poor Mr Dickens. Sarah came back in. She didn't look so pretty in a ratty old cardigan with her hair dragged back in a pony-tail which showed that her ears stuck out.

'By the way, where do you two live?' she asked. She was looking at me. I looked at Doggo who grinned sharply, his side tooth glinting.

There was a dodgy pause. 'Near the park,' I said.

'Nice,' she said. 'It's nice round there, isn't it? I'm having some toast. You?'

'Yeah.'

'Lamb?'

'She lives off air, her,' Doggo said before I could answer so I said, 'Yes please,' because actually I was quite hungry.

'Unlike *me*.' Sarah wrinkled up her nose. 'I just can't lose weight,' she said, 'well I could but I've given up trying. I adore food.' She rolled her eyes in a dreamy way. 'I love it *so much*. Like me as I am or lump it, I say.'

'Yeah,' I said.

'*Yeah*.' I thought Doggo's head would fall off with nodding.

While she was in the kitchen making toast, Doggo prowled about. He stopped to look at a framed photo on the wall, a dark photo I'd forgotten until I saw him looking. I should have remembered it was there. I'd even dusted it once, ages ago, in the days when I still used to dust.

Doggo stood with his back to me for a long time and even though he didn't say a word I knew what he was thinking. It was a picture of Zita who was meant to be my granny. I could tell from his back, from the length of time he had it turned on me, that he was thinking I was a liar. Adjusting his impression. But loads of women in the twenties looked like that, didn't they? That style, and those old photos, they make everyone look the same. I wished he'd say something so I could tell him that but he didn't say a word.

Sarah came back in with a stack of toast dripping with butter and honey.

'Hope you like honey,' she said. 'He doesn't seem to have any marmalade.' We all sat round the fire and reached for bits of toast. Doggo didn't look at me and my stomach shrank into a ball.

Sarah suddenly laughed. 'Don't you ever take your gloves off!' Her eyes danced at Doggo but he just muttered something with his mouth full.

'Cold hands, warm heart,' she said, switching the dancing on to me and I nodded but I wasn't sure what she meant. Did she mean he had the gloves on because he had cold hands and a warm heart or that he had warm hands because he had the gloves on which would mean a cold heart? I gave up wondering in the end because she was only making conversation and probably meant nothing at all.

I thought Doggo was probably sorry he'd burned the LOVE and HATE off now if he thought I was such a liar. Nobody said anything for a while, the room just filled up with toasty munching noises till I asked Sarah where she lived but she was in the middle of taking a huge bite of toast. She chewed with her eyes shut. Her lips were sticky with honey.

'Sorry,' she said, 'that is one of the best tastes on earth, don't you think?'

Doggo nodded again. There was honey and crumbs on his beard. He did look ridiculous eating with the gloves on. I nibbled the crust of my toast.

'Norwich,' Sarah said. 'Still got my flat there, but if I leave I'm thinking of maybe moving here. I don't know . . .'

'Why not?' Doggo asked. 'It's a great place.'

'What, *Sheffield*?' I said.

'I mean actually move *here*,' she said, 'this house. I think Uncle wants looking after really although he'd never put it like that. But if I was going to move I'd really prefer a place of my own to put my own stamp on. You know?'

'Yeah, your own stamp on,' I said.

At last Doggo looked at me, his eyebrow tilted up at one corner, nearly a chip of a smile, but it was too late for smiles. I'd gone stony cold at the thought of Sarah coming to stay.

'You don't seem too bothered about your uncle,' I said and I knew it was the wrong thing to say and so did Doggo judging from his expression.

'Oh I *am* . . .' Sarah said. 'I feel awful sitting here enjoying this toast so much but . . .' She licked her fingers and fanned them out, 'What can you do?'

'You visiting?' Doggo said.

'Soon as I can. I'll ring the hospital in a bit, see what's happening.'

We all stared at the plastic fire for a bit, like we were having a minute's silence for Mr Dickens.

Doggo stood up and rubbed his gloves together. 'I'll get out there and get on.'

'I wouldn't bother,' Sarah said.

'There's a few things I can be getting on with. I'll tell you what though, you could take a look at Lamb.'

He went out, letting a big blast of cold in. Thanks a million, I thought.

'So what's the matter?' Sarah said.

First I said it was nothing but I was worried about going septic. I told her I'd grazed myself.

'OK, then, I'll just have a peep.'

'Ta.' We stood there for a minute then Sarah said, 'Well you'll have to show me.' I rolled up my sleeve.

She winced. 'Oooh. What on earth . . .'

'I fell on a biro and it broke,' I said. 'There's a bit still in I think.'

'You fell on a *biro*? But, Lamb . . . all these scars.' She touched the skin on my arm.

'Can you do something or not?'

'You should really see a doctor,' she said, not meeting my eyes.

'Haven't got a doctor right now,' I said.

'You could go up to Casualty.'

'Can't you just do it?'

'Well I could clean it up for you. Put on a dressing, but that's just first aid. Anyone could do that.' She smiled, trying to lighten the mood. 'Most people would rather have a human doctor. Not that I'm not human!'

'You're not a vet either,' I said.

She went and fetched some TCP and bandages. She sterilised a pair of tweezers in a flame.

'OK,' she said. 'Here goes. I'd look away if I were you.' She held my arm down on the table and probed about with the tweezers. I bit down on my lip as I felt the steel points moving underneath my skin. She was making little breathy sighs of effort. I could smell her skin and honeyed breath. 'There,' she said, holding up a clear fragment of plastic. 'It's not too deep. If we keep it clean it should be OK.' *We*, I thought. 'You should really get a jab though. Have you had a tetanus jab lately?'

'Yes,' I said.

'That's lucky. OK, I'll just swab it then put on a dressing.' She smiled. 'It's an anomaly you know,' she said, 'it would be quite legal for a vet to do this, treat a human.' She wiped wet cotton wool across my skin. It reeked of TCP. 'But for a doctor to treat an animal, that's against the law. Did you know that?' I shook my head. I was squeezing my eyes shut and biting my lip against the antiseptic sting. She stuck on a pad of gauze. 'There,' she said. 'That should be fine.' I opened my eyes. It was a neat small dressing. Looked like nothing. Nothing to make such a fuss about at all.

'Ta.'

'Don't mention it. Just keep it clean.'

'Yes.'

'And you should get it looked at if it gets infected.' She washed her hands under the kitchen tap. 'Rightio, let's give this kitchen a spring clean. Make it nice for when he comes back.'

I could hardly refuse. It was cold in the kitchen and everything was scuzzy, grease with hairs and crumbs stuck in. There was a mug by the sink with no handle and a collection of weird toothbrushes in it like a horrid bunch of flowers. At least I suppose they were toothbrushes but strangely angled with all their bristles brown and warped. I'd rather shoot myself than put one of those in my mouth.

Sarah picked up the mug and peered. 'Defunct I think, don't you? She got a black bin bag out of the drawer. 'We'll have a clear-out,' she said and started dropping things in, bottles, soggy old Ajax cartons, rags, the mug. I just gawped wondering what on earth Mr Dickens would say when he got home.

'How long have you been together?' she said.

'Who?'

'You and Doggo.'

I turned the tap on to do the washing up. 'Oh ages,' I said, 'lost count.'

'You're so lucky,' she said chucking a heap of old cata-logues in the bag. 'It's *ages* since I was involved with anyone. There was this guy, Jeremy, lasted a couple of years but since then zilch. Or only the odd – you know.' She lifted her eyebrows and grinned. 'Maybe I'm too fat.'

'You're not fat,' I said.

'Yeah, yeah,' she laughed rubbing her hands on her thighs. 'Well maybe food is more reliable than men, anyway. Since when did a cheesecake let you down?' She stopped for a minute and gave me a long, light-blue look. 'I can see you don't agree.'

'I just don't put on weight,' I said. 'I can eat anything.'

'I'd die for that metabolism,' she said, 'ectomorph is it?'

'Dunno.'

I squirted Squeezee in and started on the dishes. The hot water felt good on my hands and through the steamy grub on the window I could just see Doggo moving about. I'd rather have been out there with him but thought I'd better leave him for a bit. Then he'd be glad to see me. I'd explain about the photo and buy him food. Hot food. We could go to a pub and he could order steak and chips or roast beef or anything he liked.

There was a smash as one glass thing in the bag broke another. 'Whoops,' Sarah said. 'Never mind. I think I might go to church this morning.'

'You go to *church*?'

'Why not?'

I just shrugged. Maybe she wanted to pray for Mr Dickens. I let the water out and rubbed at the scummy ring round the sink. She started telling me about Jeremy and why they split up which she thought was mainly because of different body clocks. 'It was like he was nocturnal,' she said, ripping a ten-year-old calendar off the wall, 'and, me, I like to be in bed by eleven. Well, earlier, really, but then I'm up at seven, bright as anything. The lark and the owl. It never works.'

'Do you mind if I just nip out?' I said. 'I forgot something.'

'Fine,' she said. She didn't seem bothered. She switched the radio on and it was *The Archers Omnibus*. 'And he didn't like *The Archers*,' she said, starting on a new black bag.

Twenty-two

The paving slabs were slippy with a skin of frost and all the shrubs in the gardens were petrified. I walked past car-washers and dog-walkers and hand-in-hand Sunday strollers. Past the Italian café with its windowful of posers drinking espresso or cappuccino and flapping newspapers, trying to look careless and European.

I stuck my hands in my pockets and watched my feet taking step after step till I got to the park. The football field was full of little boys with sore knees and cloudy breath. They have such amazing legs, fragile as twigs yet strong enough to kick a ball. You'd think they'd snap. In the playground mummies and daddies were pushing bundles of padding backwards and forwards on the swings, or running along behind children learning to balance on their wobbly bikes. Everywhere you looked someone had a life to be getting on with. Some purpose.

There was a church bell ringing and the ice on the pond had frozen into ridges like the sound of the bell. I stared at the cold of it till my eyes watered. I could feel the little silver hand dangling just to the right of my heart. I put my hand on the neat numb pad of gauze. All sealed now, square and white and safe. There were bits of bread on the ice, which the ducks had missed. I threw a stone and it bounced and skidded and sang a weird high note that was like the song of how I felt.

When I got back Sarah was out and Doggo still in the garden. I had another look at the picture of Zita that Doggo had noticed. White dress, dark fringe, maybe a little mole beside her mouth, her eyes dark stars. I *could* be related. One in four children isn't fathered by the father on the birth certificate. I heard that on the radio. I could be anyone. I look much more like Zita than Sarah does, Sarah is the opposite type, soft and blurry-edged. No one could possibly believe that she's related.

I went outside to see what kind of mood Doggo was in. He was in the act of demolishing another tree.

'Thought we were leaving that,' I said.

'Maybe I changed my plans.' He didn't look straight at me. There was a mug on the ground with a froth of chocolate round the edge. Sarah must have rushed it out to him as soon as I'd gone.

'You've got chocolate in your beard,' I said. And he may have done. That's the drawback of beards.

'You been cutting yourself up?' he said.

'*Pardon*,' I said.

'She said you've got scars right up your arm.'

'No.'

He raised an eyebrow.

'It was an accident.'

'Oh yeah. Accident prone then?' He threw a branch down and it nearly hit me. The sinews of the torn wood were pale as butter and I could faintly smell the sap.

'What else did she say about me?'

He shrugged.

'Where is she anyway?'

'Dunno. Gone out somewhere, I think. What are you, Lamb, a head-case?'

156

I couldn't believe his cheek. *Me*, a head-case. *Me*. What did he think he was?

I could tell her a few things about you, I thought, but I didn't say it. He scrunched through another branch with his secateurs. 'I'm not a head-case,' I said but he ignored me. He turned his back and hauled a pile of broken branches off across the frosty mud. 'Can I help?' I said but it was like my words were gnats or something he just wanted to swat away.

I gave up and went inside. I stood in the kitchen thinking that if Sarah walked through that door now I'd kill her. Talking about me behind my back like that. Telling Doggo such a thing. I knew what she was up to. You could see she fancied him, the way she looked at him, the smile, the dimples.

I opened the cupboard in the chest-of-drawers. There was a dinner-service I'd never looked at before. Blue and red birds like phoenixes maybe, with bits of gold in their feathers and beaks, gold rims all round the edges of everything, hundreds of pieces all matching – even a sugar bowl and a gravy boat. Imagine owning such a thing. While I was looking at an oval serving dish with a lid and twiddly knobs in the shape of birds' heads, Sarah did come in looking innocent as hell. I got up quick and shut the cupboard door.

'What were you looking for in there?' she said. I didn't answer. It wasn't as if it was her house yet. Her cheeks were scarlet from the cold. Round, like apples you could crunch. She had a carrier bag full of bleach and Flash and oven cleaner. Must have cost her a fortune. Doughnut staggered in panting, dragging his lead behind him.

'What did you tell Doggo?' I said.

'What do you mean?'

'He said you said I'd been cutting myself up. Which is a lie.'

'I'm sorry,' she said. 'It looked like it. I used to know someone who . . . I just thought . . .'

'Well you thought wrong then, didn't you?'

'What did happen then?'

'An accident. I fell through a window. Not that it's any of your business.'

She hesitated, then put her hand on my sleeve and smiled. 'OK then. Sorry.'

'Even if it *was* true why would you go rushing round telling him behind my back?' I said.

'I was just concerned, that's all. Anyway, I thought he'd know. Since you've been together so long.'

I bent down and took Doughnut's lead off, stroking his matted ears.

'Did you go to church?' I asked.

'What, with *him*?' She flopped down on a chair and Doughnut collapsed by the fire. 'I'm shattered,' she said. 'Has anyone phoned?'

'I've been out. Remember.'

'I better ring the hospital.' But she sat there and sighed a couple of times. I was obviously meant to say What's up? but I didn't. I went into the kitchen and looked at the grease of ages on the cooker, hoping it wasn't going to be me who ended up cleaning it off.

The phone rang, and nearly gave me a heart-attack. It's a specially loud phone for the hard-of-hearing and hardly ever rings, but when it does it vibrates right through you. I washed a milky saucepan up while I listened to her saying, 'Yes, oh dear, oh dear, yes, yes.'

When the call was finished she came in the kitchen and stood behind me waiting for me to ask her what it was about. Why do people do that, wait for you to ask, why don't they just come out with what they want to say? In the end I gave in and said, 'Well?'

'He's quite distressed,' she said. 'I'm going straight there. Erm . . .' She looked round. 'Lock up when you go, won't you. Say cheerio for me. Lamb – ' She tried to put her hand on my arm again but I flinched away.

'What?'

'Sorry,' she said. She had those pale eyes that are almost transparent if you look at them from the side. There was a strand of hair stuck in the corner of her mouth. 'But, Lamb, you know . . . if you ever were tempted to harm yourself in some way, you know you can get help, don't you?'

She went while my mouth was still hanging open. It was so *obvious* what she was up to. I don't know how people can stand to be so obvious. She wanted Doggo for herself. She was going to make me out to be some kind of sad case, head-case, loony. Then she could be an angel of mercy and get me help – in other words get me carted off and sectioned. Well if that's what she thought she had another think coming. I'd love to see her face if she found out Doggo was a murderer. What a laugh to see that sympathy drop away. She would run a mile.

I went back to wandering and poking about the house. Of course I *wouldn't* tell her because she'd call the police. You could see she was the law-abiding sort. Fair-haired people always seem more law-abiding to me, I don't know why.

I went into the front room where Mr Dickens' bed was since he couldn't go up the stairs. The bed was stuck incongruously in the middle of the room between armchairs and bookshelves and occasional tables. The Zimmer frame stood beside the bed with a belt dangling off it. The pillow was still dented from his head and some teeth were gaping on the floor, also a book called *The Long Goodbye* and his watch. I picked the watch up and listened to it tick. It got properly through to me then that he might be hurting and frightened. He might even die. The watch ticked quietly against my ear. If he did die, then what?

Twenty-three

Late in the afternoon, Doggo and I went back to the cellar. I thought the stupid photo issue had blown over but the first thing he did was to pick up Mr Dickens' album and start flipping through it in a slow and meaningful way. I waited for him to make some comment but he kept his head down staring at the different pictures of Zita.

'Don't they look similar,' I said in the end, 'Mr Dickens' dead wife and my gran?'

'Funny,' he said, 'it even looks like *Mr Dickens* in this one.' Why didn't he just come straight out with it and call me a liar? He didn't say another word about it but looked at me sideways and flipped the album shut.

'Let's see your arms then,' he said.

'No.'

'So it's true?'

'I fell through a window,' I said, 'when I was a kid. Cut my arms to shreds.'

He groaned and put his head in his hands. Norma whimpered and I squatted down to stroke her head. Her nose was dry and she was breathing too fast, nearly panting.

'She's not well,' I said.

'Nah.'

'I'll take her to the vet tomorrow. The proper vet.'

He looked up and nodded. 'Cheers.'

'Doggo,' I said, 'what if Sarah does move in with Mr Dickens . . .'

We sat there gloomily for a minute, imagining. But I didn't want us to be gloomy. I didn't want it to be gloomy for him, being here with me.

'Let's go out to eat,' I said, 'I'll treat you.'

'Fuck *off*.'

'Why not?'

'Where's dosh coming from? Was it a bank window you fell through?'

'Hahaha,' I said. 'While you were *discussing* me did you tell her about you?'

'Don't be so fucking stupid.'

'What *did* you do?' I said. 'I mean who did you kill? Why? I know you murdered someone so you might as well . . .'

The look on his face shut me up. He stood up so suddenly Gordon yelped. I thought I was going to faint, the way he was looking at me, but I made myself look right back into his eyes. He grabbed hold of my wrists and pulled me up.

'Get off,' I said.

'No. I get it. You like hurt, is that it? You like pain? Maybe *you'd* like to be murdered, eh? That your little fantasy?' He spoke in a hard fast whisper.

'Doggo no.'

'You want me to hurt you? Cut you up like you cut yourself?'

My heart was hammering so hard I could hardly hear him.

'Stop it.'

I would have screamed but I couldn't scream. His hands were strangling my wrists and squeezing my bad arm. My legs started to give way.

'You are a stupid bitch,' he said. His pupils were flared so huge that his eyes looked black. And I was there in them, flickering pale like two tiny flames. His breath was hot.

Then he let go and I staggered back and let myself down on the bed. He shrunk a bit, right there in front of me, his shoulders narrowing. He sat down on the deck chair, sighed and looked at me for a long time. 'OK,' he said. 'You want to know.' He rolled a cig and took a hungry drag before he spoke.

'Dave, my brother, were killed in a riot. Gang from next-door estate, beat him over head with baseball bat and that. Split his skull. He were on one of them life-support machines but he were brain dead so they switched him off. If they hadn't of switched him off he would have been a human vegetable.' He stared at the floor as he spoke. His voice sounded flat and ordinary but a little muscle jumped at the corner of his eye.

'I'm so sorry,' I said. My hands were fizzing hot as the blood prickled back into them.

'So I got my revenge, didn't I? Killed a guy.'

My voice was like paper. 'How?'

'Knifed him. Satisfied?'

He was shuddering. Finding it hard to get the fag into his mouth. I looked at his hands. He'd taken the gloves off. The bits of tape on his knuckles were curled at the edges and covered in fluff from his gloves. The burns were healing. Soon he wouldn't need the plasters at all. I imagined a knife in his hand. I couldn't think what kind of knife. A dagger? Or a flick-knife? Or a carving knife? And did he stab him once or twice or twenty times? Did he stab him through the heart or through the belly and the lungs? And how much blood?

'It were like an eye for an eye,' he said.

I couldn't think what on earth to say. It seemed ordinary, the way he said it. Like murder could actually be an ordinary thing.

'Is that how you got your scar?' I said.

He put his index finger up and tenderly stroked along the crooked brow. 'Yeah.' His stomach growled.

'You hungry?' I said.

He did a wry smile. 'I'm always fucking hungry, me.'

'Shall we go out then?'

'Nah.'

'I'll go and get some take-away then, shall I?' I said.

I went to Pizza Hut and sat in the bright cheesy glare waiting for a deep-pan with pepperoni and anchovies which he said was his favourite. I'm not so keen on the anchovies myself but you can always pick them off. There were hundreds of kids in there shrieking like trapped seagulls, and coloured balloons bobbing against the ceiling. I was trembling inside with the new knowledge. It wasn't that bad. It was the sort of murder you could understand. In the old days or in some societies it might even be considered right. A good thing. And the main thing was he trusted me. He wouldn't have told me the whole truth if he didn't trust me. He hadn't told Sarah. It was me and him now that I knew the truth. Me and him against the world. Up to me to keep him safe.

I stopped off at the off-licence for a bottle of Chianti. But when I got back Doggo had already opened another bottle of Mr Dickens' wine. It was like one of those silly balloons had popped inside me.

'Hey,' I said, 'that's not ours. I got us some, look.'

He peered at the bottle. 'Not such a fine vintage, my dear,' he said and I smiled even though I was narked. While I'd been out, he'd got himself back together. He darted a nervous look at me, but I just smiled. Wanting him to see that it was all OK.

'That's some temper you've got,' I said.

He took a slug of wine straight from the bottle. 'Who's going to miss it?' he said.

'That's not the point. He trusts me.'

'Don't talk shit,' Doggo said, 'he doesn't even know you're here.'

He took a can of dog food out of his bag and opened it with the spike on his army knife. I winced as the sharp point pierced the tin. Gordon wolfed it down but Norma didn't even lift her head.

'Tomorrow, the vet, first thing,' I said.

'Yeah.'

I drank some of the wine since it was open anyway and it got straight into my brains and I didn't care any more where it had come from. I didn't care what Doggo had done, just as long as he was there. I could not imagine being alone again. How can anyone bear to be alone? All that childish high-wire rubbish. The pizza dripped orange grease on the knees of my jeans.

The only thing that bugged me was that we could hear Sarah moving about. She put the telly on. What was she doing there? There was no reason for it. She was meant to be staying with her friend. It meant we were on edge, because any moment she might discover us. Every now and then the phone rang and you could hear her voice but not the words she said.

'You don't go up university much, do you?' Doggo said like he was throwing me a tricky catch. He flicked a bit of pepperoni to Gordon at the same time. Gordon caught the pepperoni with a snap of his teeth which was more than I did the question. There was a big creak from above and we both flinched and shut up.

'Wish she'd go away,' I whispered.

'Oh she's OK,' Doggo said.

'Do you think she's pretty?' I asked. He shrugged. 'I do,' I said, 'or she would be if she wasn't so fat.'

'She's not fat,' he said. 'She's just . . . right curvy, womanly.'

'Yeah,' I said, staring down at my skinny knees, 'I suppose she is.'

There was a long silence.

'Wonder how *he* is, poor bugger,' he said.

I nodded. While I'd been waiting for the pizza I'd watched people moving past like ghosts outside the bright window and prayed for Mr Dickens to get better and not just because of the cellar but because of himself. And because I like him. Because I was used to him sitting in his chair by the fire and telling me stories about Zita. I had liked those cosy afternoons – but they'd started to seem part of the past already. I had his watch on and the leather strap smelled of him and it still ticked away like nothing in the world was wrong.

Suddenly Norma was sick with an awful spasm as if her whole body was going to turn inside out. Lots of froth came up and hung in slippery bubbles and ribbons from her mouth.

I thought Doggo would cry, he looked so scared. I picked her up. Her little body was hot and shuddery in my arms like she was having some sort of fit. He wanted to go and see Sarah, see what she thought, maybe ring a vet. I knew she would be useless but what else could we do? We left Gordon behind and went out the side and back up the path, rang the Trumpet Voluntary and waited. Sarah arrived at the door at the same time as Doughnut and dragged him back. We stood blinking. It was like the Blackpool Illuminations in there.

'Hiya. I've changed all the bulbs,' she said. 'He had 40 watt, can you imagine, and half of *them* were dead. I didn't even know you could *get* 40 watt.'

'Norma's not well,' I said.

She lifted Norma out of my arms and carried her through. She ran her fingers under Norma's tummy and probed. I don't think she knew what on earth she was doing. Norma whimpered. Her breath reeked like something already dead and rotting. 'Sickness or diarrhoea?' Sarah asked.

'She's just puked.'

'Oh dear.' Sarah sat down and cradled Norma on her lap. 'You're not at all well, poppet, are you?'

'Will she be OK?' I said. 'Should we ring someone?'

'Sunday night . . .' Sarah said, 'she'll wait till morning. Get her to drink something or she'll get dehydrated. First thing in the morning we'll get her to the surgery.'

'I was doing that anyway,' I said.

'I'll give you a lift.'

Norma flopped across Sarah's wide denim lap. She seemed tinier than ever, just a rack of beating ribs stretched over with fur and these bright feeble eyes. We all sat and looked at her.

'We should get her home,' I said.

'All right, girl.' Sarah handed Norma to Doggo. He held her like a baby in his arms.

'How's Mr Dickens?' I asked.

Sarah sighed. 'Not too good. He can't speak properly and he's confused. Actually he keeps trying to say something about some money. Apparently it was in the sideboard. It's like he can't rest till he's sorted it out. Did he mention anything like that to you?'

I shook my head and Doggo shrugged. I went to pee and gave myself a quick wash in Mr Dickens' cloakroom with the leathery soap. I stood there trying to make it lather up and thinking how I would kill for a bath, deep and full of that milky plant stuff that Mrs Harcourt had. It would have been so brilliant to float in warm water and get my whole body sweet and clean. But I had to make do with the fossilised soap and a stiff rag of flannel.

When I came out, Doggo and Sarah were bending over Norma, their heads nearly touching. Sarah's hair looked very white next to the black of his, like a negative. They stopped what they were saying when I came back in the room.

'I'll run you home,' Sarah said, reaching for her car keys.

'Nah,' Doggo said, 'we're fine.'

'You staying here?' I asked.

'I think I will tonight,' she said. 'In case the hospital ring. *Sure* I can't give you a lift?'

We went off down the path as if we were going away. She stood at the door for a minute so we had to go along the road and wait before creeping back. It was hard, after the bright light in the house, to settle down in the chilly gloom of the cellar which smelled foul even after I'd cleaned up the sick.

The Calor heater was starting to sputter which meant the gas bottle was nearly finished. We both clammed up. It just seemed like there was nothing much to say. My arm was hurting where Doggo had squeezed it. I wanted to look but I didn't want to remind him of that subject. He had gone sullen like maybe he was regretting what he'd told me. He settled Norma down on a pile of old curtains. Gordon licked her face and gave me a look from under his grizzly eyebrows like whatever happened next it was down to me.

I brushed my teeth and while Doggo was out having a pee I quickly stripped off my jumper and jeans and got into bed. Doggo came back and took off his jacket, two sweaters and his jeans. His thighs had strong muscles in them, very darkly shadowed with hair. He paused for a minute then came across and got into bed. I couldn't say no, it was too cold for him to sleep on the chair. And anyway, there was more between us now. There was the truth. I thought the bed would tip over. It's a small bed for one let alone two.

He smelled strong but when you got used to it it wasn't bad, like old leather mixed up with ginger or something. We were crammed together, front to front, and I could feel every breath that went in and out of him, and feel his heart.

'Shame you don't do sex,' he said.

His cock got hard and twitched about between us like a wild animal. I hollowed my stomach trying to get away from it. He didn't do anything. He could have. He was so much stronger than me. I got a powerful feeling running through my veins, like love.

'Doggo,' I whispered. He stilled like he was waiting. 'Could you be, like a *couple* with someone and not do it?'

'Do what?' he said but I could hear the stick of his lip on his tooth as he smiled. Then he said, 'Dunno. What, *never*?'

'I dunno,' I said.

'Well nor do I.' He pressed his body against me so I could feel all the desire in his. I wished that I could feel it too. I did start to feel a tingle but I didn't dare to show it. There is something wrong with me. Where women are supposed to go all soft and wet, to open up, I do the opposite. I do not melt, I freeze. If we started and that happened he would hate me, he would be that disappointed. What could he do but leave?

It was dangerous being in bed with a murderer, it's only that that made my heart beat hard. He could have raped me but he didn't. He can't be that bad, can he? He can't be a really desperate man. *Unless he doesn't fancy you*, a voice said, one of the voices back again, *not next to Sarah*. Why should I want him to fancy me anyway, why should I want him to when we could never ever do it?

Once he was asleep I wriggled my arm into a comfortable position and relaxed. It was like heaven listening to the knock, knock, knock of his heart. When I was a kid I used to wait for Jesus to come knocking at my heart but he never did. The knocking of Doggo's heart was the sweetest sound I ever heard. I went to sleep with it steady against my ear. It was the best sleep I'd had since I don't know when. But when we woke up, Norma was dead.

Twenty-four

Doggo wept. He picked Norma up and held her on his lap. Her eyes were open just a shiny slit and her paws stretched out as if she was dreaming about running. A stiff pink petal of tongue poked from the side of her mouth. Gordon sat by Doggo's feet and whined. I tried to pet him but he jerked his head away. Doggo's tears fell on Norma's fur and balanced there, glistening. I didn't know what to say or do so I just made the tea as usual.

Doggo cried as hard as if someone was grabbing fistfuls of roots and wrenching them out of his guts. I took Norma off his lap and he flopped face down and sobbed into the bed. I thought, how could he stab a man and sound so cool about it, yet weep like that about a dog? I put Norma on the floor. She was cold and stiff and had probably been dead for hours. Gordon lay with his head across her neck and closed his eyes as if he was weary of the world and wanted no more of it.

Doggo cried for so long the tea got cold and I had to make some more. Eventually he sat up. His face was shiny and swollen, with snot in his moustache, and you could smell the hot salt of his tears. I got him a cold flannel to wipe his face with. He drank the tea and his shoulders kept shuddering with the aftershocks of his weeping.

'We'll have to bury her,' I said.

He nodded and looked at me as if he was grateful for the suggestion though it was obvious that was what we had to do. Doggo carried Norma outside. He dug a deep hole by the back fence. The soil wasn't frozen but he had to chop through a tangle of roots to make it deep enough, a cradle-shaped grave. The roots would grow back and grow through Norma's bones, the spaces between her ribs. She would become part of the tree. I didn't say that but hoped that Doggo was thinking it too. A good thought. When I'm dead I want to be buried under a tree like that so I can be part of it. I do not want to be cremated.

Doggo lifted Norma up very gently and held her in his arms again just like a baby. He kissed her on the side of her nose and said goodbye. I stroked her cold fur and said goodbye too. He knelt down and put her in the hole. She wouldn't go sideways because her legs were stuck stiffly out so she had to go on her back with her legs sticking up. It felt awful shovelling the earth in over her face and her front. Soon just her paws were sticking up which would have been comical if it hadn't been so sad.

Doggo kept shovelling earth on but one of Norma's paws kept sticking out like it was growing longer or something. Doggo gave up and crouched down with his muddy hands over his face. I finished off, digging up some more earth and making a mound to be sure that every scrap of her was buried.

A question leapt into my head. If Doggo had just escaped from prison how come he had the dogs? It didn't make sense. I wanted to ask but I didn't dare then. It didn't seem the right moment for a new interrogation.

A steamy rush of water emptied into the drain, showing that Sarah was up. Gordon was crying from the cellar. I was worried that Sarah might hear him but we couldn't let him out in case he tried to dig Norma up.

Sure enough, just as I was patting the earth on the mound, the door opened and Sarah stood there tying a dressing gown round her waist. Doughnut yapped and tottered down the steps.

'You're early!' she called, then to Doggo, 'What are you doing here anyway? I thought you just came weekends.'

Doggo stayed put with his back turned and I went up the garden to the kitchen steps. Sarah's dressing gown was pink towelling, shaggy with loose-pulled threads. One of her cheeks was creased with sleep and her hair was wet.

'How's your arm?' she whispered.

'Fine. But Norma died.'

'Oh my God.' She sifted her hand through her hair. 'I'm so sorry, Lamb. It's all my fault.'

'Don't think that,' I said.

'But . . .' A tear rolled down her cheek.

'It's not *your* fault,' I said. 'Nobody thinks it was your fault. But I hope you don't mind us burying her here. We haven't got a garden.'

'Course not. Oh dear . . . I'm so sorry. I should have done something.'

'She was *our* dog.'

'Just that what with Uncle . . .'

'It's OK.'

'I'm so sorry.' Sarah plonked herself down on the step. I could see the smooth white skin on the insides of her thighs disappearing into fuzzy blonde shadow and I was glad Doggo wasn't standing where I was. I couldn't believe how white and smooth her flesh was, no scars, no veins, no pimples, not even any roughness on her knees. As if she was made of dense white bread instead of flesh and gristle and bones like me.

'I can't bear it when an animal dies,' she said. 'Makes you feel so useless. That's why I'm giving up being a vet.'

'So you've decided?'

She nodded. I thought it was just as well, considering how useless she'd been. She got a crumpled tissue out of her pocket and blew her nose. 'Is that Gordon?' She tilted her head to one side. Gordon was going demented underneath us.

'I shut him in that old cellar,' I said, 'just while we were burying Norma.'

'Come in for some breakfast when you've finished,' Sarah said. 'And bring poor Gordon in with you.' When she went in she left the back door open a bit as if she was trying to be part of us which she wasn't.

Sarah made scrambled eggs which Doggo managed to wolf down despite his grief. We didn't say much. Sarah kept sniffing. I don't know why *she* was acting so upset. Norma wasn't anything to do with her.

'Do you want to visit Uncle with me?' she asked. I looked at Doggo but he was staring at the fire, chewing on the inside of his cheek. 'He's really got a soft spot for *you*,' she said to me.

'Yeah,' I said. Actually once she'd suggested visiting him I knew that of course I would. But alone, not with Sarah, because if we were standing side by side what would be the point of me?

'His speech is all . . .' she said. 'But he managed to talk about you a bit. He thinks you're too thin.'

'Not that thin,' I said taking a bite of toast.

Gordon whimpered in his sleep. 'Poor sod,' Doggo said, the first thing he'd said since we'd gone in.

'Yes. They do mourn, you know,' Sarah said, 'dogs, they do mourn. They need to grieve, just like us.'

I remembered those stories about dogs who pine to death by their masters' graves and all that weepy stuff. Though Gordon did still have Doggo – and me, sort of.

'Did you ever see that film called . . . some journey,' I said, 'about a couple of dogs and a cat – or maybe cats and a dog, who went hundreds of miles to find their owners? It was just amazing how they found the way. They went on boats and everything.'

'*The Incredible Journey*. I loved that film,' Sarah said. 'I was wearing a muff when I saw that, white fur, and after the film I suddenly thought it might be made of cat-skin. I've never worn fur since. That's when I decided I wanted to be a vet.'

'Hmmm,' I said.

There was a long pause then something amazing happened. It was like the answer to a prayer.

'I want to ask you two a favour.' Sarah sounded nervous. Doggo dragged his eyes away from the plastic fire. I got a glimpse of Sarah as he might be seeing her. Her curves straining against the pink dressing gown, her blonde hair which had dried like something from a shampoo advert. All she needed was to toss her head about a bit but she didn't, she pushed a wisp of hair behind her ears and wrinkled her creamy forehead.

'I've got to go away,' she said, 'probably just for a few days. Something's come up. I just wondered if maybe one of you, or both, would mind staying here. Looking after the place – and Doughnut. And maybe visiting Uncle, I know it's a lot to ask but I can't bear to think of him in there with no one to visit. I feel bad about it but I really need to go. I can't think of anyone else to ask.'

There was a long silence. Doggo and I did not look at each other.

'If *not* I could shut up the house and take Doughnut but I'd rather not.'

'I guess we could manage that,' I said in the end. 'Doggo?'

'Sure,' he said. 'Don't see why not. If he can stay too.' He nodded down at Gordon.

'Course,' she said, 'oh that'd be so brilliant. A weight off my mind. Thanks so much. See there's this chance of a job and if I don't . . .'

'No problem,' I said. I didn't dare catch Doggo's eye because a coat-hanger of a grin had got in my mouth and was trying to stretch it open.

'It seems such a cheek when I hardly know you,' she said.

'Really it's fine,' I said. 'Glad to help.' And after a reasonable pause. 'When are you off?'

'Well,' she pulled a face. 'If possible today. I know it's short notice. Or I *could* put it off till tomorrow.'

'Whenever,' I said. 'Soon as you like. No problem, is it, Doggo?'

She went upstairs to dress. I piled the breakfast things up and carried them into the kitchen with a sunbeam feeling inside me even though the sky was like a wad of thick grey felt and there were muddy footprints on the floor. Even though Norma was dead and Doggo was so cast down. It was hard to stop myself from singing.

Twenty-five

Outside the hospital a huddle of people in dressing gowns were smoking. Tragic. A man in a wheelchair and even a woman with a drip on a stand hunched over in the cold, sucking grey smoke into their grey skins.

When I got through the nicotine the hospital air was so hot I nearly fainted. It wasn't just the heat. It was the officialdom of the atmosphere. I hadn't been anywhere official for years. Not since the loony-bin. I nearly turned and walked straight out. But I didn't let myself. I was just a visitor, not a real part of it. Just passing through. When I'd been in hospital I'd so envied the visitors with their coats and proper outside shoes with mud on. With their proper outside lives. And now I was one too.

There was a row of artificial Christmas trees, all identical, the tinsel crackling with static. The foyer was like a station with a newsagent's, a café and a florist but instead of platforms and trains there were lifts and people milling about waiting for lifts.

I bought a card for Mr Dickens. The picture on the front was of a cat in plus-fours playing golf and inside it said, 'I heard you were below par.' Hahaha. I don't even know if Mr Dickens ever played golf in his life. I borrowed a pen from the woman in the shop and put *Love Lamb* and then stopped, wondering if I should put Doggo too. I did in the end even though it used to annoy me at school when a girl only had to snog a boy once and she'd be signing him on her Christmas cards as if they'd been happily married for fifty years.

It took ages for the lift to come and then a crowd of visitors, patients and nurses crammed in together like sardines, strange smells and wet paper full of flowers and other people's hair too near your face. It was friendly in a way though, as if we were all in it together – like wartime was meant to be. The man pressing up against me was not a visitor but a patient. His skin was as silver as fish skin and he smelt like fish too. I turned my face away from his scuzzy smile.

The ward was high up and you could see across the city for miles. Mr Dickens was in the end bed. He was lying on top of the blankets wearing green pyjamas. I think he looked pleased when he saw me. I didn't know whether to kiss him. I left it too late in the end and didn't kiss him but I got hold of his hand and half shook and half squeezed it. He wrestled with his face a bit and said, 'Lamb, I want to say . . .' but he couldn't get the next bit out. It was as if the words had turned to bubble-gum in his mouth. I didn't know what to say. The man in the next bed had a shaved head with a tube stuck in. I felt my knees going. It was so hot in there and the hygiene clung in my nostrils like cellophane so I could hardly breathe.

There were some skinny flowers in a vase but they'd been put where he couldn't see them without craning his neck and I knew the trouble he had with his neck. There was a plastic beaker with a lid and spout like a baby's training cup. It was half full of tea. I sat down in a chair. I opened the card and showed it to Mr Dickens and half his face beamed with the old familiar crinkles. The other half was smooth, as if all the lines had been ironed out. The front of his pyjama-trousers gaped a bit and it was hard to keep my eyes away from the grizzled gap even though I really didn't want to see.

'Lamb . . .' he said again. He was getting agitated. I didn't know what to do. He looked much smaller on the bed and much cleaner. Someone had shaved him but left a triangle of silver bristles on one side of his nose. Once I'd started talking I couldn't stop. I gabbled on about the garden and what Doggo was doing and told him about Norma dying and how we were spring cleaning the kitchen. It was like I was talking for England or something which is not like me at all. I told him that Doggo and I would be minding his house and his dog while Sarah was away.

A crazy idea started growing in my head then that maybe we could stay in the house for ever, Doggo and me, and live there properly. When Mr Dickens came out of hospital we could look after him and the garden and the house. Be his housekeeper and gardener. I would have to brush up a bit on housekeeping though. That would be so wonderful and safe. A proper life to live.

He closed his eyes while I was talking and I looked up and saw that big grey snowflakes had started to fall, not fall but *whirl*, sideways across the window so the miles of view were blotted out.

'Look,' I said, 'it's snowing.' Mr Dickens opened his eyes and creaked his neck round to see.

I took the photo of Zita out of my bag. 'Look who I've brought to see you,' I said. It was the picture from the wall. 'Shall I put her here?' I was going to prop the picture up but he lifted his working hand and took it. Nearly snatched it. He didn't even look he just clutched on to it like it would save him from falling. The whirl of snow outside made my stomach lurch. Mr Dickens started getting agitated and the two halves of his face were two different masks.

'TV,' he shouted.

'What?' I said. I didn't know what he meant. TV?

He said something like *Watch out*. He started shouting

that. Then *TV*. I looked across at the screen. It was switched on with no sound. A pair of hands was kneading dough.

'It's all right,' I said. Flecks of spit were making froth in one corner of his mouth. One eye started running. The man in the next bed flicked his eyes to the ceiling at me and smiled conspiratorially as if Mr Dickens had gone soft in the head. I looked away.

A nurse came up. 'Now, now, Kenneth,' she said. 'They do get agitated.' She shook her head. 'But he's all right really, aren't you, Ken?'

A hopeless look passed across his face, his eyes going dull before he closed them. The knuckles on the hand he was clutching the picture with were like yellow marbles ready to pop straight through his skin but the other hand was soft as a bird.

'What have we here? Oh isn't she lovely,' the nurse said, glimpsing Zita between Mr Dickens' fingers.

'My granny,' I said. I don't know why I said that but anyway Mr Dickens didn't seem to mind.

'You've got her eyes,' the nurse said.

See. Everyone says that.

'He's your grandad then?' the nurse said. 'Funny. I thought – '

I know what she thought, that he had no relatives other than Sarah. Well then, where *was* Sarah? Something was obviously much more important to her than Mr Dickens. She had gone swanning off after a job and now there was only me. And Mr Dickens didn't contradict her. He probably liked the thought that we might be related too.

'Well anyway, we're all right now, aren't we?' the nurse said patting his arm. 'And will you just *look* at that weather, you're in the right place here, Kenneth.'

She went away, her shoe-soles squeaking as they peeled off the floor tiles. Mr Dickens just gripped on to the picture and kept his eyes shut as if he was on some scary swooping fairground ride. I sat watching the snow lifting and dizzying outside the window for as long as I could stand it. The dough had been rolled out and made into a gingerbread house. A hand was sticking Smarties to the roof. My belly suddenly caved in realising what he might have meant. The news. He'd seen Doggo on the news. *Watch out*. I think he was asleep. I whispered goodbye and left.

When I got outside the world was broken into dots and swirls, lights trapped in fuzz and the edges between the road and path blurred over. I should rush back and warn Doggo straightaway. I slithered on the path. But Mr Dickens might *not* have meant that. He might have meant anything. Why should they put Doggo on TV now? It was weeks since he'd escaped.

The damp cold crept inside my jacket and made me shiver. The snow clogged up my eyelashes and stuck like a soft wig over my hair. I stuck out my tongue to catch a snowflake and it tasted like a cheap tin spoon.

Twenty-six

I walked straight up the front path. My footprints were the only footprints. I opened the door and walked straight in, half expecting a shout of Oi! from somewhere. But there was no shout. I had a perfect right to walk straight in, a perfect right to be there.

I hurried past the barred-up door and into the back room which was blazing with light and heat. I wanted Doggo to see the snow on my hair and eyelashes but he didn't look up and it was melting anyway. He was watching television with Gordon on his lap and Doughnut at his feet.

'Any news or anything?' I said. I didn't mind him not answering because I knew he was grieving. And if he'd seen himself on telly he'd be more wound up than this. It was just my stupid nerves. I went over and touched his shoulder. I was so glad to see him safely there, I just needed to touch him to check that he was real.

'How is he?' he said, still not looking up. But I understood from the way he was sitting, his arms round Gordon, that he was just holding himself together. If he moved his head the tears would spill out. I do know that feeling. And Mr Dickens too. He was holding himself together.

Don't we all hold ourselves together in the only ways we can?

'Not so good,' I said. I wanted to tell him my plan, about living there and caring for Mr Dickens, but it didn't feel like the right moment. There was a war film on but I couldn't concentrate.

I felt fidgety. I felt like a life-sized doll in a life-sized doll's house. I wanted to touch everything and try everything out. 'We could have dinner off *this*, look,' I said.

I'd opened the sideboard to show him the dinner-service. 'Isn't it great?' I said. 'A proper set. Everything matching.' I turned a plate upside down. 'Finest Bone China, Royal Worcester,' I read. But he didn't look impressed. He didn't look at all. His big toe was coming through his sock and the nail was shocking.

Bone china is made with real bone, did you know that? Bones are burnt into ash and then mixed in with the clay. That's why it's so thin and strong. Only doesn't it make you wonder whose bones?

I fidgeted about in the kitchen thinking about trying to cook a meal. It was so cosy being inside in the bright and warm while outside the rest of the world was torn up into confetti and flung about. I made myself leave Doggo alone and wandered all round the house. Only the back room was warm. The rest of it had a musty, mushroom smell. Sarah hadn't put new bulbs everywhere and some of it was too gloomy to bear.

I found the room Sarah had been sleeping in. I could see why she'd chosen it. Small enough to heat and there was a lethal-looking electric fire, the flex hairy as a bog-brush. She'd taken all her stuff with her except some handcream and a brush with blonde hairs stuck in the bristles.

By the window was a tall chest-of-drawers. Inside the top drawer there were balls of wool, folded material and a sewing box with rusty pins and needles. There was something half knitted with the needles still in. It was a pair of woollen leggings for a baby, fine pink wool. Still on the needles and with moth holes in. There was one of Zita's wigs in a pale lavender colour. I thought I'd put it on for Doggo to see but when I picked it up millions of dead-moth wings fluttered out and wormy bits of eaten stuff. It just came apart in my hands, leaving dry traces on my skin and making me sneeze and sneeze. I shoved it back quick and scrubbed my hands on my jeans.

In the next drawer was a jam-jar full of buttons. I tipped some out in my hand, icy thin shell-buttons and rugged coat buttons, some covered in material and some shiny. One silver one with an anchor on. There were some things there waiting to be mended. Socks for darning; a shirt with a rip and a nightdress with a broken strap. Waiting for at least sixteen years. I took the nightdress out and held it up. It was made of that peachy silk which is almost like skin. The straps were thin as spaghetti. I wonder how the strap broke? Maybe Mr Dickens ripped it in a fit of passion. I tied a knot in the strap and it was suddenly mended after all those years.

I found our bedroom up a little staircase through a narrow door. It was the tower room. You had to be very careful because some of the stairs had splintery holes in. It would have been a spiral staircase if it had gone on long enough. The room was octagonal with seven windows. All the windows had sludge-green velvet curtains that felt like sludge too. On the eighth wall there was a painted-on pretend window with a view of a stormy sea outside. My heart was beating like a boogie woogie or something. From all the real windows the view was the same. Snowstorm.

Of course it was cold and damp but not more cold and damp than the cellar. There was a nearly-double bed and under it a potty patterned with twining ivy leaves. Underneath the stormy sea was the furred-up black iron throat of a fireplace. The room was like a lighthouse room, high and round and with the sea painted there. Maybe someone else thought it was like a lighthouse and that is why the sea was painted. Maybe Zita did it. Doggo the lighthouse keeper. He would love it, I knew that much about him.

I decided to fetch some coal from the cellar and light a fire. I went down and got sheets, a slippery blue quilt, the bedside lamp from Sarah's room and the electric fire to start to warm it up till the fire was lit. Doggo mustn't see till it was ready.

I made the bed and went back downstairs. The secret of the room was nearly jumping out of my mouth but I didn't say a word about it. Doggo was gawping at something else now anyway and hardly noticed me. The film had finished but he hadn't moved a muscle. I stood there for a minute.

'What you up to?' he said at last.

'Wait and see,' I said.

I went the way I never go, the inside way down into the cellar rather than back outside in the snow. There's a door in the hall and behind it a black plunge of stairs with no light. You have to hold your breath and close your eyes and mind against the thready break of cobwebs on your face. You have to hang on to a clammy rail while your foot feels for each uneven step. But there is nothing to fear, it is only dark. And dark is only the lack of light. It's *nothing*. That's what I tell myself – but sometimes it does seem more than that. A thing in its own right, *dark*, a quality, a mood, a spirit.

Soon as I could I put on the light and gazed around the cellar. It was already hard to believe I could ever really have lived in that desperate choking gloom. I shovelled up a scuttleful of coal. The coal must have been there years, Mr Dickens only ever used the electric fire.

I got right back upstairs without Doggo seeing me, but I could not get the fire to light. The coal was damp. I thought maybe it was stale from all those years waiting in the cellar – but then that's nothing compared with the age of it. When I held a bit in my hand I remembered a picture on a classroom wall, a diagram showing how the giant club-root moss mulches down under the earth and becomes the weird light stone that burns. The black greasy sheen of it came off on my skin. But it *wouldn't* burn. I put in match after match. I wanted to make everything perfect and cosy, a surprise for Doggo, to cheer him up, but the coal reeked of cat's piss and wouldn't even smoke let alone blaze and the electric fire made a burnt-dust smell but no impression on the cold.

It got dark while I was trying to light the fire. Houses burn down accidentally all the time but I could not deliberately light this fire. I switched on the lamp and drew the curtains leaving black smears on the velvet. The wind was rumbling around whipping the snow about. I could have made it cosy in there but the coals just sat and sulked, ignoring the match flames, cold and dead right through their hearts.

After a while I heard Doggo calling me and then coming up the first stairs. I listened to him opening doors and doors. My heart was beating as if I was hiding from him – but I did want to be found. There should have been a fire though, he should have been finding me in a warm room not a cold one.

In the end he came up the nearly spiral stairs swearing when his foot went through a hole. When he came in the first thing he said was, 'Fuck, wow.' Then, 'I've buggered my foot.'

'I wanted to light the fire,' I said, 'but there's something wrong with this coal.'

He laughed. 'Ouch. Is it bleeding?' He peered down at his sock but you couldn't tell. 'That's not how you make a fire, you daft git,' he said.

'I know,' I said.

'Hang on.' He went down again, walking on the heel of his hurt foot. I waited, shivering, and heard a snapping sound from downstairs. The sky sobbed against all the windows.

Doggo came hobbling back upstairs, his arms full of wood and a newspaper.

'Clothes horse,' he said.

You can't just go round snapping up people's clothes horses, I thought, but I didn't say. I didn't feel like saying anything. But I knew for sure then. I love Doggo, I do, even though he does these things, drinking other people's wine, murdering people, snapping up their clothes horses. But he does care about teeth and cry about dogs and the sound of his beating heart is the nearest thing to heaven.

He knelt by the fireplace and told me how you build a fire, twisting newspaper into tight screws, building a wig-wam shape with the kindling, leaving spaces for air to draw through, balancing the coals. He was in his element, I could see.

'Weren't you ever a Girl Guide?' he said leaning back, wiping his black hands on his jeans.

'Me!' I said. I *was* in the Brownies but I didn't tell him that. I hated the ridiculous things you had to do like leapfrogging over papier mâché toadstools and singing about kookaburras. I am not a group person, me – although I can still tie a reef knot.

'I can see you were a Boy Scout,' I said.

He put his head right down and blew on the fire and it lit immediately but the room choked up with smoke. 'Fuck,' he said, 'blocked chimney.' It was brilliant the practical way he handled it. He raked out the burning wood on to the tiles in front and rammed a bit of clothes horse up the chimney to hook the blockage out. First there was just a sooty trickle then a shocking clot of bird bones, feathers, leaves and beaks and God knows what. I couldn't look. I went downstairs and left him to it.

It was nice down there. *Songs of Praise* on the telly, a choir shivering on a hillside, the wind blowing their skirts up as they sang a Welsh carol. I decided to make macaroni cheese because it gave instructions on the macaroni packet and we had all the necessary ingredients. I did use to cook sometimes for Mum and me but not for ages. In domestic science we made Victoria sponge and even roll-mop herrings once. You don't need to cook, not if it's just you. But it wasn't just me any more it was me and Doggo and because it was a snowstorm and we had somewhere to be, I cooked. Like a celebration.

While I was trying to make the sauce the phone rang and I nearly shot right out of my skin. It is so ridiculously loud. I nearly didn't answer it. I nearly didn't realise it was up to me to answer it. When is the last time I answered a phone?

'Thought you weren't there,' Sarah said.

'I was – um,' I said.

'Everything all right? Warm enough?'

'We're absolutely fine.'

'And how did Uncle seem?'

'Happy as, you know, Larry,' I said thinking that was maybe going a bit far.

'Really?'

'Well quite . . . settled. Comfortable, you know.'

'That's good. Did he ask you about the money? There was some in the sideboard, hidden in a serving dish or something.'

'Nope.'

'Well, if you're all fine. Is it snowing there?'

'Yeah it's wild.'

'Good job I went when I did or I'd never have got here.'

'Yeah.'

'Any problem, here's my number.' She reeled off a number but I couldn't see a pen anywhere and there was a horrible smell coming from the kitchen. 'It's really kind of you,' she said.

'No probs, got to go,' I said. 'Bye.'

A woman on the telly was saying how having cancer had converted her into a Christian and in the kitchen the cheese sauce had converted into a solid stinking lump. I tipped it in the bin. Now there would only be macaroni. But never mind. Upstairs Doggo was building us a fire and later I'd have a bath and then we would be warm together in the lighthouse room while the wind tossed the snow about outside.

Twenty-seven

D oggo made a different sauce out of tinned tomatoes and dried herbs. He opened a bottle of cold greenish wine that tasted like stone. We sat in front of the television with our plates on our laps. I lifted my glass and said, 'To Norma.' Doggo looked back at me with dazzles in his eyes. I thought the poor dog must be frozen solid by now. I wanted to ask him whose dogs they were. If Norma wasn't his, maybe he should let someone know that she was dead. But he looked so desolate I left it. Part of a relationship is knowing when to let things be.

Last of the Summer Wine was on and there were roars of laughter washing round the room like waves. Doggo kept his eyes on the telly most of the time but he didn't laugh or even smile and nor did I. In Norma's honour we were sombre – but still it felt good to me to be somewhere I had a right to be, somewhere warm and light and with another person, especially with Doggo. It made me feel more like a proper person myself.

Last Christmas in my American lady's house I'd had light and heat, telly, a bed and a deep pink bath but I had moved about that house like a woman made of smoke, someone who would vanish if you opened the door too fast.

I ate some of the macaroni and sauce. I didn't want Doggo

thinking he'd cooked for nothing, though I don't know if he'd have noticed if I hadn't. He ate a ton of the stuff, more and more helpings, shovelling it in with his eyes on the telly, slurping down the wine. He wouldn't win any prizes for his table manners, Doggo, but I don't care.

While we were waiting for his sauce to cook I'd redone the plasters on his hands. The skin was healing up, each burn drying and pursing from the outside in. Next time, maybe, we could leave the plasters off.

When his hands were done I knelt down to look at his foot. The sock was stiff with dirt and his foot filthy, the nails ragged with black stuff caked under them. The splinter from the stairs was jammed between his big and second toe with dirt and half-dried blood crusting round it. I got the washing-up bowl and filled it with warm water. I pulled out the splinter and new blood leaked out.

His feet stank. I squirted Squeezee in the water and washed them, rinsing the squiggles of dirt from between his toes, scrubbing his heels with a pan scourer till they were pink. They are thin feet. The second toe is longer than the big one. There are wide spaces between his toes and wiry black hairs on the top of each one.

I washed his feet slowly, learning every bit. He lay back with his eyes closed, flinching if it tickled or hurt but not saying a word. I found a speckled verruca, big as a five-pence piece, on his right heel. I cut his toenails which were so long they'd started curling under. I sprayed the Savlon on the leaky place where the splinter had been and then I rubbed Sarah's handcream into the whole of his feet. He didn't say a word but a blissful look spread over his face, and the feeling spread from him to me.

I've never looked at a person's feet before, not properly studied them. Doggo's feet were beautiful. As I washed them, I went over in my mind some things he'd said.

While he was frying an onion for the sauce he'd told me this: his dad, who was called Sid, was violent to his mum. One day he hit her with a fish-slice, he hit and hit and hit while Doggo and his brother sat at the table watching. Nothing they could do. When Sid had finished he went out and left her covered with stripes of bruise. And sometimes he locked her out. If she ever went out at night he locked the door and wouldn't let her back in. Doggo said he remembered her banging at the windows and shouting *Let me see my kids*, her face pale and wild behind the net curtains. Then one day she was gone. Doggo said he woke one night and her hair was against his face and it smelled sweet. It made him feel happy and safe that she was so close and he went back to sleep smiling. But in the morning she had gone.

For a long time he'd thought she was dead. Sid said they must never mention her name in that house again. Doggo cried every night for ages but in a way he was glad she'd gone. At least he didn't have to see her being hit and bullied any more and Sid never once laid a finger on his boys.

While he was talking I thought about Mrs Banks, how quiet and ordinary she is. I just can't see her shouting and banging wildly at windows or being beaten up with a fish-slice. Or running out on her little boys.

After we'd finished eating Doggo told me more. 'Sid never cooked a thing in his life before she went.' He ran his finger round his plate to get the last of the sauce. 'But when Mum was gone he did. He learned. In some ways he was a right bastard but he did try. Our best thing were banger mountain, mashed spuds with bangers stuck in top and ketchup all over. When Mum left he learned to do that and we had it every Saturday for years. He had tattoos all up his arms of bulldogs and hearts and a Union Jack. He used to stand in the kitchen in his vest with all his tattoos showing and mash those fucking spuds like he was beating the fucking shit out of someone. Nobody ever mashed spuds like my old man. They were like silk.'

'God,' I said.

It was the most Doggo had ever spoken in one go. It was the most he'd ever told me. It's a weird thing, but sometimes the more you know about someone the less you feel you know. By the time he'd stopped I was prickling with questions. I could hardly keep sitting still. I waited for him to go on but he didn't so I asked him whose dogs Gordon and Norma were. He poured out the last of the wine, hitting the bottom with his palm like it was a bottle of ketchup.

'Eh?' I said.

'Why?'

'Dunno,' I said, 'I'm interested.'

'Like you're a fount of information about you,' he said. His shoulders hunched up. I thought maybe he was about to turn nasty again. I held my breath but he looked up and grinned.

'*Fount!*' I said and threw a bit of macaroni at him. He threw it back. He was OK but he clammed up again. It was like a door had blown open then slammed shut. The news came on and I went like a ramrod with fear but there was nothing about him, or any wanted man, just the usual terrible arguments and sufferings of the world.

The water was gurgling hot in the pipes so I had a bath. I'd never had a bath at Mr Dickens' before. Even though I love bathing it wasn't a tempting prospect. The bath was disgusting with a ginger stain under the taps and the plug-hole clogged up with grey hairs and fossilised slime. The air was so cold it turned to solid steam as soon as I switched the hot tap on. I got in and lay under the steam looking at the silver hand against my scraggy tits and the hairs everywhere that shouldn't be there. My silly scratch was nearly better. It wasn't deep at all. A lot of fuss about nothing, that had been.

Soon it would be just another scar, turning from purple to silver-white.

I tried not to look at the sides of the bath, all the rings of grey and khaki and nearly black. You could probably count all the baths that had been had in it for years. I bet it hasn't been cleaned since Zita died. I bet one of those rings has bits of her in it, skin-cells and DNA and stuff. A scientist could probably clone her from a scraping of that bath.

The bottom was gritty against my bum and there was nothing nice, no oil or anything only cheap green soap which rubbed up into scum. But still it was good to be in the hot water. I let my head go under and the water gurgled in my ears. When I came up for air I heard Doggo shouting through the door for me to leave the water in.

'It's not my dirt in there,' I said when I came out.

When I got up to the lighthouse room it was warm and the fire was crackling. It was like a scene stolen from a dream, the walls shuddering with flame-light or maybe from the wind, and the snow like numb little thoughts sliding down the glass when I peeped between the curtains.

I unfolded Zita's nightie and shook it out by the fire. I wanted to try it, what it felt like to wear a nightie like that. I took off my clothes and stood there for a minute watching the firelight and shadows lick over my skin. Funny how flame-light can make the worst things look OK. Flame-light and enough wine inside you. The nightie flowed over me like cool water. There was no mirror so I couldn't get the full effect but it clung. Even though I was much thinner than Zita it clung to my tits and stroked across my goosy belly. Imagine how it would look on Sarah, silk against her curves. There were little rot holes on the front I hadn't seen before. Moth or rot but it didn't matter. It was like a new skin and I didn't feel like me at all.

I knelt down by the fire, not thinking about Sarah, thinking about Doggo, how it must have felt to watch his mum get beaten up. I poked the fire with a bit of clothes horse trying to remember my parents together. Maybe I could remember them holding hands. Their hands above me like a pink knot and the shadow stretched between them on the ground, joined up like cut-out paper dolls. I must have been so small. And they used to fly me between them. I do remember the jolt and swing as my red shoes flew up and they shouted *Wheeeee!*, my wings tugged tight between their arms, my hands squashed up in theirs, flying as if I was their own trapped bird. But no hitting. And I have never been hit that I remember, not once in my entire life. Not yet.

I felt a trickle inside me like the gradual start of a landslide thinking of the scary jolt and swing between their safe hands, the giggle and skirt flap and scuff of my shoes and me probably saying *More, more* till they were sick of it. Thinking about my mum. How after Daddy died she had red eyes and always the lump of a bunched-up hankie in her sleeve. I didn't cry of course because I was too small to know what I had lost.

I was going to get into bed but before I could, Doggo came up the stairs with a towel round his waist. He'd only stayed in the bath about a minute. His nipples were like two wet and fuzzy flowers.

His eyes flared when he saw me. 'Stand up,' he said. I wanted to crawl under the bed but I did stand up and did an idiotic twirl. 'That is . . .' he said but the words died in his mouth. The towel poked out in front of him like a tent. And he did really fancy me. He really fancied me. *Me.* 'You look so sexy,' he said. And I knew that I did, in the dim firelight in someone else's nightdress, I did. Pity it was only me inside.

'*I'm* not *sexy*,' I said and tried to laugh but it came out as a bleat. He shook his head and stepped towards me.

'Changed your mind then?' He took me in his arms and

kissed me. It was like a Hollywood kiss. I felt as if I should bend myself back in his arms, arch my body up the way they do. His damp skin got on the silk till it was practically dissolving. I opened my mouth and his tongue slipped in. I thought it would be all right but then the nightdress seemed to be disappearing and it was still me under it, my own rough skin, my own self turning into splintery wood.

His hands crawled down my back to my bum. His towel was pushing out so far I knew it was only a matter of time before it fell right off. I tried not to think. Thoughts were rushing in but I tried to stop them. I tried to think, *I can do it, I can let him do it. I love him, I can, I can*. But then one of his hands tried to go up inside the silk and I didn't want him to feel me and the towel fell off. His prick sprung up and it reminded me of Mr Harcourt. Not that it was a horrid whiskery prawn like Mr Harcourt's, it was smooth and kind of hopeful-looking, but still I couldn't touch it or let it near. I jerked away so hard my head banged his nose. I didn't mean it.

'Fuck.' He let go of me and bent over, hands cupped over his nose.

'Sorry,' I said.

He took his hands away and there was blood running from his nostrils. I hid behind my hands, feeling naked, feeling stupid, feeling scared. If he was ever going to kill me it would be now. I looked between my fingers but he hadn't moved. Standing there with a hard-on and the blood streaming down. The blood was shiny red, gorgeous in the flames.

'Sorry.'

'Stop fucking apologising.'

I picked up the towel and chucked it to him to mop the blood away. 'You should tip your head back.' There was blood all down the nightdress. I went down to fetch a cold wet flannel but when I got back the bleeding had almost stopped.

'Sorry,' I said. I couldn't think what else to say.

'*Sorry*,' he spat. He went downstairs.

I took off the nightie and threw it on the fire. It wisped into flame and bits of it flew up the chimney before the rest sizzled on the coals. The smell was of Doggo's burning blood. I put on my T-shirt and knickers and got between the cold sheets. I thought he would never come back upstairs. I lay there for ages wondering what he was doing down there, what he was thinking. Wondering if he would ever come back up. Listening for the slam of the door. But after a while he did come stumping back up.

'What is up with you?' he said. His voice had gone stuffy and thick as if he had a cold. I couldn't look at him.

'Nothing.'

'You're a fucking tease,' he said. He was so angry. I could smell it coming off his skin.

'I'm not.'

'You were begging for it.'

'I wasn't. You said it didn't matter if we didn't do it,' I said and dared to look up at him. His penis had given up hope and flopped down.

'I never said it didn't *matter*,' he said. He put some clothes on and got into bed but so far away from me he might as well have been on another planet. 'It does matter,' he said after a while. 'That's what it's all about, isn't it?'

I wanted to say, What *what's* all about? but I didn't say anything. I wanted to say, That's *not* what it's all about for *me* but I just lay there. How could I explain? I was nearly afraid to breathe.

'Why didn't you just say no?' he said. 'Christ, Lamb, you didn't have to head-butt me.'

'Didn't mean to.'

'Don't know if I *can* do without,' he said, 'not with us being so close together. And what are you doing dressing up in that fucking négligé thing and prancing about if you don't want it. Fucking tease.' I opened my mouth to say it wasn't a négligé it was a nightie but shut it again. We lay side by side in a stiff sulk.

I thought about what he'd just said. *I don't know if I can do without.* Did that mean he'd rape me or he'd leave me if I wouldn't do it with him?

I lay for ages listening to the crackling fire, the wind, to Doggo's breath and the invisible sound that snowflakes make. It felt as if the room was rocking. Doggo's breath turned from angry snuffly breath to calm breath and then to sleeping breath.

When I was sure he was asleep I slid across the cold sheet and into the edges of his warmth. I was so wide awake it was like someone had opened up my skull to the wind and snow. I moved up against Doggo until we were touching and after a while he curled round me and the weight of his warm sleeping arm came across me. I screwed up my eyes but the flames flickered right through the lids.

Twenty-eight

The phone woke me, ringing on and on for ages. I didn't move, holding my breath hoping that it wouldn't disturb Doggo but it was OK, he didn't even stir. It was morning and an odd bluish light was filtering between the curtains. There were dark splatters of blood on the pillow from Doggo's nose-bleed. I could only see his hair above the slippery quilt. Sharp quiffs of feather were poking through the material and I lay there pulling them out, wondering what kind of bird they came from.

In the end I got up. It was freezing and silent, as if the whole world had put a finger to its lips. I pulled my sweater on and went to the window and looked between the curtains. The sky was bright toothpaste-blue and the garden and the roofs, the whole city, muffled with snow. The fire had gone out, just a clag of grey cinders and a powder of silky ash all over the carpet that stuck to my footsoles.

Excitement swooped through me. On snowy days when I was a kid I used to rush out into the garden before breakfast and stamp about in my Wellingtons, making the first footprints in the whole wide world. I felt like doing the same now.

Of course it would be all right with Doggo. I would

somehow make it be all right. His sleeping breath was like a kind of charm.

I crept out and down the stairs listening to the creaking of my feet on the treads. It was as if part of me was still down there in the cellar, listening to the feet moving about above. But these feet were mine and I was *not* down there any more. This was me up here. The real me. The other one was like a kind of ghost or shadow.

The back room was sweltering because we'd left the electric fire on high all night. It stunk of dog breath. Gordon and Doughnut got up and wagged their tails but when I put my hand out to pat Gordon, he side-stepped. I know he blames me for Norma, but it was not me. I would never hurt a dog.

I opened the back door for them and they just stood and gawped. The snow had blown halfway up the door and stuck there. From their height the world had been blocked off into a frieze of glittering white. Doughnut bumped his nose on it and Gordon gave an anxious whine.

'Come on, boys,' I said and we went through to the front. The sun shining through the green stained-glass fanlight mottled my bare feet. I opened it and the cold blasted in. The snow was deep but not drifting in the front and the two dogs went out to do their stuff.

I made a tray of tea and biscuits to take up to Doggo in bed. Waiting for the kettle to boil, I remembered that during the night he'd had a nightmare. He had woken me up, twitching and whimpering and making frightened sounds like bits of chopped-up words. I'd held him. It didn't stop the dream but I liked to hold him. Maybe it was of some help, subconsciously. I whispered things like *You are safe*. He hadn't properly woken but eventually calmed down and lay quietly in my arms.

My feet were numb. Walking up the stairs with the tray

of tea I noticed how the hairs on my legs were bristling out with cold. I thought maybe I should shave them. Or just wear trousers all the time. When I was halfway upstairs the phone rang again. I hesitated, nearly left it, then put the tray on a step and went down to answer it.

It was the hospital to say that Mr Dickens was dead. He'd had another stroke in the night. They thought I was Sarah but what difference does that make? They asked me what I wanted to do and I had no idea. They asked me to ring them back later when I'd got over the shock. *Do you understand?* a woman kept saying, as if I was subnormal. I put the phone down and stood there staring at it.

I took the tea up. Doggo was still asleep but I pulled the curtains to let in the snow light. Doggo put his head out from under the covers, squinting. He had a delicate crust of dried blood round his nostrils. When he saw the tea he smiled. My stomach went soft at his smile. I climbed into bed and he flinched at my icy toes.

'Still lying?' he said and I swallowed. What did he mean *lying*? Then he said, 'The snow,' but he gave me a blade of a look.

'Deep,' I said quickly. 'We're practically snowed in.'

'You going to explain?' he said.

'I think it's to do with atmospheric conditions,' I said but he didn't laugh. I tried to but my throat was closing up.

'You going to tell me what's up with you?' he said.

'I'm gay.'

'No you're not.'

'How do you know?'

'You said so. Anyway . . . Try again.' He waited. He slurped his tea then looked at me sharply. 'You got Aids or something?'

'No!'

199

'You just don't fancy me then. That it?' he said.

'No, no,' I said more quickly than I meant, 'no it's not that.'

'You *do* fancy me.'

'Well . . . yes.'

'Ta.' He grinned. 'So what the fuck's up with you then?'

'I . . .' I couldn't bring myself to say it. He waited.

'I've run out of ideas,' he said. 'Unless you've taken holy orders.' That nearly made me laugh. He held my hand between his gentle murdering hands, stroked my fingers, pinching the ends the way I love.

I took a deep breath. 'OK then I'm frigid,' I said.

He put his head on one side. 'Frigid.' He considered the word, said it slowly like it was a strange new taste. 'Frigid. Fucking hell. Why?'

I shrugged. I was getting fed up with the subject, all the questions. 'How am I supposed to know?'

'Were you mucked about with as a kid?'

'Don't be stupid,' I said.

He let go of my hands. 'So, sex isn't an option then?'

There was no way I could answer that. I couldn't even nod or shake my head.

'What *do* you want then?' he said. 'Why are we together in this bed?'

To say *For your warmth* would have sounded stupid. *Your warmth and your heart beating by my ear and your arms around but nothing else.* That sounds too stupid to be true.

But once we got downstairs it was OK again. He was like a kid about the snow, worse than me. I borrowed a pair of Wellies from the cloakroom, maybe Zita's, and we pushed our way through the drifts of snow against the door. It was so perfect the way the snow had traced the edge of even the smallest twig and covered the muddy wreck of the garden with curves and dips of white. The sun came out even though it was frosty cold all day and everything sparkled, with shadows blue and mauve.

'Oi,' Doggo said and before I could turn round there was the splat of icy cold on my face. It stung, the ice crystals sharp against my skin.

'Ow!' I put my hand up to my cheek and he pelted me again, this time it hit my ear. I wanted to go in.

'Get me back then,' he said.

I crouched down and gathered up a handful of snow, but when I flung it, it just powdered up mid-air.

'Pathetic,' he went and threw another one that thumped against my chest. It really hurt. I felt like crying. Gordon was eating the snow. Doggo laughing like it was all some big joke. I tried to laugh too. I picked up more snow and squeezed it hard between my hands until it made a solid ball. I threw it but he jumped aside. It missed and smashed against the wall. He kept on throwing. He got me on the head and then the thigh. I couldn't believe how much it hurt like he was throwing stones at me. Like hurt is what he really wanted, to hurt me.

My hands were raw and numb and almost orange from the cold. I made another one and flung it and this time it hit. It clocked him on the cheek and bits of white stuck in his beard. He paused, I flinched – but he just laughed. 'She's got it!' he said and punched the air. He was exactly like a little kid. I got him once more but only on the arm.

'Let's make a snowman,' he said. I tried to help but my hands were frozen solid. I don't know how he stood it. He made a small ball and started rolling it about. It gathered up the snow quickly, a growing globe of white. He rolled it further down the garden and soon the perfect snow was messed with streaks of mud and mud mixed with the snow and instead of a pure white ball it was grey and stuck with torn-off leaves, bird-shit and squashed berries. He never finished it. He soon got bored. The sun went in and the sky turned to a giant pink bruise. We went inside.

He fetched a bottle of wine up from the cellar. I was thinking mulled wine would be nice, my mum used to do that sometimes but I didn't know how, so we just drank it cold. We were thawing our fingers and toes out by the fire when Doggo said, 'What about visiting Mr Dickens?'

'Tomorrow,' I said. 'He wouldn't expect us in this weather.'

But when he'd said that the snow started sliding off the roof, like a spell had broken. Yes, in the night the thaw began and snow slid with that awful whoosh and there were creakings and drips and the fire didn't want to burn, it hissed with the drops trickling down the chimney and the wind got up and boo-hooed outside.

We sat up late because going to bed was awkward. We didn't need to sleep in the same bed but I wanted to. Just to be close beside him while he dreamt. Just to be near his beating heart. I thought if I went up first he might stay downstairs and sleep by the fire or maybe in Mr Dickens' bed or Sarah's. I was nodding off before he finally got up and stretched. He shoved the dogs out for a minute, then he went upstairs. I followed. He didn't mind. At least he didn't say.

It was freezing because nobody had thought to light the fire. It was too cold to undress. With most of our clothes on we slipped between the icy sheets. Doggo immediately turned his back but didn't go straight to sleep. He didn't ask me to do anything or even kiss me. He was in one of his talking moods. He lay and talked into the dark, explained about the dogs.

When he'd got out of prison, jumping from a transfer van, he'd gone straight to his gran's. They were her dogs. She was confused and ill. She didn't know he'd escaped or even been in jail. Nothing stuck in her memory for more than five minutes. She kept saying to him, 'Look after my doggies,' because she needed to go into hospital for an operation on her hip. There was nobody else to take care of them. And if she went into hospital they'd have had to be put down or anyway, that's what she thought. Doggo promised he'd mind them for the few weeks she was in hospital and the few weeks were nearly up. I thought it was strange to take on two dogs when you're lying low. 'Too fucking right,' he said. 'Who'd think to look for a man with dogs.'

His gran had promised not to say a word. Not that anyone would have taken notice if she had, she was that loopy. After his mum had left he'd spent a lot of time with her. She had called him Doggo ever since he was a little kid, because he was so soft on dogs. Now it was up to him to tell her about Norma's death. I could see that would be hard.

'If I get taken in,' he said, 'would *you* take Gordon back to her and explain? Tell her it weren't my fault.' I said of course I would. I was honoured to be asked.

I asked him why the dogs were called such funny names. I could hear the smile in his voice as he told that his gran's sister had been called Norma and she had pretended to everyone she was married to a reclusive man called Gordon. When she was found dead there was no husband to be seen, but they did find about a million Gordon's Gin bottles, all nicely washed and stacked in the shed. Her whole marriage one weird joke. His gran had named the dogs after that marriage, in her sister's memory.

I was glad he'd told me one of his family secrets, even if it was so strange. Told me more than he'd told Sarah. I put my arms round him from the back but so lightly I don't think he would have noticed and got the wrong idea.

In the night I heard a noise. It was drips splashing on the floor by the bed. I could see a shiny wetness on the carpet. I got out of bed and put the potty in the right place to catch the drips. I lay still all the rest of the night just listening to Doggo's breath and the leaking roof.

And remembering something. The phone had rung during the evening and I'd had to answer it because Doggo was there listening. It was Sarah. We talked about the snow. It was even deeper where she was. She'd had to help dig a Shetland pony out of a field. She asked how we were getting on, how Mr Dickens was. I said everything was fine, he was rapidly improving. She said, 'Great,' sounding as if she'd been let off the hook. Well, that is what she wanted to hear, isn't it? There was no point her rushing back.

Twenty-nine

It was Mrs Banks next morning. I would have forgotten. The days were losing their order with everything in life so altered. But Doggo said something about his mum and that reminded me. I was curious to see her now I knew so much, to see if she looked different.

Walking was awful. Zita's boots were wet inside from yesterday and my jeans damp too. Everywhere snow was rushing and shushing to the ground, the paths slithery with deep fudgey slush. Gutters were blocked and cars swished along the roads sending up muddy waves of slop.

It was weird seeing her face to face. She'd turned into a different person in my head – but here she was, the ordinary same. She looked surprised to see me. Apparently I'd not come when I'd last been meant to. 'Lamb! Come in,' she said. 'Get those wet things off. Have you been ill? I've been worried. Could you give me a phone number so I could get in touch?'

Worried.

'Sorry, I haven't got a phone,' I said.

Roy was making a snowman out of green plasticine on the kitchen table. 'I maded a real one yesday,' he said, 'and I gived it a carrot for a nose and one of Daddy's cigars.'

'Daddy wasn't too impressed with that idea, was he?' She winked at me over his head.

'I made a snowman yesterday too,' I said, 'with my boyfriend.'

'You've got a boyfriend? *Good*.' She sounded almost relieved. 'What's his name?'

'Oh . . . Derek,' I said. I don't know where that came from.

'Been together long?'

'No,' I said. 'What shall I do?'

'Have a coffee before you start? Nursery's shut today so I'm taking a sickie.'

I sat down at the table. The table mat had been moved and the burns were there for anyone to see but she just poured the coffee and went on about this and that. How they might get the lounge decorated only she wanted peach and Neville wanted green, well not green, a hint of mint it's called. She got out the colour-cards to show me and I agreed that peach was better. 'I'll tell him that,' she said and grinned in a way that was so much like Doggo I had to look away.

I watched Roy making his plasticine man, black hair sticking up, tongue nipped between his teeth with such fierce concentration, his strong grubby little fingers squeezing and pressing.

'We're going to decorate the tree later, aren't we, Roy,' she said; 'so there's no point hoovering, anyway.'

'Yeah, tree,' Roy said, grinding his fist into the plasticine man. 'Now.'

'No, we've got to wait for Daddy. Shall I put Pingu on for you?'

Her mention of the tree gave me an idea. Doggo and I could have Christmas. We could get a tree and even have a Christmas dinner. We could pull crackers and watch telly and be traditional. We could be just like everybody else.

She started gabbling on again about making curtains or buying them or what about Roman blinds? but the words that were coming out of her mouth were not the ones in her eyes. I watched her face, trying to imagine her being beaten up. I listened and hardly said a word except for yeah, and mmm.

'I got my handbag back by the way,' she said suddenly, and it was like another voice cutting through. My face went hot. I'd forgotten all about the bag.

'Yeah?' I said.

I only had to stay cool. There was no way she could know I had anything to do with it. No way.

'A few days ago. All there. Someone left it on the door-step.'

'That's weird.' I gulped down the last of my coffee, thinking I'd scalp Doggo when I saw him.

'Yes,' she said, 'yes, it is weird, isn't it?' My coffee was finished so I didn't know what to do with my hands, apart from chew my nails. There was a long sloppy drip from the gutter. I shivered.

'It's funny,' she said, 'a funny thing to do, I mean, stealing the bag and then returning it. I wonder what possible motive . . .'

What did she want me to say? I mean I wouldn't mind if I had even *taken* the bag in the first place. 'Maybe you lost it,' I suggested, 'and someone found it.'

'I don't think so, Lamb. More coffee?'

I shook my head. I was practically sticking to the ceiling as it was. I got up. 'So what shall I do then?' I have never wanted to get on and clean so much in my entire life.

'I want to have a word with you first.'

I sat down again thinking, what now? I waited but she paused. I searched my mind for what I'd done but apart from the bag and a few baths – which were while I was cleaning it anyway – there was nothing. My eyes fixed on the burns but it wasn't about the burns.

She cleared her throat. 'I had a phone call from Margaret,' she said. I waited, thinking who the hell's Margaret?

'Margaret Harcourt,' she said.

'Oh.'

'She told me this frankly incredible story . . . advised me to send you packing before you got up to any of your tricks here, as she put it.'

She waited for me to say something but I just shut my eyes and felt the edge of the bath against the back of my knees and pictured the thick pink of Mr Harcourt's flesh and started to cry. It was warm runny salt on my face, wet as the melting world outside.

'Oh Lamb, I'm sorry.' Mrs Banks put her hand over mine like a soft cup. We sat there for a minute while tears ran down my face. 'Would you like to tell me about it . . . as a friend,' she said.

Friend. A friend. A fried fiend. Part of me wanted to tell her where to stick her friendship. I mean I was her cleaner. Paid peanuts to do her dirty work. But she was Doggo's mum too and in her eyes I could see Doggo's eyes.

'What did she say?' I said.

'Well, she said that you, well you *seduced* Mr Harcourt. He was ill in bed and you were poking about where you shouldn't have been, as she put it, and he challenged you and you offered him your . . . well.'

I snatched my hand away. 'That's a lie,' I said.

'I'm quite sure it is.' It was like Brands Hatch or something in my head while I tried to think. I didn't have to say anything. She couldn't make me say a word. It was none of her business anyway. I could just go. But I didn't want to go. I wanted to say something. I didn't want her thinking that.

'It wasn't like that,' I went. 'He ... Mr Harcourt ... he tried to rape me.'

'Oh Lamb.' She got hold of my hand again and squeezed.

'I was terrified and he tried it on but I fought him off then he offered me a thousand pounds to shag him. And then he . . .'

She shook her head and squeezed harder.

'Ow.'

'Sorry.'

'But I never took it. I never did it.'

'Of course you didn't.'

'It's worth a grand to me not to have done it.'

'I'm sure.' She sat there, shaking her head, the corners of her mouth pulled down. Probably wondering who to believe. Sometimes it's hard to remember what *is* the exact truth when there are so many possible versions. The easiest thing to do was cry again. She handed me a tissue and got up to put the kettle on.

'What I'm wondering,' she said after a while, 'is what we should do.' *We?* I thought. 'I mean whether we should tell her. She should know what her husband's like. Would you be prepared to face her? You could even press charges.'

'The police?' I said. 'No way.'

She looked at me for a long time. 'All right. But you can't let him get away with it.'

'I just want to forget it.'

'I've never liked Bruce,' she said. 'He's that type that undresses you with his eyes.' Roy came running in with wet all down his legs. 'Not again,' Mrs Banks said. '*Please* tell me when you get the feeling.'

She took him upstairs. I washed up the coffee cups and rolled the plasticine into a neat ball. It was raining now, thick gloopy rain so you could hardly see out of the windows. Maybe I did take money from Mr Harcourt. Not a thousand pounds. Maybe this is how it happened: I said I wanted the money first. He said, 'You obviously weren't born yesterday,' and laughed like a man of the world. He went out in his car to the cash machine. While he was gone my clothes finished drying and I put them on. He came in, put the money on the table and looked at me, a fat grin spreading on his face. I picked the money up. 'Feels good, eh?' he said. 'A thick wad like that. I bet you never held so much in your little hand before.'

He reached out for me but I kicked his shin and ran. Ran out the door and down the street. Ran until my lungs were bursting. Then I went to the Botanics. I counted the money. It wasn't a thousand pounds it was three hundred and seventy. So he had done me, just like I'd done him. Hahaha. Though he must have been mad. He could have had a girl off the street for twenty quid. But maybe it was a thrill, the thought of doing it in his very own house with the cleaning girl. The naked sylph. Who knows how his sick mind worked. Anyway, I had done him. And it served him right.

I was picking away at one of the scorched flecks when Mrs Banks came back. She saw me.

'What happened here?' I said.

'God knows,' she said. 'But I'm after a new table anyway.' She turned her back, making Roy a peanut-butter sandwich. 'Would you like a snack, Lamb?' she said.

'Gotta go,' I said.

'Oh don't go yet. I feel so awful for you.'

'Nah,' I said, 'it's not down to you.'

'Still.'

She heated up some soup in the microwave. Bright orange tomato soup like my mum used to give me when I was ill. Roy got it all down his chin and made a butterfly out of his sandwich. In the end he went off to play.

'What a mess.' She tutted at the soup splashes and peanut mush he'd left behind.

'Can I talk to you, Lamb,' she said suddenly, as if she'd dared herself. 'I've been feeling the need to talk to someone. If I don't talk to someone soon I'll burst.'

'What, *me*?' I said.

A cloud passed over her eyes. 'I'll tell you something, Lamb. Not many people know this, no one round here, for a start. I can't talk about this to anyone else. Can I trust you?'

'Dunno,' I said. 'I suppose so.'

She took a deep breath and started. 'Neville isn't my first husband. I was married before when I was only eighteen. I had two boys, less than a year between. Two under one, can you imagine?' She left me a gap to imagine it in.

I couldn't think what would be the natural thing to say. 'Where are they?' I said.

Now it was her time to cry. Not quite cry but go red and get that bright look in her eyes. She bit her lip. 'You'll probably think I'm a monster.'

I said nothing but I remembered Doggo's words, how her hair brushed his cheek, the sweet smell of it, then she was gone. The sad shine in his eyes when he told me that.

'I was a bit, *wild* as a girl. My poor parents, they did their best. I got expelled from the local school and they sent me to a private one and I got expelled from that too.'

I stared at her. 'Mrs Banks! Why?'

It was the last thing I expected. She wasn't wild at all. Her house was neat and boring and full of scatter cushions. If you ask me scatter cushions are the opposite of wild. She put her index finger in a splash of soup and drew a circle, over and over, round and round.

'I don't know what was up with me really,' she went on. 'They gave me everything. Riding lessons, dancing, holidays here, there and everywhere, whatever I wanted, but I just . . .

I got in with a gang of . . . well. My father went spare when he realised. Said it was the limit, either I stopped seeing them and pulled myself together or I left. So I left.

'To cut a long story short, I got pregnant. Seventeen and pregnant. Had the baby and another. It was a disaster. But did we do the sensible thing and call it a day? Did we heck. I loved the kids but oh God I was just a kid myself.'

'Yeah,' I said.

She told me the story that Doggo had told me, but her side of it. About how her husband had taunted her for being posh, bullied and beaten her till she could hardly think straight. About how she might have cracked up altogether or even died if she hadn't left when she did. About how she'd still been a child. Just a little girl. She kept saying that.

She also told me how it felt to leave your kids.

She talked very fast gulping her coffee and knitting her fingers together and bending them back till I was afraid one of them would snap. Tears started to race down her cheeks and I did something I would never have dreamt I'd ever do. I got up and put my arms round her from behind.

'Oh Mrs Banks,' I said. She sniffed and patted my hand and I felt a tear fall on my skin. It sat there gleaming and burning like acid. As soon as I could I took my hand away and rubbed the feeling off on my jeans. She was right on the edge of breaking down but then she sucked it all back down inside her.

'Another drink?' she said, getting up. 'And, Lamb, would you do me a favour?'

'Yeah?'

'Do stop calling me Mrs Banks, it makes me feel about a hundred. Call me Marion, *please*.'

'K,' I said even though that is well against my usual rules.

I asked her if she'd seen either of her other boys lately. I would ask that, wouldn't I? Not knowing anything about it.

I thought she'd say no. But she surprised me. She said she'd seen Martin, who is Doggo, about eighteen months ago. She stared at the window as she talked as if she was watching a film. She'd been in the park with Roy – he was playing in the sandpit and Martin came right up to the bench where she was sitting. She said he had two dogs with him and that made me smile, thinking he hadn't changed. But these were British bulldogs and he looked a hard-case which shocked her because he'd been a gentle kind of child. They'd had an awkward conversation. She wanted to pour out her heart to him but instead it was just artificial small-talk then Roy came running up. Seeing Roy gave him a shock, you could see it on his face, she said. He just went pale, then got up and went. She called after him but she couldn't chase after him because of Roy. And she just watched him walk out of her life again.

She slid her wedding ring off her finger, turned it round and put it back. 'I suppose he felt replaced,' she said. 'I was going to say I hadn't replaced him but maybe in a way I had. You can never replace someone in your heart but the fact is, in day-to-day life you can.'

I don't know why that struck me as so tragic. I looked down at my scrubby hands and bitten nails. I wondered if she even knew that David was dead. 'Have you heard anything since? From either of them?'

She opened her mouth to speak but Roy came in and started pushing his toy cars about on the floor. She put her finger to her lips and shook her head. I could have screamed. She went back to spouting rubbish like was it really worth getting a turkey or what about opting for roast beef which they all prefer but what about the mad-cow disease and blablabla.

The phone rang and it was someone coming round so I had to go. No cleaning at all but she still paid me. She lent me a brolly. 'Friday?' she called after me and I called back, 'Yeah,' as I slopped off down the sleety street.

Thirty

I didn't go straight home. Just as I was passing a bus-stop a bus stopped and I jumped on. It was so steamy inside that you couldn't see out of the windows and so packed I had to stand. Everyone doing their Christmas shopping. If Doggo and I were going to have Christmas then I needed to do some shopping too.

Clinging to a hand-rail I looked down at the tops of all the heads, all the hats and hair-dye, the dandruff, the scalps showing through perms, the bald heads and the baby hair. I knew my red streaks wouldn't be showing because there was no sun. Do you ever think that everyone's head is just as important as your own head? To them I mean. Each head is the centre of a different world. It can make you giddy to think how many million centres of the world there are.

Debenhams stunk of tinsel. A sugary voice kept inviting customers to have a special seasonal hot turkey 'n' cranberry baguette in the restaurant with a half-price hot beverage. I bought myself some presents, some brilliant things, even better than the stuff I'd lost. Levi jeans and cosy sweaters, nice underwear and some slinky white pyjamas. I hadn't planned on these but when I saw them I just couldn't resist. They are exactly like some that Zita is wearing in one of the photos. I'd never even dreamed of wearing such things before.

I floated down the escalator into the men's department to buy presents for Doggo. It felt so weird. I have not bought a Christmas present for years. I walked round and round and couldn't choose. What *do* you buy the man who has nothing?

In the end I bought him a jacket, warm, padded and supposedly waterproof. I got him a pair of gloves too because his old ones are worn out. His knuckles have almost healed but when they get cold the scars go shiny blue. I want his hands always to be warm. They had sets of stuff like after-shave and soap with manly names: Brutus and Charge. He doesn't shave so I didn't buy one with after-shave in, just with soap and deodorant. I hope he doesn't take it wrong.

I got carried away then. I went to the cosmetics department and bought some gorgeous soap, clear and pink like a big jelly sweet. It's supposed to moisturise as it gently cleanses. You could see the woman was surprised when I asked how much for the bath milk – which is the same one that Mrs Harcourt had. She said, 'Twenty-six pounds ninety-nine,' in a snooty way-out-*your*-range voice and I said, 'I'll take it. And the matching body lotion,' without even asking the price of that. She slammed it in the bag while I smiled sweetly and peeled off the notes saying, 'Keep the change.' I bought lipstick too, Damson Heart, some blusher and some smoky kohl.

I chose baubles for the tree which are like the bubbles kids blow, clear but streaked with shimmering colours. You wouldn't believe how much they cost. Then I went into another shop to find a present for Gordon. I found a *diamanté* dog collar. It made me laugh to think of Gordon with his grumpy eyebrows wearing the sparkles round his neck. I got a squeezy feeling in my ribs every time the cash-registers rang my money up, part scared and part excited. I had to stop then.

There wasn't that much cash left and I had to save enough for dinner.

It was ten days till Christmas which is a long time to wait when you have presents to give. I didn't know whether I could bear to wait or not. I walked back, my arms stretching nearly to the ground with all the carrier bags. I started going round the side of the house from habit before I remembered I had a right to be here now and I could just waltz straight up the path and through the front door.

Doggo was not there. He should have been. He was supposed to stay in except for after dark. He was supposed to stay in and hide. I was worried. Then I realised the dogs had gone. If they'd arrested him they wouldn't have taken the dogs, I was pretty sure of that. But I was cross. He was stupid going out in daylight. It was too much of a risk.

It's a good job he was out though otherwise I would have had to give him his presents then and there. I hid the things in the front room under Mr Dickens' bed. It was cold everywhere except the back room where it was so hot there was sweat running down the window. It was too quiet with even the dogs out. I put the telly on for company. I walked about the house not knowing what to do. It was drinking coffee at Mrs Banks' that made me so buzzy. Probably drinking coffee that made me buy all the stuff. I sometimes think the world would be a much more laid-back place if people weren't drinking coffee all the time.

I couldn't wait for Doggo to come back. To see him come back safe. I couldn't imagine life without him. How I spent all that time *alone*. When I shut my eyes there was no balance left but that was OK. That is OK. You don't need your own balance when there's someone there to hold you up. I wanted to tell him what his mum said. How she had cried about leaving him and I was going to find out more. I had a plan growing in me about getting them together like one of those weepy old movies. *Oh Mother, Oh Son!! Oh Happy Christmas* and an orchestra suddenly striking up from behind the sofa.

The phone rang and I jumped but didn't answer it. It kept ringing and ringing till it really got on my nerves. I didn't answer it because it would only be Sarah or the hospital and I didn't want to talk to either. I hate the phone. It gets under your skin like that, just when you're happy it rings and it could be anyone calling to smash up your happiness or peace. Imagine a world without coffee or the phone.

I left it and went to pick up the post from the mat. The envelopes were covered in footprints. There were hundreds of Christmas cards for Mr Dickens. I opened them and stuck them on the mantelpiece. Lots of holly sprigs and old-fashioned coach-and-horses and snow-scenes with church spires, all filled with wavery old people's writing. One of them had a ten-pound note in. Well he wouldn't be needing that.

On telly a woman was making a chocolate yule log out of broken biscuits. I opened the sideboard and searched but there was no money in there. I got out all the albums and scoured them for Christmas pictures but there was only the one. It was Mr Dickens and Zita standing by a tree all lit up with candles. They were young and she was wearing a flowery dress and a cardigan with sequins round the edges. Her hair was neat as a helmet and her lips like a Christmas bow. There was something at the side that looked like a pyramid of tangerines. Well, we could get a tree and tangerines. If we had a camera we could take a picture. I would get a camera, one of those with a timer, and take us by our Christmas tree, me in my white pyjamas, then one day someone would look at the picture and think, *they were happy* and maybe wish to be like us.

The phone rang again so I unplugged it.

I flicked through all the albums soaking Zita in. The more I look the more I see what they mean. I *do* look like her. I do look like her true descendant. I got to the album with the newspaper cuttings. I tried to put it back in the cupboard but I couldn't help looking. It was weird of Mr Dickens to keep those cuttings, don't you think? Kind of morbid, in the same way shutting off the room was. I thought that maybe I was starting to get phobic about that room. It was always coming into my head, it just *bothered* me so much.

I read very slowly the story that told me in fuzzy black words about how she died. The pathologist's photograph showed me the burnt black space in the room and everything quite ordinary all around. A cup with a biscuit in the saucer. A beaded lamp. And the two shins, still wearing their shoes, lying on the carpet, silly skittles.

I was cold all up my back and the ash taste was in my throat again. How can it happen? I do not understand how it happens that a person can catch fire inside where it is wet and there is no air. Can burn from the inside out.

Confront your fears is how you beat them. If you're phobic about something you have to face whatever it is, bit by bit. Like if you're phobic about mice you have to look at a picture of a mouse every day, then a real one in a cage then in the end you have to hold the mouse or even put it up your sleeve. This cures you.

I went and stood outside and touched the door. It was just a cold door and there was no sign of burning. I put my hand against the plank that was nailed across. When I looked closely I saw that it wasn't nailed on very well. Only two big nails, one each side that went through the plank and into the door frame, but I could pull and move it. The nails weren't long enough to go very far into the wood of the door frame. If I wanted to I could pull it off.

I was standing and thinking this with a cold and sinking

feeling in my guts when I heard footsteps and voices and the Trumpet Voluntary. The shock of it practically stopped my heart. I froze. Somebody laughed and pressed it again and then knocked and knocked. From the front the house looks completely dead. Lucky that Doggo had taken the dogs out so there was no barking. I glided along the wall into the back and switched off the lights and the telly and lay down on the floor. Just in time because the people came poking round the back. They knocked at the door even tried it but it was locked. I could heard the stabs and wisps of their voices going up, questions, questions but not an answer in sight.

After a while they went away but I stayed on the floor till the dog-hairs made me sneeze. I lay there for ages till I was positive they'd gone. Just as I was getting up and putting the light back on, Doggo came back. The dogs stunk of wet and Gordon shook all over me.

'What you doing?' Doggo said.

'Nothing,' I said. True. 'Where've you been?'

'I'd go fucking apeshit if I didn't get out sometimes.'

I couldn't tell him off. I was so pleased to see him I went right up to him, right into his personal space, and stood there thinking, *kiss me kiss me*. He looked at me as if I was cracked and backed away. 'You're covered in dog-hairs,' he said.

I could smell the raw cold on him. If he had kissed me his lips would have been like ice. He went through and sat by the fire to take his boots off and then there was the smell of feet to top everything. I remembered socks. I should have bought him socks.

'I was thinking about Christmas,' I said. 'We could get a tree.'

He grinned at me the way that makes my heart swoop. 'Fuck off,' he said.

'Why not?'

'We might not be here at Christmas. We're only here till Mr Dickens gets back.'

'But he's in for a couple more weeks at least.'

'How do you know?'

'Because I've been up the hospital, obviously. Yeah. He'll be in a couple of weeks yet. And Christmas is only ten days away so that means . . .'

Doggo stretched out his toes and rested them on Doughnut's back. 'That's ace. Why didn't you say? Fetch us a cup of tea.' I gave him the finger but went and filled the kettle.

'Maybe I'll come up hospital with you next time,' he said.

'You *could*.' I stared at the ghost of my face in the window. 'But it's only one visitor at a time, the ward he's on.' The kettle steamed my face away and I took him his tea.

'Ta,' he said. He looked up at me for a moment and his grey eyes scrunched my heart. 'What's up?' he said.

'Nothing.'

'And?' he said.

'And what?'

'How was my mum?'

'She said you saw her once, in the park.'

'Oh yeah.'

'What *were* you doing at her house that day?'

'Fuck knows,' he said. 'I wanted to see her, that's all. When I was inside I kept . . . she were on my mind . . . I . . . I don't fucking know.'

'You're swearing a lot,' I said. 'And hey, thanks for taking her bag back without telling *me*.'

'That's OK,' he said.

'When did you?'

'Other night when I was out with dogs.'

I opened my mouth to quiz him more but something about the set of his shoulders made me shut it again. It didn't matter anyway, what did it matter?

Thirty-one

The next night Doggo got a Christmas tree. He went out after dark and came back with a tree which he'd dug up from somewhere. Don't ask. I couldn't believe it, there were trees for sale everywhere but he'd nicked one and it wasn't even the right sort of tree. It *was* evergreen but its branches were soft and floppy, drooping down instead of sticking out sideways. I don't know how he thought we were going to fix the baubles on.

He looked so proud of himself though, carrying the tree in with a big grin stretched right across his face and trudging mud everywhere, that I only said, 'Great,' and found it a bucket. There was a big holly bush in the garden and he went berserk bringing in more and more till you couldn't move without scratching yourself. He even found some mistletoe from somewhere. He held it up and stood there and I went right over and kissed him on the lips. I don't know who was most surprised. Then we both felt stupid and pulled away. '*Fuck* off,' he said. It was a nice kiss though, I must admit.

He told me off for opening the cards. He said I should have taken them into hospital for Mr Dickens to open himself. I said that Mr Dickens had asked me to open them and tell him who they were from because there wasn't room on his locker for hundreds of Christmas cards. Which would have been true.

Doggo did most of the cooking and he wasn't bad at it. I was getting used to eating every night and my hip-bones were looking less sharp. Mr Dickens had a stockpile of tinned stuff like he'd been expecting a nuclear war or something. Fray Bentos pies, carrots, meatballs. One night Doggo made corned-beef hash which he ate with about half a bottle of HP sauce. I washed up like I usually did. We were getting into a routine like normal people. Sometimes, if Doggo insisted, we went for a pint at night but usually we just stayed home drinking wine and watching telly.

After the corned-beef hash, Doggo said he wanted to make a phone call. He wanted to phone his dad just to say he was OK. But phone calls can be traced, can't they? What if his dad rang the police. When I said that Doggo shook his head. 'He wouldn't grass on me. Christ, the stuff I'd have on him if I got going.'

It was days since I'd unplugged the phone and the peace had been wonderful. I didn't have the knot of fear in my gut that it would ring when he was there and smash everything. He hadn't even noticed. But when he saw the phone was unplugged he was put out.

'Because it was getting on my wick ringing and ringing,' I said when he asked why. He rolled his eyes and plugged it back in. I listened to him talking to his dad and it was all monosyllables, like yeah, nah, right, nah, yeah, yeah, yeah, nah, right. Not exactly riveting. Mind you lots of talking isn't, is it? If you listen, most of it is like dogs wagging their tails or rolling over on their backs or something, it's just saying *Hey I exist*. I reckon if you cut all the crap and only let people say things that mattered or actually *told* you something the world would be practically silent. After Doggo had finished I casually flipped the plug out again.

Millions more cards came for Mr Dickens. I put them all round the shelves and on the sideboard. The house started to look quite Christmasy apart from the stupid floppy tree which the baubles kept sliding off. 'Where'd you get these from?' Doggo said, picking one up and holding it up to the light. 'Found them in a cupboard,' I said. He narrowed his eyes at me like he had when I'd first worn the new Levi's. Sometimes it's like living in the middle of the Spanish Inquisition living with Doggo. It's all, 'Where did you nick that from?' or 'How much was *that*?' Sometimes I wish I hadn't bothered.

He never tried anything on with me again but one night when I couldn't sleep he said, 'Let me stroke your back.'

'K,' I said. I lay there and he stroked me and if I could have purred I would have. I lay listening to water dripping through the ceiling into the potty and feeling like I was in heaven. I nearly turned round and kissed him but I thought he would get excited again and call me a tease and I hate that because the last thing I ever am is a tease.

Next time I went to Mrs Banks' she wasn't there. I'd been ready for another morning at the table, drinking coffee, finding things out. How much she knew about Doggo and David and all that. I was so frustrated I found I was grinding my teeth as I hoovered. When I'd finished I snooped around for some evidence of something but she wasn't the type to keep a diary or save old letters or newspaper clippings. Not like Mr Dickens and his albums. There was hardly any past in the house at all. Everything was new. The earliest photo was of her wedding to Neville, and then lots of Roy as a baby. Nothing from before at all as if she'd wiped the surface of her life clean with a sponge. Yes. But you *can* only wipe the surface.

She left me a Christmas card with a robin on a letterbox and inside it ten pounds and a note:

Dear Lamb, A little bonus for you! Could you hoover up the tree needles – at this rate it'll be bald by the 25th! And there's a bit of ironing. Could you mop the kitchen floor if there's time. Help yourself to coffee etc, mince pies in tin. Lovely to talk to you the other day. See you in the New Year. Happy Christmas.
Love Marion.

Love Marion. I couldn't believe that. *Love*. Well it's just what some people put, isn't it? It doesn't really mean *love*. Anyway the ten extra quid was a nice thought. The tree had winking lights, a fairy on top and some wonky paper snowflakes that Roy must have made. And chocolate snowmen dangling from silver strings.

I did the ironing properly. I'm getting good at it. You could nearly say I like it. Getting a pile of crumpled things and straightening them out, nosing the iron into the corners and creases and that lovely hot-cloth smell rising. I ironed a little pair of Roy's pyjamas for ages, over and over again like some sort of loony. They are blue with a space ship on the front that glows in the dark which you mustn't iron so I edged the iron very carefully round it. I folded them up and they are *minute*. I ironed everything, even Mr Banks' wacky boxer shorts and the teensy triangles of Marion's knickers. I put my face in a hot-ironed sheet and sniffed and sniffed till it got cold again.

I left everything very nice and even though I didn't have a card to leave I drew a Christmas tree on a bit of paper using Roy's felt-tips and put *Happy Christmas love Lamb*. I took a mince pie with me for Doggo and walked off with a bouncy elastic feeling in my feet. But when I got back, Sarah was there.

Thirty-two

I should have seen her car outside but no, I just barged right in, calling *Doggo Doggo* like an idiot. They were in the back room. The mistletoe was hanging by the door and I looked straight at it and then at them. The holly scratched my cheek when I went in. They had mugs of coffee and were more or less sitting on top of each other. I'm sure the chairs weren't that close together before.

'Hi, Lamb,' Sarah said in an odd voice. Doggo didn't look at me.

'Hi,' I said.

'You're bleeding,' Sarah said and I put my finger up and smeared the blood away.

'How's Mr Dickens then?' Doggo turned his eyes on me and they were the bleakest eyes I've ever seen.

The room seemed to sway. 'How should I know?' I said.

'Because you've seen him.'

'He's OK.'

'Sure?' Doggo said.

'Lamb.' Sarah's voice was gently bewildered. 'He is dead.'

There was a long pause.

'Is he?' I said.

All their eyes, even Doughnut's blind eyes, were hot on me as searchlights.

'So?' I said.

'*So?*' Doggo repeated. '*So?*'

There really wasn't much else I could say. It was so hot in there that the berries were dropping off the holly. It was suffocating. I stepped over Doughnut and squeezed between their knees and switched off the fire. It was the first time it had been off for about a week. The metal cracked and sighed.

'The nurse I spoke to was rather confused,' Sarah said. 'Look for goodness sakes have a tissue and wipe that blood off.' She got one of those handy little packets of tissues out of her bag and shoved it at me. 'I was informed the morning he died, nearly a week ago. She spoke to me herself apparently.'

There was a pause. I stuck my tongue out sideways and caught a drop of blood. 'They've been trying to get in contact ever since. When someone dies you have to do something, you know, Lamb. There are procedures. You can't just ignore it.' Her voice filled up with tears and Doggo put his hand on her knee. 'I came back thinking everything was fine – but he's dead. And he's been dead a *week*.'

I couldn't say *So?* again and nothing else sprang to mind. They looked like outraged geese or something the way they were staring at me. It was hot as hell in that room anyway with the stink of dogs and all. I just banged right out of there.

I walked round the Botanical Gardens. It was nearly closing time. They lock the gates early in the winter as if they think no one would like to go there in the dark. Oh yes they would. I would. It was windy and everywhere branches were creaking and swaying, dropping their last few leaves. The light was weird and greenish and the trees were big graffiti scribbles happening on the sky. I sat on a bench and dabbed at my cheek with the tissue till the blood had dried.

What *is* up with them? I mean what *is* their problem? I

mean if someone's dead, they're dead, aren't they? What difference does it make *when* you know about it? Or if you ever know about it at all? In a war you sometimes don't know for ages or for ever. A person goes missing and just never comes back. People disappear all the time and they might be dead and they might not be dead. So what?

I would have told Doggo in the end. And Sarah. After Christmas. Of course I would. I just didn't want to spoil Christmas for anyone. Anyway, Sarah could have rung the hospital herself, why didn't she? Why did she just go swanning off and leave it all to me? Mr Dickens was *her* relation not mine. I wished I'd thought to say that. I nearly went back to shout it through the letterbox.

A squirrel came and sat by my feet with its tail curled up behind it and I fed it Doggo's mince pie. Doggo said they were only rats with fluffy tails but it was still cute the way it held the pastry in its tiny hands. It was freezing on the bench and my ears were aching with the wind in them but I didn't know where else to go.

I watched the people going past. Me alone on a bench again. A couple arm in arm with breath-feathers all round them and matching anoraks; a woman rushing along with a flowering cactus. The magpies were cawing away like football rattles. It was starting to get dark. The bell went. The bell means get out or you're locked in. I thought about letting myself get locked in but it was so cold and anyway the man with the keys had seen me. I knew he'd be waiting by the gate. I waited till I was the last person and you could hardly see the trees any more then I dawdled down to the gate. The man had a giant key like something from a pantomime. When he smiled I saw he had a missing front tooth. The gate clanged shut behind me with a sound like being locked in jail. Only I was being locked out.

I went into a shop that is full of crap. The sort of thing you'd only buy for someone else and never for yourself. I wouldn't even buy it for someone else. Bleating key-rings; crossword toilet rolls; money boxes shaped like toilets that flush when you put pennies in; willy-warmers and chocolate nipples. But it was warm in there and light. I read all the so-called funny cards but none of them even made me smile.

'Can I help you?' a person said in the end.

'How anyone that works here can ask that!' I said and stalked out feeling pleased with myself for about a nano-second.

I walked around watching shoppers with their bulging bags and their greedy bulging eyes. I went back to Mr Dickens' house but Sarah's car was still there so I went away again. I couldn't get their stupid outraged faces out of my head. So what if Mr Dickens was dead? So what?

I walked for hours. It was too cold to stop. I walked and walked and got so tired from walking. Watching the shops shut, watching the people going home, the curtains shutting, the lights coming on. I walked round to Mrs Banks' house and saw that they'd strung Christmas lights up round their porch. They rattled in the wind. The rest of the world was shut out by their curtains drawn tight.

I went back on the main road and was reading the ads in the post office for rooms and skate-boards and lost cats. Maybe I would have gone back to Mr Dickens' house. I think I would have. Where else would I go? But then a voice said, 'Jo?' I didn't even stop at first because that's not my name any more but then someone got hold of my arm and I turned. It was Simon.

'I'm not Jo, I'm Lamb,' I said speeding up. He walked along as fast as me.

'Lamb, eh? That's cool,' he said. 'Great to see you.'

'Yeah, I guess.' We were practically running by then.

'Where you rushing off to?'

'Nowhere.' I slowed down. 'Nowhere really.'

We walked along together. I felt so stupid trying not to pant.

'What are *you* doing?' I asked in the end, just for something to say.

'Nothing,' he said.

We walked on some more.

'Want to do something?' he said.

'Like what?'

'Dunno.'

'OK.'

'Cool.'

I have had more scintillating conversations.

We went to the pub. There was a quiz going on and we joined in and between us we nearly won. He knows practically everything and I turned out to know some things I didn't even know I knew like, Which French king was known as the Sun King? Louis the fourteenth. And, What fraction of an iceberg shows above water? One ninth. Where we fell down was sport otherwise we'd have won twenty quid.

Money wasn't a problem though. Unbelievably The Sticky Labels had got paid for a gig and he was out to blow his share. He was drinking Malibu and Coke which believe me is about the most disgusting drink on this earth. I was on tequila which shrinks your brain till it bounces on the sides of your skull when you move which feels quite funny at the time. He's cool really, Si, so greasy you'd think he'd crawled out of a chip-pan but with a sense of humour. He made me laugh anyway, quite something the state I was in. Or maybe it was the tequila laughing, I don't know.

Everything went quite a blur after a few drinks. We played darts with some people but were useless, he was doing pratty throws lifting one leg off the ground and swinging his arm like he was bowling in cricket. In the end we got asked to leave. It was nearly last orders anyway. We went to his flat.

I can hardly remember getting there, just a smear of coloured light whenever I turned my head. I might have been sick on the side of the road. His flat was right up the top of what seemed to be a mountain. He had to drag me up. It was shared with some other people and there were more pizza boxes than bits of furniture in there. Someone was asleep on the sofa with a cushion over his head and there was something on telly only don't ask me what. Si rolled a huge spliff but I don't think I had any in case I was sick again.

After a while we went into his bedroom. He took off his clothes. It felt *so* weird, I mean at school he was just a prize nerd with thick glasses. Everyone laughed at him but he didn't care, he didn't even notice, his head so full of astrophysics or whatever. I would have laughed my head off then if anyone had said, One day you'll go to bed with Simon.

He didn't look too bad in the half-dark. He got into bed and politely looked away while I took some things off. It was a single bed and the sheets were full of bits and smelt like they had never been washed in their lives. I felt too sick to kiss. I thought, OK then I'll have sex with him.

I don't understand this. Maybe it was the drink. Maybe it was because I didn't care what he thought of me. I don't know how or why, all I know is it worked. I lay there waiting to go frigid but I didn't. Mind you, I hardly felt a thing. I didn't scream and claw his back or any of that theatrical stuff. He wouldn't have believed me if I had. In fact I bet he would have run a mile. I tried to think about Doggo but it was too far-fetched. Doggo was like another universe. I breathed through my mouth to try and stop the reek of latex, scuzzy sheets and pizza getting to me. The only sound I made was the sound of someone having the air battered out of them for about two minutes then that was that.

I smiled into the dark. I had done it. Or had it done to me. Simon mumbled something sweet then rolled straight off and snored. I shut my eyes and thought of Doggo. It would be OK. I wanted to get up then and go straight home to him. I lay beside Simon thinking, *I should wash I should wash* and longing for a glass of water. But next thing I was waking up and it was morning. Just for a second I thought he was Doggo but everything was wrong, the shape of the room, where the light was coming from – and most of all the smell.

Simon's back was to me and I lay there looking at the most amazing array of spots I have ever seen. If there was a prize for spots he'd be a serious contender. My brain still felt too small for my skull and my mouth was so dry I could hardly move my tongue. I got up and found my clothes. He didn't even stir.

I went in the bathroom but it was untouchable in there. The towels were in a wet heap on the floor and the washbasin looked like Harris tweed or something with all its mix of different bristles and God knows what. There were empty toothpaste tubes, spot creams, disposable razors, condom packets and of course a pizza box on the floor. I drank from the tap, peed standing up and left.

It was dustbin day and a lorry was roaring, tipping up the plastic bins and munching the stinking rubbish. Why are dustbin men so cheery? I don't know. I was cheery too apart from a throbbing head. I had *done it*, sex. I felt like calling it out to the dustbin men, to the whole wide world. OK maybe I'd been half pissed and it was hardly shag of the century but still I had done it. *Me*.

I just wished it had been Doggo.

Thirty-three

Sarah's car was still there. The front door was locked. I could not believe it. They had locked me out. I stood there for ages just staring at the door. I put my finger on the doorbell but didn't press. Last thing I needed was the Trumpet Voluntary. I went round the back but they'd locked that door too. I had to go my old way. They had not locked the cellar door.

I pressed the light switch. It looked like a scene from another life in there. Or from some awful tedious dream. The camp bed where I had slept for months, the cold Calor heater, the card from Mr Dickens lying on the floor. I picked it up but it had gone soft. It was so cold, so gloomy. How could I ever have thought that was a *life*? A possible life. Cobwebs were crowding across everywhere, between everything, draped on the old high wire. What a desperately stupid idea.

The only way into the house was up the pitch-black stairs. The hand-rail was tacky and sour breath was leaking from the walls. What if they had locked the hall door too? I didn't even know if there was a lock on it. What if they had gone round, laughing, locking me out in every possible way?

But they had not. I stepped out into the hall, dazzling bright with green fan shapes of sun on the lino. I blinked, looking at the inside of the front door with the key still in the lock.

Everything was quiet. It was early. I thought they must still be asleep. The dogs looked up at me when I went through to the back and Gordon yapped half-heartedly. The fire was on and they seemed drugged by the heat. Once they'd realised it was only me they both put their heads back on their paws. Gordon has aged about a hundred years since Norma died. Maybe it's rubbed off from Doughnut. There were two empty wine bottles on the floor, one red one white. How sweet. I made tea for me and Doggo and went up the stairs. Sarah's door was shut. I climbed quietly up into the lighthouse room.

Of course they were both there in the bed. Of course I knew they would be. They were asleep. The sun was shining through the ripped curtains and it was nearly hot. They had no clothes on and their hair was mixed up light and dark. The pillowcase was still splattered with Doggo's blood.

You can see how people get murdered, can't you?

'I've brought you some tea,' I said, maybe louder than necessary.

Sarah opened her eyes first. They were the same blue as the quilt. She stared at me for a minute. I have to give it her, she was cool. 'Oh, thanks,' she said. I could see Doggo was not really asleep. His eyes were screwed up tight.

'Lamb's brought us up some tea,' Sarah said, nudging him.

She sat up and I got a flash of her tits, like big white loaves, before she pulled the quilt up to cover her. Not quilt, eiderdown. That is such a lovely word, don't you think? Eiderdown. Feathers from the eider duck.

Doggo sat up and his eyes skidded round the room avoiding mine. I handed them the tea and stood staring. The dark and the blonde, sitting up in bed with their cups of tea. They looked like an advert for something but I don't know what.

'Urm,' Sarah said. 'I urm, hope this is all right with you.'

'Oh absolutely,' I said in a phony voice I didn't even know I had. 'Actually I was off seeing an old flame last night, so call it quits, Doggo.'

He did look at me then. He practically slashed me with his eyes.

'It was urm, mainly for warmth,' Sarah said and I snorted. It would be an advert for yoghurt or some other dairy product with all her acres of white skin.

I couldn't stand there all day and smell the smells that were hanging round the bed. I had to get out of there while I could still control my face. Down in the bathroom I stripped off. I ran an inch of water in the bath and scrubbed myself all over with a scratchy flannel, scrubbed and scrubbed until it hurt and I was pink. I went downstairs and kicked and kicked at the chairs. The dogs cringed and crawled off into the corners. As if I would ever, in a million years, hurt a dog.

I was watching the telly when Sarah left. A woman in a lurex top was demonstrating how to pot on poinsettias. Doggo might have been interested if he'd been down but I wasn't about to call him. Sarah put her head round the door and said, 'I'm off now. Bye, Lamb.' I didn't answer.

She was half in the room, half out. What did she think I'd do to her if she came right in? 'Doggo said . . . he said you didn't . . .'

'Didn't what?'

'That you are more sort of . . . platonic.'

I managed to laugh. 'He said *that*, did he?'

She waited for a minute and then said, 'Well, see you then.'

'There's something you should know about Doggo,' I said. 'Something I bet he *didn't* tell you. That he's a murderer.'

She widened her eyes at me and then she laughed. 'A murderer! God, Lamb! First Uncle's happy as Larry now Doggo's a murderer. Get a grip.'

She closed the door. There was the sound of the front door then a dim choke as her car started up and drove away. My heart was racing. I should not have said that. A murderer, I should not have told her that.

Doggo came down as if nothing was wrong and started making toast. 'Want some?' he said. I didn't answer. Anyway, Sarah didn't believe me. So maybe there was no harm done. He slathered the toast with about an inch of butter and chewed so loud I had to turn the telly up. The way he was chewing was like, *hey I've got a healthy appetite, wonder why?* but I ignored him. Maybe I should have told him what I'd told her. But what would be the point of that? I did feel bad though, something inside me going dark. He chewed his way through a whole stack of toast and slurped a pot of tea.

He wiped the butter off his lips with his sleeve and said, 'So, who's this old flame then?'

'Just someone,' I said, 'no one you know.'

'Did you sleep with him?' he said.

Get that! The nerve of him. 'Like you care,' I said. *Him* asking *me*.

He still had butter on his beard. I watched his fingers on the mug and thought about all the things he'd touched lately. There was the advert on for frozen cod steaks. It made me shiver. I looked at the side of his face, the puff of moustache over his lip, the curve of long lashes. He was staring into his mug as if there was something fascinating taking place in there. I got a pang under my ribs and believe it or not, it was still love.

'So that was a lie too?' he said.

'What?'

'That you're frigid.' He gave me a very scornful look. I didn't know what to say. I didn't know any more. I didn't know the truth of that. I couldn't bear the scorn on his face when he looked at me. I had to do something. I didn't know what to do. Then I had an idea. It was a desperate idea, but it was the only one I had.

'Shut your eyes,' I said.

'What?'

'Go on. I've got a surprise only you have to shut your eyes.' He looked at me, his mug stopped halfway to his mouth. 'You needn't look so petrified,' I said.

I went in the front room and got his presents out from under Mr Dickens' bed. Still in their carrier bags and no proper wrappings but it didn't matter. I thought we would have Christmas that very minute before everything fell apart. Presents and Christmas dinner and everything. There was still time to save it, us, everything.

I could go to Tesco for food and crackers. Plenty of wine in the cellar. At least now that Mr Dickens was dead it didn't matter about the wine any more. That was one good thing. He'd probably want us to drink it. He would probably be looking down on us, if there was anywhere to look down from, saying, 'Cheers.'

'Here,' I dumped the bags at Doggo's feet. 'Happy Christmas.' He just stared. 'Open them,' I said. But he sat there like a lemon. 'Presents,' I said. 'It's Christmas.'

'It's not.'

'It is,' I said. 'It is if we want it to be.' There was no expression on his face. '*Please*, Doggo.'

He sighed and shook his head as if he thought I was cracked but he did pull the soap and deodorant out of their bag. He held them and looked at them but not at me. He put them down. OK, so maybe deodorant wasn't such a bright idea.

'Go on,' I said. He unwrapped the gloves and last of all the jacket. 'Try it on,' I said. 'I can change it if it doesn't fit.' But he didn't try it on. He let everything slide on to the floor. I wanted to say, Don't do that because of all the dog-hairs

236

everywhere but I didn't. Maybe he thought I'd stolen it. 'I've got the receipt,' I said.

The jacket was beautiful but he never said thanks and he never even smiled. I knew what would make him laugh. I got out Gordon's new collar and buckled it on him. It looked just as funny as I'd thought with the sparkles sparkling round the grumpy ginger face but no one laughed.

Doggo's eyes were on me. I looked everywhere I could except his eyes until in the end I just had to.

'What you staring at?' I said.

'I *know*.'

'Know what?'

'Know you stole that money off Mr Dickens.'

'I did not!'

'You bought these things with that money, didn't you?'

'I did *not* . . .'

'Where's it from then? When I met you you were skint as me then suddenly presents, pizzas, clothes . . . Your hair-do.'

Hair-do! I wanted to laugh. No one's called it a hair-do for about a hundred years. What was the matter with him? I mean he had *slept* with Sarah and I had said not a word about it. I was giving him presents. I was giving him Christmas.

He could have had anything he wanted from me.

'And Sarah knows you stole it,' he said. 'Out of that sideboard.'

'What?'

'She even saw you looking in there. Fuck it, Lamb. I can't believe you'd do that after how nice she's been, sorting your arm out and letting us be here . . .'

And shagging you, I thought but I didn't say. 'I did *not*,' I said instead. 'And anyway what about all the wine? You steal all the time. What about the tree?' I thought there was nothing he could say to that and I was right. I looked at the tree and one of the baubles slid down and plopped on to the floor. I didn't even bother to pick it up. There were only about two left on and I'd never even taken a photo. I'd never even got a camera.

You can just picture it, can't you. Me out of the way and them with their chairs pulled close together, knees touching, oh what a thrill, talking about me and making up stories when they knew nothing about me. You can just imagine them getting closer and closer till they closed right over the space where I'd been.

If they think I would steal money from Mr Dickens then they don't know the first thing about me. I can't believe Doggo could think that of me. I thought of telling him about Mr Harcourt and how I got the money but why *should* I? Anyway he wouldn't have believed me. Why doesn't anyone believe a single thing I say?

There were no more possible words so I just slammed out of there. He never even said thank you. I thought, sod this trying and trying to make things nice. All that effort and to be told I am a thief. To be told that by a murderer who *I* am hiding from the law. And Sarah with her great big curves all cosied up in my bit of bed with my Doggo.

I was walking so fast there were practically sparks coming off my jeans. I could have gone then. I had it in me to go, just go, but it was like there was a voice saying *Do not give up*. And for once I listened. I stopped walking away. I stopped dead and swivelled on my heel.

Thirty-four

I went into Tesco like any normal person and bought the dinner. Rolled turkey breast, which only takes an hour, with cranberry sauce, spuds, sprouts and a pudding. Also a bottle of Cognac and some crackers. And that was all the money blown. In some ways a relief.

When I got back Doggo had taken the dogs out and left all his presents dumped on the floor. He's so ungrateful. And he should *not* go out like that. I'm always telling him. I picked everything up and hung the jacket over the back of a chair. I chucked the deodorant in the bin.

I set the table and turned the telly off for once and started on the food. Things like peeling potatoes and cutting little crosses in the sprouts I haven't done for years but I remembered how. I managed to fix the baubles back on the tree. There was no star on top and no fairy and that was a mistake but there was nothing I could think of to use instead so I left it bare.

I put on the white pyjamas even though it was daytime and they *were* like Zita's. I looked at the picture and at myself in the bathroom mirror. It was weird how similar we were. I made sure the little silver hand was showing between the buttons. Then I had a good idea. I took the photo of Zita in her white pyjamas and pegged it to the top of the Christmas

239

tree with a clothes peg. The perfect angel.

I put mascara on and drew a thick line of smoky kohl right round my eyes and in the bathroom light my red streaks showed. I did my lips damson and fetched some claret from the cellar and opened it so it had time to breathe. The time went on and the house filled up with cooking smells but there was still no Doggo. I was starting to think, what if he never came back? What then? But at last he did.

He walked in and looked round the room and at that moment I realised I'd forgotten candles. Candles on the table would have been the finishing touch. And maybe one of those table decorations with fir-cones sprayed gold. We could have done without the two wet dogs though. Doggo had a strange expression on his face. I couldn't tell you what it meant.

I poured out some wine and handed it to him. 'Happy Christmas,' I said.

'Fuck off,' he said but he knocked it back then shrugged and grinned. 'Not bad,' he said, 'a perky vintage.' He avoided looking at his presents and I didn't look either. He didn't mention the pyjamas even though I was standing beside the tree with Zita's picture on top so there was no way he could have missed the likeness.

We drank the wine too quickly and I thought maybe we'd need some more. We pulled a cracker. He wouldn't at first but I kept poking him with it till he got hold of the end and pulled. The snap made Gordon bark and put a tang of fireworks in the air. Doggo got the big end and inside was a pair of tacky ear-rings.

'Here,' he said chucking them at me, 'Happy Christmas.' I ignored the sarcastic edge in his voice and put them on even though they were dangly plastic carrots. We pulled another cracker and put the hats on. He read out the jokes which were those elephant ones like How does an elephant get down from a tree? Sit on a leaf and wait till autumn. Hahaha. But we never ate the dinner.

'Lamb, maybe you could give what's left of dosh back?' he said. 'Then we could forget it. I know Sarah would.'

His hat was orange and purple and why would anyone put orange and purple together in a hat? It was half over one eye and he pushed it up.

'It was not Mr Dickens' money,' I said keeping my voice level. 'It was mine. I told you.'

'Yeah right.' His fists were bunched up, the scars shiny. Scars he made because of *me*. To please *me*. Listen, what he did with Sarah meant nothing. Just fucking someone, that's not special or clever, is it? Animals do it all the time. Even I'd done it now and sure enough it did mean nothing.

'Let's go to bed,' I said. I don't know why I said it. But anyway he shook his head. 'What's up, shagged out?' I said. I didn't mean to say that. It must have been the wine catching up with last night's tequila. He took the paper hat off and scrunched it into a ball. It didn't matter. There were four more crackers left with four more hats inside.

'You're doing my head in,' he said in a voice like a tyre going down. 'You are one screwed-up person.'

Me!

'You need help,' he said.

I laughed.

'Sarah says,' he started but realised that was maybe not the thing to say. I stared at him, pityingly, shaking my head. I didn't say a word because remember, not speaking is more powerful than speaking. When I met Doggo he was sneaking about in his mum's house with her stolen bag and then trying to piss off in a puff of smoke. He is a murderer on the run. A wanted man. And *he* thinks *I* need help.

'Why didn't you say about Mr Dickens?' he said.

Well what's *that* got to do with anything?

'What else have you lied about?' he went on. 'Or maybe, what have you *not* lied about?'

Lies. What are lies? Everybody lies, they do it all the time. Can you honestly say you have never lied? Haha. Trick question. Say yes you're a liar, say no you're a liar too. There is nothing wrong with lying. It doesn't mean you're out of control. Lying *is* control.

'OK then,' he said. 'Where *did* you get money? And don't say savings.'

'Why?' I said.

'What do you mean, why?'

'What does it matter?'

That stumped him. I spilt some wine on my pyjama trousers and it spread like a fast purple bruise.

'Why do you care anyway?'

He leant forward and put his hands over his face for a minute then he took them away. 'Fuck knows,' he said, looking at the carpet, 'but I do.'

'Do what?'

'Care.'

Oh.

There was a long period of quiet. Doughnut groaned in his sleep. Bubbling sounds from the kitchen, a creak from the fire. Maybe a smell of something burning. I tried to think of what to say but then he started off again.

'Tell me one thing,' he said. 'How's research going? Lighthouses, was it? Or fashion? Sarah said Mr Dickens said it was fashion. That's why you had his album, with the pictures of his wife. Or was it your nan?'

'So?' I said.

What difference does it make anyway? Lighthouses or fashion or nothing at all?

'Quit saying *so* to everything.'

'Why?'

242

His eyes rolled up to the ceiling and the scars on his fists stretched tight. '*And* she said you'd made out we'd been living together for years.' A burning smell *was* coming from the kitchen. I got up. 'Is anything you've told me true?' he said. 'And *did* you shag another guy last night? Was it another lie – that you're frigid? Funnily enough I believed that one. I felt right sorry for you. *Joanna Vinier.*'

I wish he hadn't said that. I was all right up to that point. But Joanna Vinier is someone else entirely. I went into the kitchen and found that the potatoes which were meant to be par-boiling had gone into a mush and welded themselves to the bottom of the pan. I chucked the pan in the bin. When I looked back Doggo was putting Gordon's lead on. The *diamanté* collar glinted in the plastic flame-light.

'I'm off,' Doggo said.

'Don't go out,' I said, 'you might get caught.'

'What if I do. Makes more fucking sense inside than you do.'

'What about the Christmas dinner?'

He didn't bother to answer. 'Please,' I said but he just shrugged on his old jacket not the new one.

'Come on, lads,' he said. Doughnut hauled himself up.

'K. Be like that,' I said.

I went back in the kitchen and turned the oven off. All that stupid fucking turkey smell filling up the house. Who cares anyway? He slammed the door so hard I thought the house would fall down but it didn't it just stood there all around me and I was very small. The vegetable knife was on the side, the steel glinting like a friend. I picked it up. The new scar on my arm was ridged and red. It would be so easy. Just to let the pressure off, just to ease it up a bit. But what if he came straight back in? Anyway the knife was blunt. I banged it down and picked the new gloves off the floor, lovely gloves, black fleece. What's up with him anyway slamming the door like that and not wearing the new gloves even though it's freezing cold?

I stood in the room for a long time. There are so many sounds in a house. The sounds of it holding itself up, wall by wall, the thin sounds of hidden wires, the plumbing sounds. The pyjamas were ruined by the wine and my head was throbbing. I picked up a new cracker and tried to pull it but I couldn't pull it by myself, I couldn't rip my arms far enough apart. I could have gone out too. I looked at the new coat and thought about putting it on and going out. I could be like a spy and follow Doggo wherever he went. But what would be the point? I took off my paper hat and tore it to shreds.

I went into the hall and stood looking at the barred-up room. It really got to me that the room was barred up and empty. I do think it a weird and sinister thing to do, bar up a room like that.

Sometimes you do things without thinking, don't you? As if you are watching yourself but quite detached from the decision. I stood outside the room where Zita burnt to death. I got hold of the plank of wood and pulled. There was no struggle. It came off straightaway as if it wanted to. So simple after all that time. I stood there with it in my arms and then I put it down. I put my hand on the door-handle and turned it. The door opened and I stepped inside.

And there was nothing. There was no carpet or hole in the floor or stink of old fire. No lampshades or bookshelves, no vases. Nothing, not even a light bulb to switch on. Just nothing. The day was dark with sleet falling. You could hear it tutting like a million tongues. The room was dark with the curtains pulled. I walked across the bare floor and opened the curtains. The window was licked by wet grey tongues. The light that came through was a dirty wavery light and the room was empty. I got a feeling in my chest like a door opening and then pain.

I thought there would be something. Some sort of leftover something even if it was only smell. But it was clean and blank. Rain shadows wobbled and slid on the walls and the floor. I started to sweat. My heart went like a rat in a cage, trying to scrabble out of my ribs.

The grate was a black and empty throat.

I hurt so much. My back and my belly with a body memory of hurt. Like a dream of being awake and remembering and my body did remember. I went on my knees.

The memory came and my mouth dribbled blood when I bit my tongue. The sleet was stinging in the chimney-throat. The door was miles away and there was no way I could move. Wind blew out of the grate like black breath. I shut my mind but it rushed over me and the rat fled right out of my chest and disappeared across the floor and down a hole.

Thirty-five

The place I was was bed and it was dark. Ice branched in my veins. My head was empty as a room and my chest was, till my heart came back. Wind rattled the glass all night, it crept through cracks and chinks, whistled between my ribs, flapped my lungs like curtains while my sad heart throbbed.

Then what?

I don't know. I think Doggo said *OK now OK now* or something and there were arms around me and my face against a beating chest. When I did come back I was thin as sticks and shaking. Doggo dripped some brandy in my mouth. It tasted of electric light.

Is that real? From now on is as real as it gets. As real as you are, anyway.

One day I sat up and drank tea. Doggo was sitting on the bed looking comical in Sarah's dressing gown. I was so light and thin I didn't want to spoil the light thin cleanness with food but he made me eat a bit. I started to speak and this is what I said:

A girl had a baby. She was sixteen. She didn't even know she was pregnant. There were the signs but she didn't read them. Part of her knew but part of her didn't. She was sick sometimes and she felt thumps inside her when she was trying to sleep. She never got that big.

She was working hard at school. She wanted to be a doctor. She had hung on to that even when her mum had died. Her mum's friends had taken her in until she finished school. The date of the birth was the 1st of June, the same day as her GCSE science.

She woke up and the bed was wet. Then she got an outrageous pain. It started in her spine and spread round both ways till she was in a vice. She tried to shout but her voice wouldn't come. Then it stopped hurting and she was OK.

It was five o'clock in the morning. Pink light was coming through the curtains. A bird was singing. She got up. The pain again. She went on her knees and shoved her face in the pillow. When the pain stopped there was a hard wriggle inside her and she knew. She had a flashback to a broken greenhouse window and the moon. A boy saying it would be OK.

The pains went on and on. The time went past like it had nothing to do with real time any more, hands skidding on the clock face and the ticking speeding up and down. Wet came out of her mouth and sweat from everywhere but she was shivering.

Then it changed, like she was sharpening. On her hands and knees on the fluffy white rug. She screamed silent mouth shapes into the bed. Everything felt as if it was pushing back, the whole room gathering back around her haunches as she pushed and pushed against the bulge and split of the whole world cramming down.

And then it changed again. She put her hand between her legs and felt a hot wet thing like heavy fruit. Then more pain and the whole thing came slithering out. Floppy like something rubber. Tiny and covered in blood. She knew biology. She knew about the umbilical cord and how you have to cut it. She tried to cut it with her nail scissors but they slipped on the blood. The afterbirth came like a horrible butcher thing and she couldn't look. The white rug was bright red.

She got through the cord with the scissors and tied the belly stump with some silver gift tape left over from a birthday gift. The baby was a boy and he was moving a bit but not crying. She wrapped him in a T-shirt and put him in a drawer.

You'd think she'd rehearsed all this a million times. She had a shower and poppies bloomed around her feet. She nicked a sanitary towel and put her school uniform on. The skirt was loose. She got a black bin bag and put all the bloody stuff in. She put the sheets and towels in the washing machine. She put the baby in a carrier bag. She put the bin bag in the dustbin and took the bag down the road to the medical centre. There was no one about. Inside the bag there was movement and maybe the faintest mew of sound. She put the bag on the step beside a bottle of milk. The bottle had beads of wet outside and she realised how dry she was.

She walked back and it was already getting hot.

After her exam she walked back and the bag was still there. It had dropped off the step. She stood and looked and looked at it, just a creamy bag, perfectly still in the shadow with a beer can and some fag-ends. Someone had put a washed-up milk bottle on the step but the bag had fallen off the step like rubbish.

Please believe this. She didn't mean for that to happen. Someone was meant to find the bag and take it in. She stood and stared and willed herself to pick the bag up but she couldn't. She was too scared to look. The heat beat right through her. The whole street was throbbing. She was not brave enough to pick up the bag and look inside. She turned away and left it.

After that, well after that her life was ended. Who could

live with themselves after that? That was Joanna Vinier. That life was over with. That was her. Just stopped.

You see, you cannot even bear to dream if you've done something like that. You cannot bear to believe in a life that would let a bag fall off a step like that and not get carried in and saved. How anyone could even joke about a God in a life like that.

I didn't look at Doggo's face, I just looked at the blue quilt with the little feathers poking their sharp ends through and sometimes I pulled one right out. Weird how the details come back – pink light, poppies, an empty bottle.

When I had finished we were silent. Then Doggo said, 'What happened to baby?' There were tears in his eyes. I could not believe that. Actual tears. I couldn't answer because I don't know. I could never bear to know. I couldn't watch the news or listen to it or read it because I didn't want to know the worst and I still don't.

'Maybe someone did find him and he lived,' he said. Then he got up and went out. I listened to him going down the stairs and the front door banging shut. You can't blame him for walking out like that.

It might not seem possible that I forgot that. But I did. That is the truth. Maybe not forget, exactly. More like detach. More like lock up behind a door. I lay and ached and ached so much I thought I'd bleed to death but there was no blood at all. I thought it couldn't hurt so much to die.

At the moment of getting dark, Doggo came in. I never thought he would. I thought he'd gone. I turned my face towards him. The pillow was cold from tears and drool. The sky was purple with full dark clouds. Doggo poked the fire and I heard the hiss of flames on damp new coals. I had this stupid thought. You could paint the ceiling purple and stick on moons and stars.

He sat on the edge of the bed and I felt myself tilt towards him. He cleared his throat a few times and finally said, 'Fuck, Lamb.' He reached out and took my hand. His was like ice. 'I'm right sorry,' he said. I lay still, feeling his hand warm up in mine, waiting for him to go on, to say *Sorry but . . .* something or other, *Sorry but that's it I'm off* or something. At that moment I almost didn't care.

Then looking not at me, but at the fire, he said, 'I've been walking about thinking about what you said. And thinking it must have broke your fucking heart.' His voice choked up. 'You poor, poor frightened kid.'

Everything stopped for a second. What? The sky froze, the world did but then he moved and it started off again. He lay beside me and held me tight. Held so tight it was not just comfort for me but like he was clinging on to something too. The words kept going on and on in my head, echoes and echoes of words I could hardly believe had been said. *Me* a poor kid. The rough wet wool of his jumper rubbed my face raw. *Me* a poor kid. *Me.* I never thought of it like that.

Thirty-six

In the middle of the real Christmas Day Doggo cooked the pudding. It wouldn't catch fire even with brandy poured on. We were in bed in the lighthouse room with the fire in the grate and the world going on outside the windows. Doggo splashed more and more brandy on the pudding and struck match after match but it wouldn't burn. The smell of the matches caught in my throat. I stared at the pretend window with the ship tossing on the stormy waves and wished we were in a real lighthouse with nothing but sea outside. Nothing but waves for miles.

When I took a spoonful of pudding I saw that it was flickering blue. A spoonful of dark pudding and flames so pale we hadn't seen them. Maybe it had been burning all along. I stopped before the flames got in my mouth and waited for them to go out. Then I stuffed my mouth with the scorchy pudding. It made me remember the thin bite of a silver threepence between my teeth. Get the threepence get a wish. *To be in a real lighthouse with Doggo, just me and Doggo and nothing around us but sea. And nobody able to get us ever.* But you don't get silver threepences in shop puddings. Wishes aren't for sale.

We went downstairs and watched telly, drinking bottle after bottle of wine. Doggo was smoking but I only had one puff. I couldn't stand the telly for long, all the raucous noise and falseness, so I went back to the lighthouse room and watched the soft flap of the flames instead. I was trying to concentrate. Trying to keep myself together, to keep *us* together. And I think it would have worked.

But then a letter came for Doggo. He never looked at the post but I sometimes picked it up. There was no surname just Doggo and the address. I opened it.

23rd Dec

Dear Doggo,

I keep trying to phone, is the phone out of order? Obviously we need to speak about what happened. I hope you don't regret it, I don't. I know it's awkward with Lamb. She really is disturbed, isn't she? I don't want to do anything to upset her. We don't want her to harm herself again. Is it really true you're just platonic because if it is . . . well I'd like to see you. As in seeing you. I'm coming to Sheffield on the 29th. I won't come round – I feel too awkward with Lamb being there. Daft isn't it when it's actually my house now! But I won't come round till we've sorted this thing out. Meet me by the statue in the Botanics at one o'clock.

Please be there, love Sarah.

I took the letter straight upstairs and fed it to the flames. *Her house.* How could someone like her own a house? It was hard to remember that Mr Dickens was really dead, even though the funeral was over and the will had obviously been read. I kept his watch strapped to my wrist and sometimes put it up to my ear to hear its tick.

We settled back into nearly our old routine. The grey days rolled past. Doggo went back to making wild plans for the garden though I don't know why. I think it was a kind of game. We slept in the same bed and he held me every night but he never tried anything. I wouldn't have minded if he had but now he knew the truth about me why would he? It was almost a relief he knew. No more pretending.

Another letter came. This time short.

29th Dec

Dear Doggo,
I waited for an hour. What happened? I need to speak to you. If you don't ring me I'll call round, awkward or not.
Love Sarah.

She gave a number, not a Sheffield one thank God.

But days went past and she didn't come. I watched television with Doggo in the evenings and sometimes during the day while he was in the garden. Not really watched, just let it go on in front of me while my mind was somewhere else. But sometimes hooked me back. One night there was a programme about spontaneous combustion.

It was late and Doggo was asleep in his armchair with a glass of wine tilting perilously in his hand. I nearly got up and switched the telly off but then I didn't. The programme was trying to explain the phenomenon. Some scientists were doing an experiment to try and duplicate the effect of spontaneous combustion. They didn't use a person but a pig. They wrapped it in cloth and set fire to the cloth. The flames melted the pig's flesh which soaked into the cloth and it burnt like a candle. The cloth was the wick and the fat was the wax. It burnt for hours at an amazingly high temperature, higher even than cremation fires, and the blaze didn't spread away from the pig. When in the end the fire died down the pig was burnt up, even the bones were gone. Except for the ends of the legs where there is less fat. The bottoms of the legs don't burn because they are not fat enough and it is the same with humans.

From this they deduce that there is no such phenomenon as spontaneous combustion. In all reported cases it could have happened like this: the person sets themselves alight somehow, maybe they fall asleep with a lit cigarette, or maybe a spark jumps from the fireplace where they're drunk or dozing and they don't wake up till too late.

Which means there is no such thing as spontaneous combustion. The impossible idea of catching fire from the inside out. It just can't happen. I am so glad. I wish I could tell Mr Dickens that.

Doggo woke up just as it finished. He blinked at me then swigged his wine. He reminded me of Mr Dickens at that moment, jerking back to consciousness and carrying on.

Sarah still didn't come and the days went past in a muffled way as if we were living under a grey blanket. Some days it hardly got light and those days I came down and waited for the post, made sure the phone remained unplugged then went back to bed. Doggo brought me plates of honey sandwiches with the crusts cut off. It was all I would eat. No crusts, nothing hard, just sticky fraying bread and endless cups of tea. He threw the crusts out for the birds and every day he told me which ones he'd seen, robins, blue tits, blackbirds, even a jay.

I thought about my mum a lot but never without crying. I do know she didn't mean to die. I thought about the baby. He must have been found eventually. And I'd gone missing. Someone must have put two and two together and known that it was me. That he was mine. That I had dumped him. If I rang the friends they'd tell me. Tell me if he had lived or died but that I couldn't bear to know.

Maybe someone did find him in time and he survived. It might be. Spartan people used to put their new-born babies out on a hill so that the weaklings would die. Only those who were tough enough to survive were allowed to grow up to be Spartans. Maybe that baby was a tough one.

After some time the edges of the blanket lifted and let a little light in. I recovered enough to have baths and walk round the garden and then to go out, even though my legs were wobbly as new legs and the world was sharp enough to hurt my eyes. I started thinking about other people for a change and that was a relief. There had been no more letters from Sarah and that was good. I thought that she had given up. Maybe she had gone away. She once said she wanted to go to the States to think. Why is thinking easier in the States? Maybe she'd done that.

We had no money. I decided to go back to Mrs Banks. A tingling on the back of my hand was the memory of her tear. I wanted to be in her warm kitchen, sitting at her table with her, drinking coffee with Roy playing about around us. Maybe doing a bit of ironing, bringing a few pounds home. That seemed so long ago. But it wasn't really long at all.

And one day the sun came out like something lost and found again. I put on my jacket and stood outside the back door with dazzles in my eyes. Doggo was out there, digging, the sun shining on his clean black hair. I stood watching but he didn't see. The berries on the holly bush were stabs of red. A blackbird opened his yellow beak and did a thrill of song. I didn't tell Doggo I was going, I just went.

Thirty-seven

It was dustbin day again and there were Christmas trees put out, trails of needles on the wet path and a golden scatter of empty chocolate money. Some of the trees still had wisps of tinsel on. I didn't like to see the trees shoved out like that, like rubbish. Doggo had planted ours, though it didn't look too good.

I stood outside Mrs Banks' house for a while before I rang the bell. I didn't know what to expect from her, having not turned up for ages. I could have been replaced for all I knew.

But she opened the door and said, 'Lamb!' as if she was glad to see me. 'I'd given you up!'

'I'm sorry,' I said and started to stumble out some excuse but she wasn't listening.

'Look,' she said, 'I know, blow the cleaning, why don't I take you out to lunch?'

I stared at her and she laughed. 'I feel like going out, stuck in the house all over Christmas. Neville's taken Roy to his granny's for a day or two. I'm at a loose end. What about it?'

I shrugged. 'K.'

She looked down at her pink track-suit. 'I'll just get ready.'

She ran up the stairs. *I* wasn't ready. Luckily I was wearing my new jeans that weren't too bad but my hair needed doing again and, when I looked in her mirror, I saw that my face was the colour of celery. I looked away and stood breathing in the smell of her house which I have always liked, coffee and washing-powder and child.

She came downstairs, wearing a short black dress as if she was going to a cocktail party and carrying her high-heeled shoes.

'Like it?' she said, pushing her feet into her shoes and twirling round in front of me. It wasn't the sort of thing I'd be seen dead in but it looked OK on her. 'My New Year's resolution is to wear nice things when I feel like it, not save them up for special occasions that never happen anyway. What's yours?' She squinted into the hall mirror and drew on some sugar lips.

I hadn't even thought about resolutions so I said, 'None.'

'Then we'll have to think of one for you.' She fluffed her hair up, sprayed on some shocking perfume and off we went.

She took me to the Italian place with all the posers in the window. We stood there waiting for a table, sipping our mineral water and posing. Or I did. She was quite normal. And actually when you got in there everyone was normal. It was very kind of her but I wanted to say, Why me? I mean it's pretty sad, having lunch with your cleaner. Where were her proper friends? But she was happy and bubbly and I didn't want to burst her bubble.

Me, I was feeling . . . the way you feel when you've had flu and haven't been out for ages and the outside world seems so full on you can hardly stand it. Like *please*, turn it all down. I was like a snail who'd lost its shell. Everything was frost and salt and stinging me.

She told me I'd like *crostini misti* and she was right. It was all sorts of different-coloured stuff on toast. She chose a neon salad thing and we had fizzy wine. I was so empty that it bypassed my stomach altogether and fizzed straight on up to my brain. I thought, well why *not* me? Why shouldn't it be me in here?

She asked me about my Christmas. I didn't say I spent it in bed with her son eating spoonfuls of flames and spewing up my memory. I just said, 'K.'

'Nice presents?' she said.

'Some ear-rings,' I said with a straight face, picturing the plastic carrots.

'I've got a little something for you,' she said, bending down and fishing in her bag. 'It *is* only little.' She handed me a box wrapped in red foil.

Maybe it's normal to buy your cleaner a present? And maybe it's the thing to do to take her out to lunch? Then you can just happen to drop it in the conversation, *Took the cleaner to Nonna's for a perk*. My cheeks went hot. I didn't even want the present but I unwrapped it. It was a silver brooch shaped like a frisking lamb.

'Ta,' I said and stuffed it in my pocket.

'I couldn't resist it,' she said.

'I've not got you one,' I said.

She waved her hand as if she didn't expect anything. I looked down and saw I had shredded the label off the wine bottle. I sat on my hands.

'What's the matter?' she said. The waiter came and topped up our wine glasses. I crunched a bit of toast with some salty black stuff on but I couldn't swallow.

'Lamb . . . I hope you didn't mind the way I went on the other week. I thought . . .' She stopped and her eyes went bright.

'What?' I said through the mouthful of food. I didn't need this. I had enough tears of my own thank you very much.

'It's just that I, well I find you easy to talk to,' she said. 'You're a good listener. I don't . . .' She stopped and wrestled with her face until she won. 'I don't have that many friends,' she said, 'I'm not that type, but sometimes, well you meet someone and you feel a sort of link with them, a connection. Know what I mean?'

The anger puffed right out of me and left me smaller than before. I did know what she meant and I managed to swallow the food in my mouth. I know because that is just how I felt about Doggo. Because I don't have that many friends believe it or not, hahaha. But when I met Doggo it was different. I recognised him. As if he was made of the same kind of stuff.

She swallowed some wine. 'You strike me as rather brave,' she said, 'very prickly and private. To tell you the truth you remind me a bit of myself when I was younger.' She stopped and summoned up a smile. 'What my poor parents did to deserve me.'

The restaurant was clattering with so much noise my head was aching. Marion pushed away her plate and got out some fags. Consulate. I didn't know she smoked.

I looked away while she struggled with her lighter. The people walking past outside had cold-weather skins and long plumes of private breath. Normally it would be me out there and someone else sitting where I was. I would be scurrying along with my face down, not sitting and gazing out with a glass of wine in my hand. I saw the sorry shadow of myself flit by.

Marion finally managed to light up. She smoked like someone who has only just learned, spitting the smoke out immediately before it could reach her tonsils but still choking.

'I wanted to be a doctor once,' I said. I don't know what made me say that then.

'Really?' She held the cigarette as far away as possible. 'Well you still could be. How old are you, eighteen, nineteen?'

'Twenty. No qualifications.'

'Well, you're obviously bright. Start now and in less than ten years you could *be* a doctor.'

'Ten years!' I said. I mean, that is a *decade*.

'Ten years will go past anyway,' she said. 'You can either be a doctor at the end of it or not. You'd still be much younger than I am now.'

I stared at her. Maybe it was the wine that made that sound like sense. It would kill Doggo if I told him that. Me a doctor with a stethoscope and everything. Can you see it? *Me*.

'*That* can be your resolution,' she said. 'Look into it.'

My mind was whirling. A waiter came and took away our plates. She ordered two cappuccinos. We sat there for a minute not saying anything. I wanted to ask her about Doggo but didn't know how, and then we both tried to say something at once.

She laughed but only a whisk of a laugh before her face went bleak and she leant forward. 'I really appreciated being able to talk to you the other day,' she said. 'It's oh . . . leaving children it's . . . you never really leave them . . . it's – '

The waiter came with the cappuccinos. 'All right, ladies?' he said. 'Enjoy.' The coffees had smiley faces sprinkled in cocoa on top of the froth.

'Like, like a bit of yourself has gone,' she said. 'You *can* leave them but you leave a bit of yourself too and it never stops hurting.'

My hand went to my ribs. Oh, so that is what it is.

We were quiet for a moment. She made a little gulping sound. I scooped the froth off my coffee and licked it off the spoon. There was a chocolate coffee bean on the saucer. I put it in my pocket to give to Doggo.

'One of my sons is dead,' she said, 'the other was convicted of his murder.'

The window glass warped in and out.

'No!'

'What?' She was shocked out of her wave of grief.

'I mean . . . that is awful. God.'

It was almost impossible to sit still. My legs were jumping

under the table as if they wanted to run. I wanted to lean across the table and slap her. Beat the truth out of her. It couldn't be true. It was a lie.

She shut her eyes and a tear squeezed out. 'They never, they never got on. They were you know chalk and cheese. David he was . . . he was like his dad, Martin more like oh what does it matter anyway. They were tooth and nail all their lives then there was a girl. Martin's girl, all this is from the papers, Lamb, can you imagine learning about your children from the papers?' She stopped and bit her lip. I shook my head. I couldn't speak, my mouth gone so dry my tongue was stuck to the roof of my mouth.

'Apparently she'd been two-timing Martin with David for ages. That was more than it sounds. Because there'd always been this rivalry. Martin followed them back to David's one night, after they'd been to some club or other. There was a fight. David shut Martin out. Martin came back later and fired up the house. It wasn't just David he killed, it was the girl too. And she was pregnant though they don't know whose . . .'

I so much wanted to run. I so much wanted to hurl the wine bottle at the window and hear it smash. To kick the table over, slam a chair down on her head. But I did nothing. Someone on another table was laughing, a ridiculous spasm of sound. She had not touched her coffee. The smiley face had gone. She saw me staring at it and took a sip. A thin brown moustache clung on her upper lip.

'I'm sorry,' I managed to say.

She knitted her jittering fingers together. 'Martin was arrested and charged with arson and murder. Found guilty. Well he was guilty. No question. Life sentence.'

A shudder of chill went right through me. Arson. *Doggo?* A *girl, pregnant. Arson.* If I shut my eyes I could picture his face in the firelight, his gorgeous peachy skin. What lies he'd told. I thought I would vomit. I went to the toilet and stared at myself in the mirror and the pupils of my eyes were like bullet holes. The ash taste in my mouth. I rested my forehead against the cold glass till my heart stopped thumping and the sickness went away. I drank some water from the tap and went back and sat down.

Marion was puffing at another fag. There were blobs of mascara on her cheeks and a waiter was eyeing her warily.

'Let's go,' I said.

'Yes.' She forced her lips into the most miserable smile I have ever seen. 'But hang on, Lamb.'

I didn't want to hang on another minute, or know another thing, but I forced my body to fold back on the chair.

'I wanted to say . . . a few months ago Martin escaped from Rampton. Then a couple of weeks later my bag went missing and my keys, I thought maybe . . . I thought maybe he'd traced me and had come to me for . . . I don't know. There were descriptions of him in the paper, maybe you saw? Height and everything, the scar and the LOVE-HATE on his knuckles.'

'Love-hate?' I said.

'He's got LOVE-HATE tattooed on his knuckles. "The LOVE-HATE Man" the papers called him, dangerous. Do not attempt to apprehend and all that nonsense.'

She kept on talking but my mind had gone still like a pond, a stone sinking straight to the bottom. The LOVE-HATE Man. So the burning off was part of his disguise. I thought he burnt it off for me.

She was still going on while parts of me were falling away, like fragments of a shell. 'And when my bag went missing I had this what you might call a gut feeling that it was *him*. I didn't go to the police or tell Neville, I just waited. And this is daft, Lamb, forgive me, but for some reason I had an inkling that you knew something about it too.' She looked at me with a brief flare of hope in her eyes.

'And then the bag turned up with only the keys missing. I searched through it but there was no message, nothing. I know I should have changed the locks. But I don't want to change the locks. Whatever he's done. I don't want to lock him out.' She started to really blub then and two waiters scurried over and smoothed us out of there after smoothing payment out of her credit card first.

I walked with her back to her house. She wept as she walked along and people looked away quick. My mind was still and blank. He had lied to me. He had lied. He had lied and I had trusted him. All that story about the riot, the stabbing, revenge for his brother's death. All lies and *I* had trusted him. *Me*.

We walked like two mad women. I left her at her door even though she wanted me to come in. I couldn't spend any more time with her. Her heart was breaking in front of me and how could I stand that?

Thirty-eight

I walked about for ages, faster and faster. I could not go back. How could I go back? How could I bear to see him? The liar. How he had lied to me. How I'd *believed* him. And *he'd* called *me* a liar. God, it could nearly make you laugh.

I walked past the house again and again, the door shut smug behind the scraggy trees. But I didn't go in. I went to the Botanics and sat on a wet bench among the dead sticks of the rose garden. It wasn't all dead sticks, there was one straggly white rose browning at the edges, sagging under its own wet weight.

A man with a damp moustache sat down next to me. 'Cheer up, might never happen,' he said. 'Spare a fag?' I told him that I didn't smoke. He said he'd climbed Mount Kilimanjaro without any oxygen once. And who knows, maybe he did. Who cares. I gave him the chocolate coffee bean.

In the end there was nothing I could do except go back. I stepped through the door. There were a couple of envelopes on the mat, a brown one, bill, there had been lots of those. I left it. The other was a creamy square. I picked it up. I walked through into the back but no one was there, not even the dogs. The telly wasn't on and Doggo wasn't in his chair. A false flame flickered in the fire. A sinking in my gut said he'd gone. Just gone. Why wouldn't he?

I went upstairs and stood in the lighthouse room looking at the phony storm. His stuff was still there. The real fire was hot. If he'd gone, he hadn't been gone long, someone had tended it and lately. Anyway, he would have taken his stuff. He would only be outside, that's all. Only in his stupid garden. I knelt down beside the fire. The tidy writing on the envelope was Sarah's. I could hardly be bothered to open it but I did.

9th Jan

Dear Doggo,
OK, I get the message. I feel exploited by you and by Lamb. You are living in my house but won't even phone me. I've had flu but I'm better now. I'm coming back. While I was in bed with flu I had lots of time to think. Lamb said something crazy before I left that morning. She said you were a murderer. I just laughed. I was still high from . . . well you know. And after all her other terrible lies. But all those hours in bed alone, aching and coughing, I started to think. And I remembered some-thing too, something about an escaped prisoner, someone dangerous, some connection with Sheffield. I'm sure this is crazy and I'm going to end up feeling incredibly stupid, but I don't care. If you don't ring me when you get this I'm phoning the police. Please ring and tell me how stupid this all is.
Love (believe it or not) Sarah.

I screwed it up and chucked it in the fire. How stupid. How hysterical. *Get a grip*, I would have said if I could see her. She would never do it. Call the police. Why would she? What a liar. Love. *Believe it or not.* If she loved him, she wouldn't. What good would that do? Anyway she would wait a few days, give him a few days. What if the letter got delayed in the post? What if it got lost?

I went downstairs and into the room that was once Zita's. I looked at the floor and the walls. A sunbeam jittered on the dusty floor. There really was no sign that anybody had ever burned to death in that room. No sign and no smell at all. It was just an empty room. It didn't affect me one bit.

Of course he was in the garden with the dogs. He was smoking a fag, his back turned to me. I stood and watched him for a while. He was lost in thought. He looked just the same. I stared at him and thought, *you lied to me*. I refocused and tried to see him differently. As a liar, the murderer of his brother, a girl, an unborn child. A person who lived with that. *A liar*. But no matter how long I stared at him, I couldn't. He was wearing an old sweater unravelling at the sleeves and all he looked was dear and familiar to me.

'Hi,' I said.

'Fuck.' He clutched his chest. 'Nearly gave me a heart-attack.' He grinned as if he was really pleased to see me. I looked with interest at his grin. Funny how that contraction of muscles, that naked slash of teeth, means *happy*, means *friends*.

'This is where fountain goes.' He walked across the mud and pointed. 'And then a kind of stream leading down to pond. Here.' I stood there staring at him. He was moving like a puppet but you couldn't see the strings. 'With goldfish,' he said and squinted at me. 'What's up?'

'I've been talking to your mum.'

'That where you've been? And maybe a little bridge across. Or would that be too . . .'

'Proper talking,' I said, 'about *everything*.'

'Oh yeah?' He ground his fag out in the mud. 'Come here.' He held his arms out but I didn't move. His eyes were naked metal in the sun. I could have stopped there. He was just a grinning puppet but the grin was falling off. I looked past him at the mound where Norma was buried. I saw he'd made

266

a cross with twigs and poked it in the earth. Words shrivelled in my mouth.

'What?' he said.

My lips moved for a moment before I could speak. '*You*. You killed your brother?'

He didn't look down or away when I said it, he kept his darkening eyes on mine.

'Yeah, she read all about it in the papers,' I said. 'They call you the LOVE-HATE Man.'

The scars on his knuckles showed shiny through the frayed cuffs of his sweater. His shoulders rose. We just stood there as if time had stopped and the weird thing is I had a sudden vision of the fountain. The fountain, the stream, the pond, even a flicker of goldfish. Just how it would be.

'Didn't mean to kill him,' he said in a flat voice. 'I was off my head. Didn't mean it.'

'K,' I said, 'if you say so. What was all that about a knife? All that stuff you told me, about revenge? *You called me a liar!*' I couldn't stop myself from shouting when I got to that.

'Lamb . . .'

'I'm going to get some milk.'

I don't know if we even needed milk, all I knew is I couldn't bear to be near him a moment longer. I walked fast with that smoke taste rising in my throat again. I didn't give a toss where I walked, I didn't even look, just let my legs scissor scissor scissor, slicing the air to rags.

I ended up in the park. I didn't notice where I was until it started raining, soaking through my clothes, but I just kept on walking. Trust. I had trusted him. Trust, the word gone dull, the rusting T of truth. Thinking about burning. Of all the people in the world for me to fall in love with, someone who'd done arson. Foul word, like arsey person. I stopped and spat to try and get the taste out of my mouth. And he had lied to me. Called *me* a liar. Falling in love, yes that is what I'd done. And *trusting* and he had lied to me. Worse than that. I had *believed* him. The river was tumbling towards me over its stones, dragging its ripped-off roots and branches, a lost football bouncing madly on the top.

I couldn't stop walking until my head was sorted and if it never got sorted then I'd walk till I dropped. And who would care? People were panicking about as if they thought it would kill them to get wet. The rain turned to hail and the hail stabbed cold needles in my scalp and face and tiny nuggets bounced up around my feet. Good. It stung, good.

How *can* you ever know another person? Or even know yourself. How can you trust? The hail turned to sleet and it was like walking through interference on the telly, long white streaks rushing at my eyes. If you can't trust then you're alone. I had to blink even to see and a runner came past, face wet red, stuttering through my lashes. But you can never trust.

My fingers vanished, my scalp froze, my boots squelched, bubbles squeezing out between the laces. But it came suddenly clear to me. Like light filtering between my ribs. I wanted him. The liar. I wanted him. Whatever. We were both liars, *so?* At least we knew that. Most people don't, do they, most people, *you*, you lie and think you get away with it. Don't you? Don't you? At least I *know* with Doggo now. At least he knows. He must not go. He might be gone already or be going now.

I swivelled and ran back the other way. Spikes of ice lashed at my back. There was no one else out. The swings swung empty in the playground. The swollen yellow river hurtled past and I ran to keep up.

He was not in the garden and not downstairs. The dogs were there and on the table a bit of paper, I thought it was a note but it was just an address. I picked it up. Underneath written *My gran*. Nothing else, nothing personal, nothing about love, not even my name. I thought he'd gone. Just gone. Leaving me to take Gordon back. Leaving me alone.

But even if he *was* here I'd be alone because I could not trust him. There is nothing for it but to be alone. You're no less alone if someone's with you. You only think you are. That is what a voice was saying. I didn't know if it was true, is it true? Please, is it true?

No. I wanted him. He was a wanted man. We were both liars and we knew it. So that was OK. That was a kind of trust. We'd always *know* that we were lying. That is more honest, I think. I stood at the bottom of the stairs and yelled his name over and over again. I would have yelled for ever, yelled till I dropped dead, but then the front door opened behind me.

I felt so stupid, the echoes of my shouts shuddering in the air. I turned round as he stepped in and banged the door shut. He flicked the Yale lock down and stood with his back against the door as if he was keeping someone out. His curls had turned to glittering tendrils. Gordon pattered past me to welcome him back.

We stood there for a minute our breath all foggy in the air.

'So?' I said in the end.

'Thought you'd fucked off,' he said.

A hectic shiver ran up my spine. 'Thought you had.'

We stood there, water running off us and pooling on the floor. A green stain from the fanlight tinged his hair and his face was shadowed so I couldn't read it.

'Where've you been?' My teeth were chattering. A drop of water slithered down between my shoulder blades.

'You're fucking freezing,' he said. 'Come on.' He got hold of my arm and pulled me through into the back room which was hot and orange from the fire. He turned it up as high as it would go and a drop fell from his hair and sizzled on the metal edge.

'Where?'

'Botanics.'

'*Botanics?*'

'Fucking well looking for you, weren't I.'

'Oh,' I said. Then, 'Why did you lie to me?'

He looked down. There was nothing he could say. Nothing he needed to say. Of course he couldn't have told me what he'd done. There are things too awful to be told. Things too awful to believe you've done yourself, to live with. Lies you have to tell. Every word of *me* a lie, to start with.

He looked up. 'You should get that off,' he said, nodding at my denim jacket which was black with wet. 'Before you fucking die of cold.'

'Trying to scare me with all this swearing?' I said.

He half smiled, his shoulders raising a fraction. He was wearing his new jacket and I bet he was dry inside because it was such a good jacket for this weather. 'Will you . . . will you stay here?' he said.

'Why? Where you going?'

'My mum's.' He said it as if it was a normal and every-day thing for him to say. But I caught the tension in his cheek and knew the effort it was taking to keep his expression bland. I do know that feeling when your throat bulges and your mouth twists down. I looked away. Doughnut was flopped in his usual position on the floor, one ear turned inside out so you could see the pink silk lining.

'Don't,' I said.

'I can't fu . . . I can't leave it.'

'Don't,' I said again, but I knew he would and that he had to and that it was the right thing for him to do.

'I'm off,' he said, turning again.

'I'm coming with you,' I said.

'No.'

'I am. You can't stop me.'

He shrugged and a drop of rain trickled from his hair into his beard.

We didn't take the dogs for once. The rain gurgled in the gutters and surged up with every passing car, sloshing the pavement, splashing our already soaking legs. We held hands. The rain made them slippy but we both clung on, our fingers intermeshed.

He speeded up the nearer we got and I know it was in case he lost his nerve. He didn't even pause at the gate but went right on up the path nearly dragging me. He let go of my hand and lifted his finger to the bell. 'Sure?' I said. His eyes met mine and I jumped at his expression. His finger trembled as he pressed. We listened to the soft sugary ding-dong and then nothing. Not a stir from inside.

'She's not fucking there,' he said.

Let's go then, I wanted to say. But I knew she would be there. After the state she was in over lunch. She would be there.

'Try again,' I said.

He pressed and made the bell go dingdongdingdongdingdong. The rain clung in his beard. His eyes, fixed on the door, were that strange sky grey. No shades today. We stood there frozen in the streaming rain. A bird sang, a sudden crazy streak of sound. Then we heard movement inside and the door opened and she was there.

Her face was blotchy red from weeping and her hair standing on end. She looked from Doggo to me and back again. A ripple passed across her face. Her mouth opened and then closed. She breathed in sharply and grabbed his hands in both of hers as if she would pull him back inside her and then dropped them as if they burnt. Her fingers flexed and fought with the urge to embrace or the urge to tear apart.

I looked at my feet and felt the moment stretch and ache until it was not bearable. I sneaked a look at her face and wished I hadn't. It was as if all the invisible secret things, the inside things, the things no one else should ever be allowed to see, had crept out and were crawling over her features. It was not fair to look.

'I'll go,' I said. 'Doggo ... *Martin* ...' My teeth were chattering so much I could hardly make the words. 'See you later . . .' But no one was listening. Doggo looked nowhere but his mother's face.

I left them. I walked away back down the path and heard the door click shut behind them as they went in.

Thirty-nine

When I turned the bath taps on the room filled up with steam. Taking off the wet clothes was like peeling off dead skin. I gasped as I stepped into the scalding bath but made myself slide right down. The water held me like a cradle or like arms. But I could not relax with all the helter pelter skelter in my head.

I was thinking that we would have to run. When he got back from Marion's. Whatever happened there. Whatever was happening. She wouldn't shop him, call the police, I was pretty sure of that. But Sarah . . . we would have to go before she turned up again or sent another stupid threatening letter. We would have to run. What was up with her trying to mess everything up? It would be OK, on the run, together. Me and Doggo. It would be fine.

The rain was streaming down the windows and the grey light mixing with the steam ran down the mirror and the walls. Tears ran down my face, mixing with the wetness in the bath and in the air. I don't know what I was crying for. I didn't want to. I didn't mean to. Crying is no good, it only makes you ugly and wet – but in all the wetness what difference would a few tears make? I lay and watched the world get dark.

I do not want to be alone. I'm *not* alone with Doggo there. Even if we do nothing else but lie.

273

I thought, what if he does not come back?

I knew I should get up and pack my stuff and as soon as he returned we should go out into the horrid night. Go out, go anywhere. But while my mind thought that my body just lay there in the cooling water.

Of course he would come back. He had to. And after a long time I did hear his feet come stomping up the stairs. He came right into the bathroom and put the light on. I slid under the water, deep as I could. He said nothing. I couldn't stand the dripping quiet. Something needed to be said.

'Could you put the hot on?' He turned the tap, sat on the end of the bath and stared at me. I stared straight back. 'So?' I said.

He looked as if he'd been crying again but who was I to talk? He sat there for a minute, dabbling a finger in the water. 'Can I get in?'

'I'll call you when I get out.'

'No, with you, I mean,' he said.

'*With* me?'

His fists were loose, his hair was long, his face was so so sad. I thought, why not? The water was hotting up again and he turned off the tap. Then he took off his clothes and I tried not to stare at how beautiful he is. And that is true. Beautiful to me.

He stepped in and his skin was cold against mine at first and it was strange and squashed, with knees and elbows everywhere and water spilling out and sloshing on the floor. He got behind me and I lay back, my head against his chest. His heart boomed through me. We lay there as if we'd gone into a trance but in the end I had to ask what happened.

He didn't answer for a moment. The tap dripped circles that broke and warped when they hit the angles of our knees. He started telling me what I didn't even want to hear. About how he hadn't meant to kill his brother. How he'd been off his head. How he'd been going to see his mum when he first met me to tell her he was sorry.

'And now you have,' I said.

'Yeah.' He took a long breath in. '*Sorry*, that's such a . . . such a crap word, isn't it?' he said.

'No,' I said.

'But it sounds so . . . you do . . . you do terrible things . . . and then you say *sorry* like you think everything will then be OK.'

'What did she say?'

'You know how Catholics confess?' he said. 'I knew a Catholic guy inside. You're not Catholic, are you?'

I did know what he meant. It is a sweet lie, make-believe, a funny sort of fairy-tale, that you can ever be forgiven. If we could believe that maybe we would be all right.

'But what did she *say*?'

'I'm turning myself in.'

'No.'

'She's coming with me. Tomorrow. Going to stand by me. Pay for a brief and that.'

My heart was jumping. I could see it through the wet skin between my ribs. 'She's forgiven you?'

'Nah. How could she?'

The phone rang and I nearly shot out of my skin. I'd thought it was unplugged. He must have plugged it in while I was out. We lay and listened until it stopped.

'Doggo, we have to get away from here,' I said. 'Now.'

'Nah. Like I said. I'm turning myself in. I've had enough. And I promised.'

'Promised who?'

'Her.'

'No,' I said. 'Don't. Please. She'll understand.'

'Sorry.'

'No, Doggo. You can't. You don't have to do that. We can go away somewhere. Please. What about *me*?'

'If I give myself up that'll go good for me. I can't hide out for ever.'

'You can,' I said. 'Of course you can.'

'I've had enough.'

But I would not let him. There was no way.

I tried to get out of the bath but he started soaping me. First my arms and every finger and under my arms and then my belly and my tits, round and round making them glitter with all the suds. He stroked the scars on the insides of my wrists.

'Don't ever cut yourself again,' he said. 'Promise?'

'K,' I said. True or not, who knows?

His hands carried on down me, soaping and stroking until I got a feeling in my belly like I have never felt before. Even though I was under the water it felt like flames. I started to melt then thought, he touched *her* like that. He touched Sarah there.

'Come on,' he said. He got out and I went under for a minute and came up blinking. He held a towel up for me, it was cold and damp. The air was bitter on my skin. 'Let's get upstairs,' he said.

The lighthouse room was flickering bright and warm. The wind was roaring in the trees outside and sounding like the sea. He put me on the bed. He lay on top and kissed me. I thought, this is the same place that he lay and kissed Sarah and didn't only kiss her either. I waited to turn to stone. I let him kiss me, let him touch. This was now and it was me. My head was so tired with the thoughts. The way he was touching was really getting through to me.

And then we did it. My body did not stop me. I didn't get turned on enough to lose myself, who wants to lose themselves? But I watched him and felt him, the weight of

276

him, the heat of him, the bucking strength against me, inside me. I breathed his breath, his film of sweat wiped off on me. And it was making love, him making love. *Really*. To me.

He came with a groan like being killed. I held him tight. My heart was beating. This was what I wanted, me and him, and this was what I'd got. A bird shrieked outside the window and made me start.

'Frigid, eh?' he said. He grinned and kissed me on my forehead. It was useless to explain. He was hot and heavy like someone drugged. He soon fell asleep. I slid down and put my head on his belly. The flesh was like a hammock slung between the hips. I lay there looking at his cock curled up like a mouse in a black nest and breathing in the sweet and scuzzy stink of sex.

I knelt up and gazed at his face. The long lashes, the pale jag of scar through his eyebrow. His sleeping throat was white and smooth. Beneath the line where the black beard started, shockingly soft, tender as a baby's skin. In his sleep he stirred and smiled. I was lulled by a lazy pulse beating by his collar bone. I touched it with my finger and he woke.

'I'll get some tea,' I whispered.

In the kitchen I looked at knives. Mr Dickens' terrible blunt bent knives. I picked one up and pressed my finger against the blade. Nothing but a dent. That was Doggo's lie. He didn't really stab. Why did he say that? Burning would make more sense. Zita burnt and Mr Dickens. Doggo's brother burnt to death. If someone burned Doggo it would be revenge for that. In some societies that would be considered right.

I would not have burnt him though. Never. I struck a match and watched it burn, held it till the flame licked my fingertip – weird how it felt cool – and dropped it on the floor. We had to go. I lit another. *We had made love*. Doggo had made love to me. The flame flapped against the dirty floor and died. And made love to Sarah too.

We really had to go.

I made some tea. Soon as we'd had the tea I'd persuade him that we had to leave. There would be a way. We were two of a kind, Doggo and me, and belonged together, that was obvious. Of course it was. It would be the two of us, together on the run. Even running for our whole lives would be better than any other life I could imagine. Because now we were lovers and I could persuade him. I know I could have done.

I took the tea up. He was asleep again, his eyelids twitching in another dream. I bent down to kiss him but before I touched him with my lips there was a sudden blurt of Trumpet Voluntary. I jerked upright, sloshing the tea. He woke with a start. 'Christ,' he said, 'who's that?'

'Dunno,' I said. My heart was going like a hammer. The Trumpet Voluntary went again and then there was a banging, a serious banging, and the sudden smash and splinter of the door. The dogs were going berserk down there. Doggo leapt up and pulled a pair of jeans on. His hair was wild and his cheek creased from the bed. He knew and I knew straightaway.

'Run down and out the back,' I said.

'Don't be fucking stupid.'

He sounded calm for someone about to be arrested. We could hear them getting in downstairs. He pulled me to him and hugged me hard. Our two hearts banged together like prisoners through walls and then he let me go. Feet were coming up the stairs.

'Take dogs to my gran's,' he said.

'Martin Wickerson? It's the police, Martin. Are you there?'

'OK,' he shouted, 'I'm coming down.'

'Are you armed?'

'Don't be fucking stupid.'

'Write to me,' I said.

'Where?'

'I dunno.' My mind jumped.

'Martin?'

'OK.'

'Your gran's.'

'*What?*'

'We're coming up.'

'I'm *coming.*'

He gave me a long wild look, a shrug, a miserable smile and went down ahead of me. There were four policemen. Two in uniform and two not. Four to catch one man. A man hunt, men hunting a man. And catching him. We all trooped down into the back room. Gordon wagged his tail when he saw Doggo and sat beside his feet. They handcuffed Doggo. They went through all the rigmarole they have to say. He looked small and shifty, his eyes cast down. Then they turned to me.

'Name?'

'Zita,' I said.

'Surname?' The policeman had a dewdrop on his nose. He waited, pencil poised.

'Innocent.'

Doggo turned his face away before it could explode.

The policeman raised an eyebrow. 'Zita Inn-o-cent,' he said, raising an eyebrow as he wrote it. 'Girlfriend?'

'Just a mate,' Doggo said.

'And what are you doing here – Zita?'

'I'm Sarah's friend. This is her house.'

'Either of you know someone known as' – he squinted at his pad – 'Lamb?'

'No.'

'Nah.'

'Address, Zita? We'll have to ask you to make a statement.'

I gave them the Harcourts' address. It was what came into

my head. Well they don't know a Zita Innocent, do they?

'Are you aware Mr Wickerson is an escaped criminal?'

'He's *not*,' I said.

'How well do you know Mr Wickerson, Zita?'

I shrugged.

'How long have you known him?'

'We just met,' Doggo said.

Then they took him away.

'I . . . I'll see you,' I said, as they led him out. Stars came in his eyes, and one trickled down his cheek. 'I'll wait for you. Yeah?'

Our eyes met. 'Yeah,' he mouthed and then he looked away.

'We'll certainly need your statement, miss,' the policeman said.

'Yeah.'

'Bye, *Martin*,' I said. 'See you soon.'

He said nothing. That was OK. I could see he couldn't speak. I followed them down the hall to the front door and watched them go off down the path. The rain had stopped. Doggo looked so small between the four policemen. He didn't once look back at me.

They opened the back door of a police car and he climbed in. I watched the two cars drive away, listened to the engine sounds blending with all the sounds of the world out there till they had died away.

I bang-shut the door and then it's only me. I listen to the shadow of the bang, the echo. My echo twitches on the floor in front of me. The house, Sarah's house, settles round me, sighs. Not *only* me. There are the dogs. Gordon looks up at me and yaps, head cocked. What now?

I get my stuff. Some photo albums, some plastic ear-rings, a silver lamb. Doggo's new coat, which he forgot. I put it on, though it's still damp and the sleeves are much too long. I'll wear it till I give it back. I fasten the dogs' leads, pick up Doggo's gran's address. She's alone too. I think she will be glad to see me, with her bad hips and her failing mind. She will be very glad.

Before I leave I build a fire. Boxes, a camp bed, ladders, deck chairs, magazines. Remembering what Doggo said about how to build a fire, leaving air space, piling on plenty of kindling before the heavier denser stuff. On the cellar floor I build a fire, which I could light before I leave. That would serve Sarah right.

I light a match, watch the wobble of the flame and blow it out. Because if the house burned down, the lighthouse room would be gone. And I don't want that. Even though I'll never see that room again, or be in it, I'll want to, need to, know it's there.

I step outside where the air is fresh and sweet after the rain. A bird sings, maybe thinking it is spring. I look at the wreck of the garden one last time. Out of the mud a skinny snowdrop droops. I wish Doggo had seen.

A NOTE ON THE AUTHOR

Lesley Glaister was born in Wellingborough. She teaches a Master's Degree in Writing at Sheffield Hallam University. She is the author of the novels *Honour Thy Father*, which won the Somerset Maugham and a Betty Trask award, *Trick or Treat*, *Digging to Australia*, *Limestone and Clay*, *Partial Eclipse*, *The Private Parts of Women*, *Easy Peasy* and *Sheer Blue Bliss*. She lives in Sheffield.